THE AFTERGLOW

MORE WILDSIDE CLASSICS

Please see www.wildsidepress.com for a complete list!

THE AFTERGLOW

GEORGE ALLAN ENGLAND

WILDSIDE PRESS

THE AFTERGLOW

This edition published in 2006 by Wildside Press, LLC.
www.wildsidepress.com

CHAPTER I

DEATH, LIFE, AND LOVE

Life! Life again, and light, the sun and the fresh winds of heaven, the perfect azure of a June sky, the perfume of the passionate red blooms along the lips of the chasm, the full-throated song of hidden birds within the wood to eastward—life, beauty, love—such, the sunrise hour when Allan and the girl once more stood side by side in the outer world, delivered from the perils of the black Abyss.

Hardly more real than a disordered nightmare now, the terrible fall into those depths, the captivity among the white barbarians, the battles and the ghastly scenes of war, the labors, the perilous escape.

All seemed to fall and fade away from these two lovers, all save their joy in life and in each other, their longing for the inevitable greater passion, pain and joy, their clear-eyed outlook into the vast and limitless possibilities of the future, their future and the world's.

And as they stood there, hand in hand beside the body of the fallen patriarch—he whose soul had passed in peace, even at the moment of his life's fulfillment, his knowledge of the sun—awe overcame them both. With a new tenderness, mingled with reverent adoration, Stern drew the girl once more to him.

Her face turned up to his and her arms tightened about his neck. He kissed her brow beneath the parted masses of her wondrous hair. His lips rested a moment on her eyes; and then his mouth sought hers and burned its passion into her very soul.

Suddenly she pushed him back, panting. She had gone white; she trembled in his clasp.

"Oh, your kiss—oh, Allan, what is this I feel?—it seems to choke me!" she gasped, clutching her full bosom where her heart leaped like a prisoned creature. "Your kiss—it is so different now! No, no—not again—not yet!"

He released her, for he, too was shaking in the grip of new, fierce passions.

"Forgive me!" he whispered. "I—I forgot myself, a moment. Not yet—no, not yet. You're right, Beatrice. A thousand things are pressing to be done. And love—must wait!"

He clenched his fists and strode to the edge of the chasm, where, for a while, he stood alone and silent, gazing far down and away, mastering himself, striving to get himself in leash once more.

Then suddenly he turned and smiled.

"Come, Beta," said he. "All this must be forgotten. Let's get to work. The whole world's waiting for us, for our labor. It's eager for our toil!"

She nodded. In her eyes the fire had died, and now only the light of comradeship and trust and hope glowed once again.

"Allan?"

"Yes?"

"Our first duty—" She gestured toward the body of the patriarch, nobly still beneath the rough folds of the mantle they had drawn over it.

He understood.

"Yes," murmured he. "And his grave shall be for all the future ages a place of pilgrimage and solemn thought. Where first, one of lost Folk issued again into the world and where he died, this shall be a monument of the new time now coming to its birth.

"His grave shall lie here on this height, where the first sun shall each day for ages fall upon it, supreme in its deep symbolism. Forever it shall be a memorial, not of death, but life, of liberty, of hope!"

They kept a moment's silence, then Stern added.

"So now, to work!" From the biplane he fetched the ax. With this he cut and trimmed a branch from a near-by fir. He sharpened it to a flat blade three or four inches across. In the deep red sand along the edge of the Abyss he set to work, scooping the patriarch's grave.

In silence Beatrice took the ax and also labored, throwing the sand away. Together, in an hour, they had dug a trench sufficiently deep and wide.

"This must do, for now," said Stern, looking up at last. "Some time he shall have fitting burial, but for the present we can do no more. Let us now commit his body to the earth, the Great Mother which created and which waits always to give everlasting sleep, peace, rest."

Together, silently, they bore him to the grave, still wrapped in the cloak which now had become his shroud. Once more they gazed upon the noble face of him they had grown to love in the long weeks of the Abyss, when only he had understood them or seemed near.

"What is this, Allan?" asked the girl, touching a fine chain of gold about the patriarch's neck, till now unnoticed.

Allan drew at the chain, and a small golden cylinder was revealed, curiously carven. Its lightness told him it was hollow.

"Some treasure of his, I imagine," judged he.

"Some record, perhaps? Oughtn't we to look?"

He thought a moment in silence, then detached the chain.

"Yes," said he. "It can't help him now. It may help us. He himself would have wanted us to have it."

And into the pocket of his rough, brown cassock, woven of the weed-fiber of the dark sea, he slid the chain and golden cylinder.

A final kiss they gave the patriarch, each; then, carefully wrapping his face so that no smallest particle of sand should come in contact with it, stood up. At each other they gazed, understandingly.

"Flowers? Some kind of service?" asked the girl.

"Yes. All we can do for him will be too little!"

Together they brought armfuls of the brilliant crimson and purple blooms along the edge of the sands, where forest and barren irregularly met; and with these, fir and spruce boughs, the longer to keep his grave freshly green.

All about him they heaped the blossoms. The patriarch lay at rest among beauties he never had beheld, colors arid fragrances that to him had been but dim traditions of antiquity.

"I can't preach," said Stern. "I'm not that kind, anyway, and in this new world all that sort of thing is out of place. Let's just say good-by, as to a friend gone on a long, long journey."

Beatrice could no longer keep back her grief. Kneeling beside the grave, she arranged the flowers and the evergreens, on which her tears fell shining.

"Dust unto dust!" Stern said. "To you, oh Mother Nature, we give back the body of this friend, your son. May the breeze blow gently here, the sun shine warm, and the birds forever sing his requiem. And may those who shall come after us, when we too sleep, remember that in him we had a friend, without whom the world never again could have hoped for any new birth, any life! To him we say good-by—eternally! Dust unto dust; good-by!"

"Good-by!" whispered the girl. Then, greatly overcome, she arose and walked away.

Stern, with his naked hands, filled the shallow grave and, this done, rolled three large boulders onto it, to protect it from the prowling beasts of the wild.

Beatrice returned. They strewed more flowers and green boughs, and in silence stood a while, gazing at the lowlier bed of their one friend on earth.

Suddenly Stern took her hand and drew her toward him.

"Come, come, Beatrice," said he, "he is not dead. He still lives in our memories. His body, aged and full of pain, is gone, but his spirit still survives in us—that indomitable sold which, buried alive in blindness and the dark, still strove to keep alive the knowledge and traditions of the upper world, hopes of attaining it, and visions of a better time to be!

"Was ever greater human courage, faith or strength? Let us not grieve. Let us rather go away strengthened and inspired by this wonderful life that has just passed. In us, let all his hopes and aspirations come to reality.

"His death was happy. It was as he wished it, Beatrice, for his one great ambition was fully granted—to know the reality of the upper world, the winds of heaven and the sun! Impossible for him to have survived the great change. Death was inevitable and right. He wanted rest, and rest is his, at last.

"We must be true to all he thought us, you and I—to all he believed us, even demigods! He shall inspire and enlighten us, O my love; and with his memory to guide us, faith and fortitude shall not be lacking.

"Now, we must go. Work waits for us. Everything is yet to be planned and done. The world and its redemption lie before us. Come!"

He led the girl away. As by mutual understanding they returned to where the biplane lay, symbol of their conquest of nature, epitome of hopes.

Near it, on the edge of the Abyss, they rested, hand in hand. In silence they sat thinking, for a space. And ever higher and more warmly burned the sun; the breeze of June was sweet to them, long-used to fogs and damp and dark; the boundless flood of light across the azure thrilled them with aspiration and with joy.

Life had begun again for them and for the world, life, even there in the presence of death. Life was continuing, developing, expanding—life and its immortal sister, Love!

CHAPTER II

EASTWARD HO!

Practical matters now for a time thrust introspection, dreams and sentiment aside. The morning was already half spent, and in spite of sorrow, hunger had begun to assert itself; for since time was, no two such absolutely vigorous and healthy humans had ever set foot on earth as Beatrice and Allan.

The man gathered brush and dry-kye and proceeded to make a fire, not far from the precipice, but well out of sight of the patriarch's grave. He fetched a generous heap of wood from the neighboring forest, and presently a snapping blaze flung its smoke-banner down the breeze.

Soon after Beatrice had raided the supplies on board the Pauillac—fish, edible seaweed, and the eggs of the strange birds of the Abyss—and with the skill and speed of long experience was getting an excellent meal. Allan meantime brought water from a spring near by. And the two ate in silence, cross-legged on the warm, dry sand.

"What first, now?" queried the man, when they were satisfied. "I've been thinking of about fifteen hundred separate things to tackle, each one more important than all the others put together. How are we going to begin again? That's the question!"

She drew from her warm bosom the golden cylinder and chain.

"Before we make any move at all," she answered, "I think we ought to see what's in this record—if it is a record. Don't you?"

"By Jove, you're right! Shall I open it for you?"

But already the massively chased top lay unscrewed in her hand. Within the cylinder a parchment roll appeared.

A moment later she had spread it on her knee, taking care not to tear the ancient, crackling skin whereon faint lines of writing showed.

Stern bent forward, eager and breathless. The girl, too, gazed with anxious eyes at the dim script, all but illegible with age and wear.

"You're right, Allan," said she. "This is some kind of record, some direction as to the final history of the few survivors after the great catastrophe. Oh! Look, Allan—it's fading already in the sunlight. Quick, read it quick, or we shall lose it all!"

Only too true. The dim lines, perhaps fifteen hundred years

old, certainly never exposed to sunlight since more than a thousand, were already growing weaker; and the parchment, too, seemed crumbling into dust. Its edges, where her fingers held it, already were breaking away into a fine, impalpable powder.

"Quick, Allan! Quick!"

Together they read the clumsy scrawl, their eyes leaping along the lines, striving to grasp the meaning ere it were too late.

TO ANY WHO AT ANY TIME MAY EVER REVISIT THE UPPER WORLD

Be it known that two records have been left covering our history from the time of the cataclysm in 1920 till we entered the Chasm in 1957. One is in the Great Cave in Medicine Bow Range, Colorado, near the ruins of Dexter. Exact location, 106 degrees, 11 minutes, 3 seconds west; 40 degrees, 22 minutes, 6 seconds north. Record is in left, or northern branch of Cave, 327 yards from mouth, on south wall, 4 feet 6 inches from floor. The other—

"Where? Where?" cried Beatrice. A portion of the record was gone; it had crumbled even as they read.

"Easy does it, girl! Don't get excited," Allan cautioned, but his face was pale and his hand trembled as he sought to steady and protect the parchment from the breeze.

Together they pieced out a few of the remaining words, for now the writing was but a pale blur, momentarily becoming dimmer and more dim.

... Cathedral on ... known as Storm King ... River ... crypt under ... this was agreed on ... never returned but may possibly ... signed by us on this 12th day ...

They could read no more, for now the record was but a disintegrating shell in the girl's hands, and even as they looked the last of the writing vanished, as breath evaporates from a window-pane.

Allan whirled toward the fire, snatched out a still-glowing stick, and in the sand traced figures.

"Quick! What was that? 106-11-3, West—Forty—"

"Forty, 22, north," she prompted.

"How many seconds? You remember?"

"No." Slowly she shook her head. "Five, wasn't it?"

Eagerly he peered at the record, but every trace was gone.

"Well, no matter about the seconds," he judged. "I'll enter these data on our diary, in the Pauillac, anyhow. We can remember the ruins of Dexter and Medicine Bow Range; also the cathedral on Storm King. Put the fragments of the parchment back into the case, Beta. Maybe we can yet preserve them, and by some chemical means or other bring out the writing again. As it is, I guess we've got the most important facts; enough to go on, at any rate."

She replaced the crumbled record in the golden cylinder and once more screwed on the cap. Allan got up and walked to the airplane, where, among their scanty effects, was the brief diary and set of notes he had been keeping since the great battle with the Lanskaarn.

Writing on his fish-skin tablets, with his bone stylus, dipped in his little stone jar of cuttle-fish ink, he carefully recorded the geographical location. Then he went back to Beatrice, who still sat in the midmorning sunlight by the fire, very beautiful and dear to him.

"If we can find those records, we'll have made a long step toward solving the problem of how to handle the Folk. They aren't exactly what one would call an amenable tribe, at best. We need their history, even the little of it that the records must contain, for surely there must be names and events in them of great value in our work of trying to bring these people to the surface and recivilize them."

"Well, what's to hinder our getting the records now?" she asked seriously, with wonder in her gray and level gaze.

"That, for one thing!"

He gestured at the Abyss.

"It's a good six or seven hundred miles wide, and we already know how deep it is. I don't think we want to risk trying to cross it again and running out of fuel en route! Volplaning down to the village is quite a different proposition from a straight-away flight across!"

She sat pensive a moment.

"There must be some way around," said she at last. "Otherwise a party of survivors couldn't have set out for Storm King on the Hudson to deposit a set of records there!"

"That's so, too. But—remember? 'Never returned.' I figure it this way: A party of the survivors probably started for New York, exploring. The big, concrete cathedral on Storm King—it was new in 1916, you remember—was known the country over as the most massive piece of architecture this side of the pyramids. They must have planned to leave one set of records there, in case the east, too, was devastated. Well—"

"Do you suppose they succeeded?"

"No telling. At any rate, there's a chance of it. And as for this Rocky Mountain cache, that's manifestly out of the question, for now."

"So then?" she queried eagerly.

"So then our job is to strike for Storm King. Incidentally we can revisit Hope Villa, our bungalow on the banks of the Hudson. It's been a year since we left it, almost—ten months, at any rate. Gad! What marvels and miracles have happened since then, Beta—what perils, what escapes! Wouldn't you like to see our little nest again? We could rest up and plan and strengthen ourselves for the greater tasks ahead. And then—"

He paused, a change upon his face, his eyes lighting with a sudden glow. She saw and understood; and her breast rose with sudden keen emotion.

"You mean," whispered she, "in our own home?"

"Where better?"

She paled as, kneeling beside her, he flung a powerful arm about her, and pulled her to him, breathing heavily.

"Don't! Don't!" she forbade. "No, no, Allan—there's so much work to do—you mustn't!"

To her a vision rose of dream-children—strong sons and daughters yet unborn. Their eyes seemed smiling, their fingers closing on hers. Cloudlike, yet very real, they beckoned her, and in her stirred the call of motherhood—of life to be. Her heart-strings echoed to that harmony; it seemed already as though a tiny head, downy—soft, was nestling in her bosom, while eager lips quested, quested.

"No, Allan! No!"

Almost fiercely she flung him back and stood up.

"Come!" said she. "Let us start at once. Nothing remains for us to do here. Let us go—home!"

An hour later the Pauillac spiralled far aloft, above the edge of the Abyss, then swept into its eastward tangent, and in swift, droning flight rushed toward the longed-for place of dreams, of rest, of love.

Before them stretched infinities of labor and tremendous struggle; but for a little space they knew they now were free for this, the consummation of their dreams, of all their hopes, their happiness, their joy.

CHAPTER III

CATASTROPHE!

Toward five o'clock next afternoon, from the swooping back of the air-dragon they sighted a far blue ribbon winding among wooded heights, and knew Hudson once more lay before them.

The girl's heart leaped for joy at thought of once again seeing Hope Villa, the beach, the garden, the sun-dial—all the thousand and one little happy and pleasant things that, made by them in the heart of the vast wilderness, had brought them such intimate and unforgetable delight.

"There it is, Allan!" cried she, pointing. "There's the river again. We'll soon be home now—home again!"

He smiled and nodded, watchful at the wheel, and swung the biplane a little to southward, in the direction where he judged the bungalow must lie.

Weary they both were, yet full of life and strength. The trip from the chasm had been tedious, merely a long succession of hours in the rushing air, with unbroken forest, hills, lakes, rivers, and ever more forest steadily rolling away to westward like a vast carpet a thousand feet below.

No sign of man, no life, no gap in nature's all-embracing sway. Even the occasional heap of ruins marking the grave of some forgotten city served only to intensify the old half-terror they had felt, when flying for the first time, at thought of the tremendous desolation of the world.

The shining plain of Lake Erie had served the first day as a landmark to keep them true to their course.

That night they had stopped at the ruins of Buffalo, where they had camped in the open, and where next morning Stern had fully replenished his fuel-tanks with the usual supplies of alcohol from the debris of two or three large drug-stores.

From Buffalo eastward, over almost the same course along which the hurricane of ten months ago had driven them, battling at random with the gale, they steered by the compass. Toward mid-morning they saw a thin line of smoke arising in the far north, answered by still another on the hills beyond, but to these signs they gave no heed.

Already they had seen and scorned them during their first stay at the bungalow. They felt that nothing more was to be seriously feared from such survivors of the Horde as had escaped the great Battle of the Tower—a year and a half previously.

"Those chaps won't bother us again; I'm sure of that!" said Allan, nodding toward the smoke-columns that rose, lazily blue, on the horizon. "The scare we threw into them in Madison Forest will last them one while!"

Still in this confident, defiant mood it was that they sighted the river again and watched it rapidly broaden as the Pauillac, in a long series of flat arcs, spurned the June air and whirled them onward toward their goal.

Nearer the Hudson drew, and nearer still; and now its untroubled azure, calm save for a few cat's-paws of breeze that idled on the surface, stretched almost beneath them in their rapid flight.

"We're still a little too far north, I see," the man judged, and swept the biplane round to southward.

The ruins of Newburgh lay presently upon their right. Soon after the crumbled walls of West Point's pride slid past in silence, save for the chatter of the engines, the whirling roar of the pro-peller-blades' vast energy.

No boat now vexed the flood. Upon its bosom neither steam nor sail now plowed a furrow. Along the banks no speeding train flung its smoke-pennant to the wind. Primeval silence, universal calm, wrapped all things.

Beatrice shuddered slightly. Now that they were nearing "home" the desolation seemed more appalling.

"Oh, Allan, is it possible all this will ever be peopled again—alive?"

"Certain to be! Once we get those records and begin trans-planting the Merucaans, the rest will be only a matter of time!"

She made no answer, but in her eyes shone pride that he could know such visions, have such faith.

Already they recognized the ruins of Nyack, and beyond them the point in the river behind which, they knew, lay Hope Villa, nestling in its gardens, its little sphere of cultivation hewn from the very heart of the dense wilderness.

Allan slackened speed, crossed to the eastern bank, and jock-eyed for a safe landing.

The point slipped backward and away. There, right ahead, they caught a glimpse of the long white beach where they had fished and bathed and built their boat-house, and whence in their little yawl they had ten months before started on their trip of exploration—a trip destined to end so strangely in the Abyss.

"Home! Home!" cried Beta, the quick tears starting to her

lids. "Oh, home again!"

Already the great plane was swooping downward toward the beach, hardly a mile away, when a harsh shout escaped the man.

"Look! Canoes! My God—what—"

As the drive of the Pauillac opened up the concave of the sand and brought its whole length to view, Stern and the girl suddenly became aware of trouble.

There, strung along the beach irregularly, they all at once made out ten, twenty, thirty boats. Still afar, they could see these were the same rough bancas such as they had seen after the battle—bancas in one of which they two had escaped up-river!

"Boats! The Horde again!"

Even as he shouted a tiny, black, misshapen little figure ran crouching out onto the sand. Another followed and a third, and now a dozen showed there, very distinct and hideous, upon the white crescent.

Stern's heart went sick within him A terrible rage welled up—a hate such as he had never believed possible to feel.

Wild imprecations struggled to be voiced. He snapped his lips together in a thin line, his eyes narrowed, and his face went gray.

"The infernal little beasts!" he gritted. "Tried to trap us in the tower—cut our boat loose afterward—and now invading us! Don't know when they're licked, the swine!"

Beatrice had lost her color now. Milk-white her face was; her eyes grew wide with terror; she strove to speak, but could not.

Her hand went out in a wild, repelling gesture, as though by the very power of her love for home she could protect it now against the incursion of these foul, distorted, inhuman little monsters.

Stern acted quickly. He had been about to cut off power and coast for the beach; but now he veered suddenly to eastward again, rotated the rising-plane, and brought the Pauillac up at a sharp tilt. Banking, he advanced the spark a notch; the engine shrilled a half-tone higher, and with increased speed the aero lifted them bravely in a long and rising swoop.

He snatched his automatic from its holster on his hip and as the plane swept past the beach, down-stream, let fly a spatter of steel jacketed souvenirs at the fast-thickening pack on the sand.

Far up to the girl and him, half heard through the clatter of the motors, they sensed a thin, defiant, barbarous yell—a yapping chorus, bestial and horrible.

Again Stern fired.

He could see quick spurts of water jet up along the edge of the sand, and one of the creatures fell, but this was only a chance shot.

At that distance, firing from a swift-skimming plane, he knew he could do no execution, and with a curse slid the pistol back again into its place.

"Oh, for a dirigible and a few Pulverite bombs, same as we had in the tower!" he wished. "I'd clean the blighters out mighty quick!"

But now Beatrice was pointing, with a cry of dismay, down, away at the bungalow itself, which had for a moment become visible at the far end of the clearing as the Pauillac scudded past.

Even as Stern thought: "Odd, but they're not afraid of us—a flying-machine means nothing to them, does not terrify them as it would human savages. They're too debased even to feel fear!"—even as this thought crossed his brain he, too, saw the terrible thing that the girl had cried out at sight of.

"My God!" he shouted. "This—this is too much!"

All about the bungalow, their home, the scene of such happy hours, so many dreams and hopes, such heart-enthralling labors, hundreds of the Horde were swarming.

Like vicious parasites attacking prey, they overran the garden, the grounds, even the house itself.

As in a flash, Stern knew all his work of months must be undone—the fruit-trees he had rescued from the forest be cut down or broken, the bulbs and roots in the garden uptorn, even the hedges and fences trampled flat.

Worse still, the bungalow was being destroyed! Rather, its contents, since the concrete walls defied the venomous troop.

They knew, at any rate, the use of fire, and not so swiftly skimmed the Pauillac as to prevent both Stern and Beatrice seeing a thin but ominous thread of smoke out-curling on the June air from one of the living-room windows.

With an imprecation of unutterable hate and rage, yet impotent to stay the ravishment of Hope Villa, Stern brought the machine round in a long spiral.

For a moment the wild, suicidal idea possessed him to land on the beach, after all, and charge the little slate-blue devils who had evidently piled all the furnishings together in the bungalow and were now burning them.

He longed for slaughter now; he lusted blood—the blood of the Anthropoid pack which from the beginning had hung upon his flank and been as a thorn unto his flesh.

He seemed to feel the joy of rushing them, an automatic in each hand spitting death, just as he had mown down the

Lanskaarn in the Battle of the Wall, down below in the Abyss. Even though he knew the inevitable ends poisoned spear-thrust, a wound with one of those terribly envenomed arrows—he felt no fear.

Revenge! If he could only feel its sweetness, death had no terrors.

Common sense instantly sobered him and dispelled these vain ideas. The bungalow, after all, was not vital to his future or the girl's. Barring the set of encyclopedias on metal plates, everything else could be replaced with sufficient labor. Only a madman would risk a fight with such a Horde in company with a woman.

Not now were he and Beatrice entrenched in a strong tower, with terrible explosives. Now they were in the open, armed only with revolvers. For the present there was no redress.

"Beta," cried he, "we're up against it this time for fair—and we can't hit back!"

"Our bungalow! Our precious home!"

"I know." He saw that she was crying: "It's a rotten shame and all that, but it isn't fatal."

He brought the Pauillac down-wind again, coasting high over the bungalow, whence smoke now issued ever more and more thickly.

"We're simply hamstrung this time, that's all. Where those devils have come from and how many there may be, God knows. Thousands, perhaps; the woods may be full of em. It's lucky for us they didn't attack while we were there!

"Now—well, the only thing to do is let 'em have their way for the present. Eventually—"

"Oh, can't we ever get rid of the horrid little beasts for good?"

"We can and will!" He spoke very grimly, soaring the machine still higher over the river and once more coming round above the upper end of the beach. "One of these days there's got to be a final reckoning, but not yet!"

"So it's good-by to Hope Villa, Allan? There's no way?"

"It's good-by. Humanly speaking, none."

"Couldn't we land, blockade ourselves in the boat-house, and—"

Her eyes sparkled with the boldness of the plan—its peril, its possibilities. But Allan only shook his head.

"And expose the Pauillac on the beach?" he asked. "One good swing with a war-club into the motor and then a week's siege and slow starvation, with a final rush—interesting, but not practical, little girl. No, no; the better part of valor is to recognize force majeure and wait! Remember what we've said already? 'Je recule pour mieux sauter?' Wait till we get a fresh start on these hell-hounds; we'll jump 'em far enough!"

The bungalow now lay behind. The whole clearing seemed alive with the little blue demons, like vermin crawling everywhere. Thicker and thicker now the smoke was pouring upward. The scene was one of utter desolation.

Then suddenly it faded. The plane had borne its riders onward and away from the range of vision. Again only dense forest lay below, while to eastward sparkled the broad reach where, in the first days of their happiness at Hope Villa, the girl and Allan had fished and bathed.

Her tears were unrestrained at last; but Allan, steadying the wheel with one hand, drew an arm about her and kissed and comforted her.

"There, there, little girl! The world's not ended yet, even if they have burned up our home-made mission furniture! Come, Beatrice, no tears—we've other things to think of now!"

"Where away, since our home's gone?" she queried pitifully.

"Where away? Why, Storm King, of course! And the cathedral and the records, and—and—"

CHAPTER IV

"TOMORROW IS OUR WEDDING-DAY"

Purple and gold the light of that dying day still glowed across the western sky when the stanch old Pauillac, heated yet throbbing with power, skimmed the last league and swung the last great bend of the river that hid old Storm King from the wanderers' eager sight.

Stern's eyes brightened at vision of that vast, rugged head-land, forest-clad and superb in the approaching twilight. Beatrice, weary now and spent—for the long journeys, the excitements and griefs of the day had worn her down despite her strength—paled a little and grew pensive as the massive structure of the cathedral loomed against the sky-line.

What thoughts were hers now that the goal lay near—what longings, fears and hopes, what exultation and what pain? She shivered slightly; but perhaps the evening coolness at that height had pierced her cloak. Her hands clasped tightly, she tried to smile but could not.

Allan could notice nothing of all this. His gaze was anxiously bent on the earth below, to find a landing for the great machine. He skimmed the broad brow of the mountain, hardly a hundred feet above the spires of the massive concrete pile that still reared itself steadfastly upon the height facing the east.

All about it the dense unbroken forest spread impenetrable to the eye. Below the bold breast of the cliff a narrow strip of beach appeared.

"Hard job to land, that's one sure thing!" exclaimed the man, peering at the inhospitable contours of the land. "No show to make it on top of the mountain, and if we take the beach it means a most tremendous climb up the cliff or through the forest on the flank. Here is a situation, Beatrice! Now—ah—see there? Look! that barren ridge to westward!"

Half a mile back from the river on the western slope of the highlands, a spur of Storm King stretched water-worn and bare, a sandy spit dotted only sparsely with scrub-pine.

"It's that, or nothing!" cried the man, banking in a wide sweep.

"Can you make it? Even the clearest space at this end is ter-ribly short!"

Allan laughed and cut off power. In the old days not for ten thousand dollars would he have tried so ticklish a descent, but now his mettle was of sterner stuff and his skill with the machine developed to a point where man and biplane seemed almost one organism.

With a swift rush the Pauillac coasted down. He checked her at precisely the right moment, as the sand seemed whirling up to meet them, swerved to dodge a fire-blasted trunk, and with a shout took the earth.

The plane bounced, creaked, skidded on the long runners he had fitted to her, and with a lurch came to rest not ten yards from an ugly stump dead ahead.

"Made it, by Heaven!" he exulted. "But a few feet more and it wouldn't have been—well, no matter. We're here, anyhow. Now, supper and a good sleep. And tomorrow, the cathedral!"

He helped the girl alight, for she was cramped and stiff. Presently their camp-fire cheered the down-drawing gloom, as so many other times in such strange places. And before long their evening meal was in course of preparation, close by a great glacial boulder at the edge of the sand-barren.

In good comradeship they ate, then wheeled the biplane over to the rock, and under the shelter of its wide-spreading wings made their camp for the night. An hour or so they sat talking of many things—their escape from the Abyss, the patriarch's death, their trip east again, the loss of their little home, their plans, their hopes, their work.

Beatrice seemed to grieve more than Stern over the destruction of the bungalow. So much of her woman's heart had gone into the making of that nest, so many thoughts had centered on a return to it once more, that now when it lay in ruins through the spiteful mischief of the Horde, she found sorrow knocking insistently at the gates of her soul. But Allan comforted her as best he might.

"Never you mind, little girl!" said he bravely. "It's only an incident, after all. A year from now another and a still more beautiful home will shelter us in some more secure location. And there'll be human companionship, too, about us. In a year many of the Folk will have been brought from the depths. In a year miracles may happen—even the greatest one of all!"

Her eyes met his a moment by the ruddy fire-glow and held true.

"Yes," answered she, "even the greatest in the world!"

A sudden tenderness swept over him at thought of all that had been and was still to be, at sight of this woman's well-loved face irradiated by the leaping blaze—her face now just a little wan with long fatigues and sad as though with realization, with some compelling inner sense of vast, impending responsibilities.

He gathered her in his strong arms, he drew her yielding body close, and kissed her very gently.

"Tomorrow!" he whispered. "Do you realize it?"

"Tomorrow," she made answer, her breath mingling with his. "Tomorrow, Allan—one page of life forever closed, another opened. Oh, may it be for good—may we be very strong and very wise!"

Neither spoke for the space of a few heart-beats, while the wind made a vague, melancholy music in the sentinel tree-tops and the snapping sparks danced upward by the rock.

"Life, all life—just dancing sparks—then gone!" said Beatrice slowly. "And yet—yet it is good to have lived, Allan. Good to have lighted the black mystery of the universe, formless and endless and inscrutable, by even so brief a flicker!"

"Is it my little pessimist tonight?" he asked. "Too tired, that's all. In the morning things will look different. You must smile, then, Beta, and not think of formless mystery or—or anything sad at all. For tomorrow is our wedding-day."

He felt her catch her breath and tremble just a bit.

"Yes, I know. Our wedding-day, Allan. Surely the strangest since time began. No friends, no gifts, no witnesses, no minister, no—"

"There, there!" he interrupted, smiling. "How can my little girl be so wrong-headed? Friends? Why, everything's our friend! All nature is our friend—the whole life-process is our friend and ally! Gifts? What need have we of gifts? Aren't you my gift, surely the best gift that a man ever had since the beginning of all things? Am I not yours?

"Minister? Priest? We need none! The world-to-be shall have got far away from such, far beyond its fairy-tale stage, its weaknesses and fears of the Unknown, which alone explain their existence. Here on Storm King, under the arches of the old cathedral our clasped hands, our—mutual words of love and trust and honor—these shall suffice. The river and the winds and forest, the sunlight and the sky, the whole infinite expanse of Nature herself shall be our priest and witnesses. And never has a wedding been so true, so solemn and so holy as yours and mine shall be. For you are mine, my Beatrice, and I am yours—forever!"

A little silence, while the flames leaped higher and the shadows deepened in the dim aisles of the fir-forest all about them. In the vast canopy of evening sky clustering star-points had begun to shimmer.

Redly the camp-fire lighted man and woman there alone together in the wild. For them there was no sense of isolation nor any loneliness. She was his world now, and he hers.

Up into his eyes she looked fairly and bravely, and her full lips smiled.

"Forgive me, Allan!" she whispered. "It was only a mood, that's all. It's passed now—it won't come back. Only forgive me, boy!"

"My dear, brave girl!" he murmured, smoothing the thick hair back from her brow. "Never complaining, never repining, never afraid!"

Their lips met again and for a time the girl's heart throbbed on his.

Afar a wolf's weird, tremulous call drifted down-wind. An owl, disturbed in its nocturnal quest, hooted upon the slope above to eastward; and across the darkening sky reeled an unsteady bat, far larger than in the old days when there were cities on the earth and ships upon the sea.

The fire burned low. Allan arose and flung fresh wood upon it, while sheaves of winking light gyrated upward through the air. Then he returned to Beatrice and wrapped her in his cloak.

And for a long, long time they both talked of many things—intimate, solemn, wondrous things—together in the night.

And the morrow was to be their wedding-day.

CHAPTER V

THE SEARCH FOR THE RECORDS

Morning found them early astir, to greet the glory of June sunlight over the shoulder of Storm King. A perfect morning, if ever any one was perfect since the world began—soft airs stirring in the forest, golden robins' full-throated song, the melody of the scarlet tropic birds they had named "fire-birds" for want of any more descriptive title, the chatter of gray squirrels on the branches overhead, all blent, under a sky of wondrous azure, to tell them of life, full and abundant, joyous and kind.

Two of the squirrels had to die, for breakfast, which Beta cooked while Allan quested the edges of the wood for the ever-present berries. They drank from a fern-embowered spring a hundred yards or so to south of their camp in the forest, and felt the vigorous tides of life throb hotly through their splendid bodies.

Allan got together the few simple implements at their disposal for the expedition—his ax, a torch made of the brown weed of the Abyss, oil-soaked and bound with wire that fastened it to a metal handle, and a skin bag of the rude matches he had manufactured in the village of the Folk.

"Now then, en marche!" said he at length. "The old cathedral and the records are awaiting a morning call from us—and there are all the wedding preparations to make as well. We've got no time to lose!"

She laughed happily with a blush and gave him her hand.

"Lead on, Sir Knight!" she jested. "I'm yours by right of capture and conquest, as in the good old days!"

"The good new days will have better and higher standards," he answered gravely. "Today, one age is closed, another opened for all time."

Hand in hand they ascended the barren spur to eastward, and presently reached the outposts of the forest that rose in close-ranked majesty over the brow of Storm King.

The going proved hard, for with the warmer climate that now favored the country, undergrowth had sprung up far more luxuriantly than in the days of the old-time civilization; but Stern and Beatrice were used to labor, and together—he ahead to break or cut a path—they struggled through the wood.

Half an hour's climb brought them to their first dim sight of the massive towers of the cathedral, rising beyond the tangle of trees, majestic in the morning sun.

Soon after they had made their way close up to the huge, lichen-crusted walls, and in the shadow of the gigantic pile slowly explored round to the vast portals facing eastward over the Hudson.

"Wonderful work, magnificent proportions and design," Stern commented, as they stopped at last on the broad, debris-littered steps and drew breath. "Brick and stone have long since perished. Even steel has crumbled. But concrete seems eternal. Why, the building's practically intact even today, after ten centuries of absolute abandonment. A week's work with a force of men would quite restore it. The damage it's suffered is absolutely insignificant. Concrete. A lesson to be learned, is it not, in our rebuilding of the world?"

The mighty temple stood, in fact, almost as men had left it in the long ago, when the breath of annihilation had swept a withering blast over the face of the earth. The broad grounds and driveways that had led up to the entrance had, of course, long since absolutely vanished under rank growths.

Grass flourished in the gutters and on the Gothic finials; the gargoyles were bearded with vines and fern-clusters; the flying buttresses and mullions stood green with moss; and in the vegetable mold that had for centuries accumulated on the steps and in the vestibule—for the oaken doors had crumbled to powder—many a bright-flowered plant raised its blossoms to the sun.

The tall memorial windows and the great rose-window in the eastern facade had long since been shattered out of their frames by hail and tempest. But the main body of the cathedral seemed yet as massively intact as when the master-builders of the twentieth century had taken down the last scaffold, and when the gigantic organ had first pealed its "Laus Deo" through the vaulted apse.

Together they entered the vast silent space, and—awed despite themselves—gazed in wonder at the beauties of this, the most magnificent temple ever built in the western hemisphere.

The marble floor was covered now with windrows of dead leaves and pine-spills, and with the litter from myriads of birds'-nests that sheltered themselves on achitraves and galleries, and on the lofty capitals of the fluted pillars which rose, vistalike, a hundred feet above the clear-story, spraying out into a wondrous complexity of ribs to sustain the marvelous concrete vaultings full two hundred feet in air.

Through the shattered windows broad slants of sunshine fell athwart the walls and floor. Swallows chirped and twittered far aloft, or winged their swift way through the dusky upper spaces, passing at will in or out the mullioned gaps whence all the painted glass had long since fallen.

An air of mystery, of long expectancy seemed brooding everywhere; it seemed almost as though the spirit of the past were waiting to receive them—waiting now, as it had waited a thousand years, patiently, inexorably, untiringly for those to come who should some day reclaim the hidden secrets in the crypt, once more awaken human echoes in the vault, and so redeem the world. "Waiting!" breathed Stern, as if the thought hung pregnant in the very air. "Waiting all these long centuries—for us! For you, Beatrice, for me! And we are here, at last, we of the newer time; and here we shall be one. The symbol of the pillars, mounting, ever mounting toward the infinite, the hope of life eternal, the majesty and mystery of this great temple, welcome us! Come!"

He took her hand again and now in silence they walked forward noiselessly over the thick leaf-carpet on the pavement of rare marble.

"Oh, Allan, I feel so very small in here!" she whispered, drawing close to him. "You and I, all alone in this tremendous place built for thousands—"

"You and I are the world today!" he answered very gravely; and so together they made way toward the vast transept, arched with a bewildering lacery of vaultings.

All save the concrete had long vanished. No traces now remained of pews, or railings, altars, pulpits, or any of the fittings of the vast cathedral.

Majestic in its naked strength, the building stood in light and shadow, here banded with strong sun, there lost in cool purple shade that foiled the eye far up among the hanging miracles of the roof.

At the transept-crossing they stood amazed; for here the flutings ran up five hundred feet inside the stupendous central spire, among a marvelous filigree of windows which diminished toward the top—a lacework as of frost-patterns etched into the solid substance of the fleche.

"Higher than that, more massive and more beautiful the buildings of the future shall arise," said Allan slowly after a pause. "But they shall not serve creed or faction. They shall be for all mankind, for the great race still to come. Beauty shall be its heritage, its right.

" 'And loveliness shall crown the waiting world As with a garland of immortal joy!'

"But come, come, Beatrice—there's work to do. The records, girl! We mustn't stand here admiring architecture and dreaming dreams while those records are still undiscovered. Down into the crypt we go, to dig among the relics of a vanished age!"

"The crypt, Allan? Where is it?"

"If I remember rightly—and at the time this cathedral was built I followed the plans with some care—the entrance is back of the main southern cluster of pillars over there at the transept-crossing. Come on, Beta. In a minute we can see whether thousand-year-old memories are any good or not!"

Quickly he led the way, ax and torch in hand, and as they rounded the group of massive buttresses whence sprang the pillars for the groin-vaults aloft, a cry of satisfaction escaped him, followed by a word of quick astonishment.

"What is it, Allan?" exclaimed the girl. "Anything wrong? Or—"

The man stood peering with wide eyes; then suddenly he knelt and began pawing over the little heap of vegetable drift that had accumulated along the wall.

"It's here, all right," said he. "There's the door, right in front of us—but what I don't understand is—this!"

"What, Allan? Is there anything wrong?"

"Not wrong, perhaps, but devilish peculiar!"

Speaking, he raised his hand to her. The fingers held an arrow-head of flint.

"There's been a battle here, that's sure," said he. "Look, spear-points—shattered!"

He had already uncovered three obsidian blades. The broken tips proved how forcibly they had been driven against the stone in the long ago.

"What? A—"

His fingers closed on a small, hollow shell of gold.

"A molar, so help me! All that's left of some forgotten white man who fell here, at the door, a thousand years ago!"

Speechless, the girl took the shell from him and examined it.

"You're right, Allan," she answered. "This certainly is a hollow gold crown. Any one can see that, in spite of the patina that's formed over the metal. Why—what can it all mean?"

"Search me! The patriarch's record gave the impression that this eastern expedition set out within thirty years or so of the catastrophe. Well, in that short time it doesn't seem possible there could have developed savages fighting with flints and so on. But that there certainly was a battle here at this door, and that the cathedral was used as a fort against some kind of invasion is positively certain.

"Why, look at the chips of concrete knocked off the jamb of the door here! Must have been some tall mace-work where you're standing, Beta! If we could know the complete story of this expedition, its probable failure to reach New York, its entrapment here, the siege and the inevitable tragedy of its end—starvation, sorties, repulses, hand-to-hand fighting at the outer gates, in the nave, here at the crypt door, perhaps on the stairs and in the vaults below—then defeat and slaughter and extinction—what a tremendous drama we could formulate!"

Beatrice nodded. Plain to see, the thought depressed her.

"Death, everywhere—" she began, but Allan laughed.

"Life, you mean!" he rallied. "Come, now, this does no good, poking in the rubbish of a distant tragedy. Real work awaits us. Come!"

He picked up the torch, and with his primitive but serviceable matches lighted it. The smoke rose through the silent air of the cathedral, up into a broad sunlit zone from a tall window in the transept, where it writhed blue and luminous.

A single blow of Allan's ax shattered the last few shreds of oaken plank that still hung from the eroded hinges of the door. In front of the explorers a flight of concrete steps descended, winding darkly to the crypt beneath.

Allan went first, holding the torch high to light the way.

"The records!" he exclaimed. "Soon, soon we shall know the secrets of the past!"

CHAPTER VI

TRAPPED!

Some thirty steps the way descended, ending in a straight and very narrow passage. The air, though somewhat chill, was absolutely dry and perfectly respirable, thanks to the enormously massive foundation of solid concrete which formed practically one solid monolith six hundred feet long by two hundred and fifty broad—a monolith molded about the crypt and absolutely protecting it from every outside influence.

"Not even the Great Pyramid of Ghizeh could afford a more perfect—hello, what's this?"

Allan stopped short, staring downward at the floor. His voice reechoed strangely in the restricted space.

"A skeleton, so help me!"

True indeed. At one side of the passage, lying in a position that strongly suggested death in a crouching, despairing attitude—death by starvation rather than by violence—a little clutter of human bones gleamed white under the torch-flare.

"A skeleton—the first one of our vanished race we've ever found!" exclaimed the man. "All the remains in New York, you remember, down in the subway or in any of the buildings, were invariably little piles of impalpable dust mixed with coins and bits of rusted metal. But this—it's absolutely intact!"

"The dry air and all—" suggested Beatrice.

Stern nodded.

"Yes," he answered. "Intact, so far. But—"

He stirred the skull with his foot. Instantly it vanished into powder.

"Just as I thought," said he. "No chance to give a decent burial to this or any other human remains we may come across here. The slightest disturbance totally disintegrates them. But with this it's different!"

He picked up a revolver, hardly rusted at all, that lay near at hand.

"Cartridges; look!" cried Beatrice, pointing.

"That's so, too—a score or more!"

Lying in an irregular oval that plainly told of a vanished cartridge-belt, a string of cartridges trailed on the concrete floor.

"H-m-m-m! Just for an experiment, let's see!" murmured the engineer.

Already he had slipped in a charge.

"Steady, Beatrice!" he cautioned, and, pointing down the passage, pulled trigger.

Flame stabbed the half-dark and the crashing detonation rang in their ears.

"What do you think of that?" cried Stern exultantly. "Talk about your miracles! A thousand years and—"

Beatrice grasped him by the arm and pointed downward. Astonished, he stared. The rest of the skeleton had vanished. In its place now only a few handfuls of dust lay on the floor.

"Well, I'll be—" the man exclaimed. "Even that does the trick, eh? H-m! It would be a joke, now, wouldn't it, if the records should act the same way? Come on, Beta; this is all very interesting, but it isn't getting us anywhere. We've got to be at work!"

He pocketed the new-found gun and cartridges and once more, torch on high, started down the passage, with the girl at his side.

"See here, Allan!"

"Eh?"

"On the wall here—a painted stripe?"

He held the torch close and scrutinized the mark.

"Looks like it. Pretty well gone by now—just a flake here and a daub there, but I guess it once was a broad band of white. A guide?"

They moved forward again. The strip ended in a blur that might once have been an inscription. Here, there, a letter faintly showed, but not one word could now be made out.

"Too bad," he mused. "It must have been mighty important or they wouldn't have—"

"Here's a door, Allan!"

"So? That's right. Now this looks like business at last!"

He examined the door by the unsteady flicker of the torch. It was of iron, still intact, and fastened by a long iron bar dropped into massive metal staples.

"Beat it in with the ax?" she queried.

"No. The concussion might reduce everything inside to dust. Ah! Here's a padlock and a chain!"

Carefully he studied the chain beneath bent brows.

"Here, Beta, you hold the torch, so. That's right. Now then—"

Already he had set the ax-blade between the padlock and the staple. A quick jerk—the lock flew open raspingly. Allan tried to lift the bar, but it resisted.

A tap of the ax and it gave, swinging upward on a pivot. Then a minute later the door swung inward, yielding to his vigorous push.

Together they entered the crypt of solid concrete, a chamber forty feet long by half as wide and vaulted overhead with arches, crowning perhaps twenty feet from the floor.

"More skeletons, so help me!"

Allan pointed at two more on the pavement at the left of the entrance.

"Why—how could that happen?" queried Beta, puzzled. "The door was locked outside!"

"That's so. Either there must be some other exit from this place or there were dissensions and fightings among the party itself. Or these men were wounded and were locked in here for safe-keeping while the others made a sortie and never got back, or—I don't know! Frankly, it's too much for me. If I were a story-writer I might figure it out, but I'm not. No matter, they're here, anyhow; that's all. Here two of our own people died ten centuries ago, trying to preserve civilization and the world's history for future ages, if there were to be any such. Two martyrs. I salute them!"

In silence and awed sympathy they inspected the mournful relics of humanity a minute, but took good care not to touch them.

"And now the records!"

Even as Stern spoke he saw again a dimly painted line, this time upon the floor, all but invisible beneath the dust of centuries that had come from God knows where.

"Come, let's follow the line!" cried he.

It led them straight through the middle of the crypt and to a sort of tunnel-like vault at the far end. This they entered quickly and almost at once knew they had reached the goal of their long quest.

In front of them, about seven feet from the floor, a rough white star had been smeared. Directly below it a kind of alcove or recess appeared, lined with shelves of concrete. What its original purpose may have been it would be hard to say; perhaps it may have been intended as a storage-place for the cathedral archives.

But now the explorers saw it was partly filled with pile on pile of curiously crinkled parchment not protected in any way from the air, not covered or boxed in. To the right, however, stood a massive chest, seemingly of sheet-lead.

"Some sense to the lead," growled Stern; "but why they left their records open to the air, blest if I can see!"

He raised the torch and flared the light along the shelves, and then he understood. For here, there, copper nails glinted dully, lying in dust that once upon a time had been wood.

"I'm wrong, Beta; I apologize to them," Stern exclaimed. "These were all securely boxed once, but the boxes have gone to pieces long since. Dry-rot, you know. Well, let's see what condition the parchments are in!"

She held the torch while he tried to raise one, but it broke at the slightest touch. Again he assayed, and a third time. Same result.

"Great Scott!" he ejaculated, nonplused. "See what we're up against, will you? We've found 'em and they're ours, but—"

They stood considering a minute. All at once a dull metallic clang echoed heavily through the crypt. Despite herself, the girl shuddered. The eerie depths, the gloom, the skeletons had all conspired to shake her nerves.

"What's that?" she whispered, gripping Allan by the arm.

"That? Oh—nothing! Now how the deuce are we going to get at these—"

"It was something, Allan! But what?"

He grew suddenly silent.

"By Jove—it sounded like—the door—"

"The door? Oh, Allan, quick!"

A sudden, irresistible fear fingered at the strings of the man's heart. At the back of his neck he felt the hair begin to lift. Then he smiled by very strength of will.

"Don't be absurd, Beatrice," he managed to say. "It couldn't be, of course. There's no one here. It—"

But already she was out of the alcove. With the torch held high in air, she stood there peering with wide eyes down the long blackness of the crypt, striving to pierce the dark.

Then suddenly he heard her cry of terror.

"The door, Allan! The door! It's shut!"

CHAPTER VII

THE LEADEN CHEST

Not at any time since the girl and he had wakened in the tower, more than a year ago, had Allan felt so compelling a fear as overswept him then. The siege of the Horde at Madison Forest, the plunge down the cataract, the fall into the Abyss and the battle with the Lanskaarn had all taxed his courage to the utmost, but he had met these perils with more calm than he now faced the blank menace of that metal door.

For now no sky overhung him, no human agency opposed him, no counterplay of stress and strife thrilled his blood.

No; the girl and he now were far underground in a crypt, a tomb, walled round with incalculable tons of concrete, barred from the upper world, alone—and for the first time in his life the man knew something of the anguish of unreasoning fear.

Yet he was not bereft of powers of action. Only an instant he stood there motionless and staring; then with a cry, wordless and harsh, he ran toward the barrier.

Beneath his spurning feet the friable skeletons crumbled and vanished; he dashed himself against the door with a curse that was half a prayer; he strove with it—and staggered back, livid and shaken, for it held!

Now Beatrice had reached it, too. In her hand the torch trembled and shook. She tried to speak, but could not. And as he faced her, there in the tomblike vault, their eyes met silently.

A deathly stillness fell, with but their heart-beats and the sputtering of the torch to deepen it.

"Oh!" she gasped, stretching out a hand. "You—we—can't—"

He licked his lips and tried to smile, but failed.

"Don't—don't be afraid, little girl!" he stammered. "This can't hold us, possibly. The chain—I broke it!"

"Yes, but the bar, Allan—the bar! How did you leave the bar?"

"Raised!"

The one word seemed to seal their doom. A shudder passed through Beatrice.

"So then," she choked, "some air-current swung the door shut—and the bar—fell—"

A sudden rage possessed the engineer.

"Damn that infernal staple!" he gritted, and as he spoke the ax swung into air.

"Crash!"

On the metal plates it boomed and echoed thunderously. A ringing clangor vibrated the crypt.

"Crash!"

Did the door start? No; but in the long-eroded plates a jagged dent took form.

Again the ax swung high. Cold though the vault was, sweat globuled his forehead, where the veins had swelled to twisting knots.

"Crash!"

With a wild verberation, a scream of sundered metal and a clatter of flying fragments, the staple gave way. A crack showed round the edge of the iron barrier.

Stern flung his shoulder against the door. Creaking, it swung. He staggered through. One hand groped out to steady him, against the wall. From the other the ax dropped crashing to the floor.

Only a second he stood thus, swaying; then he turned and gathered Beta in his arms. And on his breast she hid her face, from which the roses all had faded quite.

He felt her fighting back the tears, and raised her head and kissed her.

"There, there!" he soothed. "It wasn't anything, after all, you see. But—if we hadn't brought the ax with us—"

"Oh, Allan, let's go now! This crypt—I can't—"

"We will go very soon. But there's no danger now, darling. We're not children, you know. We've still got work to do. We'll go soon; but first, those records!"

"Oh, how can you, after—after what might have been?"

He found the strength to smile.

"I know," he answered, "but it didn't happen, after all. A miss is worth a million miles, dear. That's what life seems to mean to us, and has meant ever since we woke in the tower, peril and risk, labor and toil—and victory! Come, come, let's get to work again, for there's so endlessly much to do."

Calmer grown, the girl found new courage in his eyes and in his strong embrace.

"You're right, Allan. I was a little fool to—"

He stopped her self-reproach with kisses, then picked up the torch from the floor where it had fallen from her nerveless hand.

"If you prefer," he offered. "I'll take you back into the sunlight, and you can sit under the trees and watch the river, while I—"

"Where you are, there am I! Come on, Allan; let's get it over with. Oh, what a coward you must think me!"

"I think you're a woman, and the bravest that ever lived!" he exclaimed vehemently. "Who but you could ever have gone through with me all that has happened? Who could be my mate and face the future as you're doing? Oh, if you only understood my estimate of you!

"But now let's get at those records again. Time's passing, and there must be still no end of things to do!"

He recovered his ax, and with another blow demolished the last fragment of the staple, so that by no possibility could the door catch again.

Then for the second time they penetrated the crypt and the tunnel and once more reached the alcove of the records.

"Beatrice!"

"What is it, Allan?"

"Look! Gone—all gone!"

"Gone? Why, what do you mean? They're—"

"Gone, I tell you! My God! Just a mass of rubbish, powder, dust—"

"But—but how—"

"The concussion of the ax! That must have done it! The violent sound-waves—the air in commotion!"

"But, Allan, it can't be! Surely there must be something left?"

"You see?"

He pointed at the shelves. She stood and peered, with him, at the sad havoc wrought there. Then she stretched out a tentative finger and stirred a little of the detritus.

"Catastrophe!" she cried.

"Yes and no. At any rate, it may have been inevitable."

"Inevitable?"

He nodded.

"Even if this hadn't happened, Beatrice, I'm afraid we never could have moved any of these parchments, or read them, or handled them in any way. Perhaps if we'd had all kinds of proper appliances, glass plates, transparent adhesives, and so on, and a year or two at our disposal, we might have made something out of them, but even so, it's doubtful.

"Of course, in detective stories, Hawkshaw can take the ashes right out of the grate and piece them together and pour chemicals on them and decipher the mystery of the lost rubies, and all that. But this isn't a story, you see; and what's more, Hawkshaw doesn't have to work with ashes nearly a thousand years old. Ten centuries of dry-rot—that's some problem!"

She stood aghast, hardly able to believe her eyes.

"But—but," she finally articulated, "there's the other cache out there in Medicine Bow Range. The cave, you know. And we have the bearings. And some time, when we've got all the leisure in the world and all the necessary appliances—"

"Yes, perhaps. Although, of course, you realize the earth is seventeen degrees out of its normal plane, and every reckoning's shifted. Still, it's a possibility. But for the present there's strictly nothing doing, after all."

"How about that leaden chest?"

She wheeled about and pointed at the other side of the alcove, where stood the metal box, sullen, defiant, secure.

"By Jove, that's so, tool Why, I'd all but forgotten that! You're a brick, Beta! The box, by all means. Perhaps the most important things of all are still in safety there. Who knows?"

"Open it, Allan, and let's see!"

Her recent terror almost forgotten in this new excitement, the girl had begun to get back some of her splendid color. And now, as she stood gazing at the metal chest which still, perhaps, held the most vital of the records, she felt again a thrill of excitement at thought of all its possibilities.

The man, too, gazed at it with keen emotion.

"We've got to be careful this time, Beatrice!" said he. "No more mistakes. If we lose the contents of this chest, Heaven only knows when we may be able to get another glimpse into the past. Frankly, the job of opening it, without ruining the contents, looks pretty stiff. Still, with care it may be done. Let's see, now, what are we up against here?"

He took the torch from her and minutely examined the leaden casket.

It stood on the concrete floor, massive and solid, about three and a half feet high by five long and four wide. So far as he could see, there were neither locks nor hinges. The cover seemed to have been hermetically sealed on. Still visible were the marks of the soldering-iron, in a ragged line, about three inches from the top.

"The only way to get in here is to cut it open," said Allan at last. "If we had any means of melting the solder, that would be better, of course, but there's no way to heat a tool in this crypt. I take it the men who did this work had a plumber's gasoline torch, or something of that sort. We have practically nothing. As for building a fire in here and heating one of the airplane tools, that's out of the question. It would stifle us both. No, we must cut.

That's the best we can do."

He drew his hunting-knife from its sheath and, giving the torch back to Beatrice, knelt by the chest. Close under the line of soldering he dug the blade into the soft metal, and, boring with it, soon made a puncture through the leaden sheet.

"Only a quarter of an inch thick," he announced, with satisfaction. "This oughtn't to be such a bad job!"

Already he was at work, with infinite care not to shock or jar the precious contents within. In his powerful hands the knife laid back the metal in a jagged line. A quarter of an hour sufficed to cut across the entire front.

He rested a little while.

"Seems to be another chest inside, of wood," he told the girl. "Not decayed, either. I shouldn't wonder if the lead had preserved things absolutely intact. In that case this find is sure to be a rich one."

Again he set to work. In an hour from the time he had begun, the whole top of the lead box—save only that portion against the wall—had been cut off.

"Do you dare to move it out, Allan?" queried the girl anxiously.

"Better not. I think we can raise the cover as it is."

He slit up the front corners, and then with comparative ease bent the entire top upward. To the explorer's eyes stood revealed a chest of cedar, its cover held with copper screws.

"Now for it!" said the man. "We ought to have one of the screw-drivers from the Pauillac, but that would take too much time. I guess the knife will do."

With the blade he attacked the screws, one by one, and by dint of laborious patience in about an hour had removed all twenty of them.

A minute later he had pried up the cover, had quite removed it, and had set it on the floor.

Within, at one side, they saw a formless something swathed in oiled canvas. The other half of the space was occupied by eighty or a hundred vertical compartments, in each of which stood something carefully enveloped in the same material.

"Well, for all the world if it doesn't look like a set of big phonograph records!" exclaimed the man. He drew one of the objects out and very carefully unwrapped it.

"Just what they are—records! On steel. The new Chalmers-Enemarck process—new, that is, in 1917. So, then, that's a phonograph, eh?"

He pointed at the oiled canvas.

"Open it, quick, Allan!" Beatrice exclaimed. "If it is a phonograph, why, we can hear the very voices of the past, the dead, a full thousand years ago!"

With trembling fingers Stern slit the canvas wrappings.

"What a treasure! What a find!" he exulted. "Look, Beta—see what fortune has put into our hands!"

Even as he spoke he was lifting the great phonograph from the space where, absolutely uninjured and intact, it had reposed for ten centuries. A silver plate caught his eye. He paused to read:

METROPOLITAN OPERA HOUSE,
New York City.

This Phonograph and these Records were immured in the vault of this building September 28, 1918, by the Philavox Society, to be opened in the year 2000.
Non Pereat Memoria Musicae Nostrae.

"Let not the memory of our music perish!" he translated. "Why, I remember well when these records were made and deposited in the Metropolitan! A similar thing was done in Paris, you remember, and in Berlin. But how does this machine come here?"

"Probably the expedition reached New York, after all, and decided to transfer this treasure to a safer place where it might be absolutely safe and dry," she suggested. "It's here, anyhow; that's the main thing, and we've found it. What fortune!"

"It's lucky, all right enough," the man assented, setting the magnificent machine down on the floor of the crypt. "So far as I can see, the mechanism is absolutely all right in every way. They've even put in a box of the special fiber needles for use on the steel plates, Beta. Everything's provided for.

"Do you know, the expedition must have been a much larger one than we thought? It was no child's play to invade the ruins of New York, rescue all this, and transport it here, probably with savages dogging their heels every step. Those certainly were determined, vigorous men, and a goodly number at that. And the fight they must have put up in the cathedral, defending their cache against the enemy, and dying for it, must been terrifically dramatic!

"But all that's done and forgotten now, and we can only guess a bit of it here and there. The tangible fact is this machine and these records, Beatrice. They're real, and we've got them. And the quicker we see what they have to tell us the better, eh?"

She clapped her hands with enthusiasm.

"Put on a record, Allan, quick! Let's hear the voices of the past once more—human voices—the voices of the age that was!" she cried, excited as a child.

CHAPTER VIII

TILL DEATH US DO PART

"All right, my darling," he made answer. "But not here. This is no place for melody, down in this dark and gloomy crypt, surrounded by the relics of the dead. We've been buried alive down here altogether too long as it is. Brrr! The chill's beginning to get into my very bones! Don't you feel it, Beta?"

"I do, now I stop to think of it. Well, let's go up then. We'll have our music where it belongs, in the cathedral, with sunshine and air and birds to keep it company!"

Half an hour later they had transported the magnificent phonograph and the steel records out of the crypt and up the spiral stairway, into the vast, majestic sweep of the transept.

They placed their find on the broad concrete steps that in the old days had led up to the altar, and while Allan minutely examined the mechanism to make sure that all was right, the girl, sitting on the top step, looked over the records.

"Why, Allan, here are instrumental as well as vocal masterpieces," she announced with joy. "Just listen—here's Rossini's 'Barbier de Seville,' and Grieg's 'Anitra's Dance' from the 'Peer Gynt Suite,' and here's that most entrancing 'Barcarolle' from the 'Contes d'Hoffman'—you remember it?"

She began to hum the air, then, as the harmony flowed through her soul, sang a few lines, her voice like gold and honey:

> *Belle nuit, o nuit d'amour, souris a nos ivresses!*
> *Nuit plus douce que le jour, o belle nuit d'amour!*
> *Le temps fuit et sans retour emporte nos tendresses;*
> *Loin de cet heureux sejour le temps fuit sans retour!*
> *Zephyrs embrases, versez-nous vos caresses!*
> *Ah! Donnez-nous vos baisers!*

The echoes of Offenbach's wondrous air, a crystal stream of harmony, and of the passion-pulsing words, died through the vaulted heights. A moment Allan sat silent, gazing at the girl, and then he smiled.

"It lives in you again, the past!" he cried. "In you the world shall be made new once more! Beatrice, when I last heard that 'Barcarolle' it was sung by Farrar and Scotti at the Metropolitan, in the winter of 1913. And now—you waken the whole scene in me again!

"I seem to behold the vast, clear-lighted space anew, the tiers of gilded galleries and boxes, the thousands of men and women hanging eagerly on every silver note—I see the marvelous orchestra, many, yet one; the Venetian scene, the moonlight on the Grand Canal, the gondolas, the merrymakers—I hear Giulietta and Nicklausse blending those perfect tones! My heart leaps at the memory, beloved, and I bless you for once more awakening it!"

"With my poor voice?" she smiled. "Play it, play the record, Allan, and let us hear it as it should be sung!"

He shook his head.

"No!" he declared. "Not after you have sung it. Your voice to me is infinitely sweeter than any that the world of other days ever so much as dreamed of!"

He bent above her, caressed her hair and kissed her; and for a little while they both forgot their music. But soon the girl recalled him to the work in hand.

"Come, Allan, there's so much to do!"

"I know. Well now—let's see, what next?"

He paused, a new thought in his eyes.

"Beta!"

"Well?"

"You don't find Mendelssohn's 'Wedding March,' do you? Look, dearest, see if you can find it. Perhaps it may be there. If so—"

She eyed him, her gaze widening.

"You mean?"

He nodded.

"Just so! Perhaps, after all, you and I can—"

"Oh, come and help me look for it, Allan!" she cried enthusiastic as a child in the joy of his new inspiration. "If we only could find it, wouldn't that be glorious?"

Eagerly they searched together.

"'Ich Grolle Nicht,' by Schumann, no," Stern commented, as one by one they examined the records. "'Ave Maria,' Arcadelt-Liszt—no, though it's magnificent. That's the one you sing best of all, Beta. How often you've sung it to me! Remember, at the bungalow, how I used to lay my head in your lap while you played with my Samsonesque locks and sang me to sleep? Let's see—Brahms's 'Wiegenlied.' Cradle-song, eh? A little premature; that's coming later. Eh? Found it, by Jove! Here we are, the March itself, so help me! Shall I play it now?"

"Not yet, Allan. Here, see what I've found!"

She handed him a record as they sat there together in a broad ribbon of mid-morning sunlight that flooded down through one of the clearstory windows.

"'The Form of the Solemnization of Matrimony, by Bishop Gibson,'" he read. And silence fell, and for a long minute their eyes met.

"Beatrice!"

"I know; I understand! So, after all, these words—"

"Shall be spoken, O my love! Out of the dead past a voice shall speak to us and we shall hear! Beatrice, the words your mother heard, my mother heard, we shall hear, too. Come, Beatrice, for now the time is at hand!"

She fell a trembling, and for a moment could not speak. Her eyes grew veiled in tears, but through them he saw a bright smile break, like sunlight after summer showers.

She stood up and held out her hand to him.

"My Allan!"

In his arms he caught her.

"At last!" he whispered. "Oh, at last!"

When the majesty and beauty of the immortal marriage hymn climbed the high vaults of the cathedral, waking the echoes of the vacant spaces, and when it rolled, pealing triumphantly, she leaned her head upon his breast and, trembling, clung to him.

With his arm he clasped her; he leaned above her, shrouding her in his love as in an everlasting benison. And through their souls thrilled wonder, awe and passion, and life held another meaning and another mystery.

The words of solemn sacredness hallowed for centuries beyond the memory of man, rose powerful, heart-thrilling, deep with symbolism, strong with vibrant might—and, hand in hand, the woman and the man bowed their heads, listening:

"Dearly beloved, we are gathered here to join together this man and this woman in holy matrimony—reverently, discreetly, advisedly, soberly. Into this holy estate these two persons present now come to be joined."

His hand tightened upon her hand, for he felt her trembling. But bravely she smiled up at him and upon her hair the golden sunlight made an aureole.

The voice rose in its soul-shaking question—slow and powerful:

"Wilt thou have this woman to thy wedded wife, to live together in the holy estate of matrimony? Wilt thou love her, comfort her, honor, and keep her in sickness and in health, and keep thee only unto her, so long as ye both shall live?"

Allan's "I will!" was as a hymn of joy upon the morning air.

"Wilt thou have this man to thy wedded husband, to live together in the holy estate of matrimony? Wilt thou serve him, love, honor, and keep him in sickness and in health, and keep thee only unto him, so long as ye both shall live?"

She answered proudly, bravely:

"I will!"

Then the man chorused the voice and said:

"I, Allan, take thee, Beatrice, to my wedded wife, to have and to hold from this day forward for better, for worse, for richer, for poorer, in sickness and in health to love and to cherish, till death us do part, and thereto I plight thee my troth."

Her answer came, still led by the commanding voice, like an antiphony of love:

"I, Beatrice, take thee, Allan, to my wedded husband, to have and to hold from this day forward for better, for worse, for richer, for poorer, in sickness and in health to love and to cherish, till death us do part, and thereto I give thee my troth!"

Already Allan had drawn from his little finger the plain gold ring he had worn there so many centuries. Upon her finger he placed the ring and kissed it, and, following the voice, he said:

"With this ring I thee wed, and with all my worldly goods I thee endow. In the name of the Father, and of the Son, and of the Holy Ghost. Amen."

Forest, river, sky and golden sunlight greeted them as they stood on the broad porch of the cathedral, and the clear song of many birds, unafraid in the virgin wilderness, made music to their ears such as must have greeted the primal day.

Suddenly Allan caught and crushed her in his arms.

"My wife!" he whispered.

The satin of her skin from breast to brow surged into sudden flame. Her eyes closed and between her eager lips the breath came fast.

"Oh, Allan—husband! I feel—I hear—"

"The voice of the unborn, crying to us from out the dark, 'O father, mother, give us life!'"

CHAPTER IX

AT SETTLEMENT CLIFFS

Ten days later the two lovers—now man and wife—were back again at the eastern lip of the Abyss. With them on the biplane they had brought the phonograph and records, all securely wrapped in oiled canvas, the same which had enveloped the precious objects in the leaden chest.

They made a camp, which was to serve them for a while as headquarters in their tremendous undertaking of bringing the Merucaans to the surface, and here carefully stored their treasure in a deep cleft of rock, secure from rain and weather.

They had not revisited the bungalow on the return trip. The sight of their little home and garden, now totally devastated, they knew would only sadden them unnecessarily.

"Let it pass, dearest, as a happy memory that was and is no more," Stern cheered the girl as he held her in his arms the first night of their stay in the new camp, and as together they watched the purple haze of sunset beyond the chasm. "Some day, perhaps, we may go back and once more restore Hope Villa and live there again, but for the present many other and far more weighty matters press. It will be wisest for a while to leave the East alone. Too many of the Horde are still left there. Here, west of the Ohio River Valley, they don't seem to have penetrated—and what's more, they never shall! Just now we must ignore them—though the day of reckoning will surely come! We've got our hands full for a while with the gigantic task ahead of us. It's the biggest and the hardest that one man and one woman ever tackled since the beginning of time!"

She drew his head down and kissed him, and for a little while they kept the silence of perfect comradeship. But at last she questioned:

"You've got it all worked out at last, Allan? You know just the steps to take? One false move—"

"There shall be no false moves. Reason, deliberation, care will solve this problem like all the others. Given some fifteen hundred people, at a depth of five hundred miles, and given an airplane and plenty of time—"

"Yes, of course, they can be brought to the surface. But after that, what? The dangers are tremendous! The patriarch died at the first touch of sunlight. We can't afford to take chances with the rest!"

"I've planned on all that. Our first move must be to locate a rocky ledge, a cave, or something of the sort, where the transplanting process can be carried out. There mustn't be any exposure to the actual daylight for a long time after they're on the surface. The details of food and water have all got to be arranged, too. It means work, work, work! God, what work! But—it's our task, Beta, all our own. And I glory in it. I thank Heaven for it—a man's-size labor! And if we're strong and brave enough, patient and wise enough, we're bound to win."

"Win? Of course we'll win!" she answered, her faith in him touching the sublime. "We must! The life of the whole world's at stake!"

Night came, and redder glowed the firelight in the gloom. They spoke of life, of love, of destiny; and over them seemed to brood the mystery of all that was to be.

The very purpose of the universe enwrapped itself about their passion, and the untroubled stars kept vigils till the dawn.

Daylight called them to begin the epic campaign they had mapped out—the rescue of a race.

After a visit to the patriarch's grave, which they decked anew with blossoms and fresh leaves, they prepared for the journey in search of a suitable temporary home for the Folk.

Nine o'clock found them once more on the wing. Stern laid a southerly course along the edge of the Abyss. He and Beatrice had definitely decided that the new home of humanity was not to be the distant regions of the East, involving so long and perilous a journey, but rather some location in the vast, warm, central plain of what had once been the United States.

They judged they were now somewhere in the one-time State of Indiana, not far from Indianapolis. So much warmer had the climate grown that for some months to come at least the Folk could without doubt accustom themselves to the change from the hot and muggy atmosphere of the Abyss to the semitropic heat.

The main object now was to discover suitable caves near a good water supply, where by night the Folk could prosecute their accustomed fisheries. Agriculture and the care of domestic animals by daylight would have to be postponed for some time, possibly for a year or more. Above all, the health of the prospective colonists must be safeguarded.

It was not until nearly nightfall of the next day, and after stops had been made at the ruins of two considerable but unidentified towns—for fuel, as well as to fit up an electric search-light and hooded lamps to illuminate the instruments in the Abyss—that the explorers found what they were seeking.

About half past five that afternoon they sighted a very considerable river, flowing westward down a rugged and irregular valley, in the direction of the chasm.

"This can't be the Ohio," judged Stern. "We must have long since passed its bed, now probably dried up. I don't remember any such hilly region as this in the old days along the Mississippi Valley. All these formations must be the result of the cataclysm. Well, no matter, just so we find what we're after."

"Where are we now?" she asked, peering downward anxiously. "Over what State—can you tell?"

"Probably Tennessee or northern Alabama. See the change in vegetation? No conifers here, but many palms and fern-trees, and new, strange growths. Fertile isn't the name for it! Once we clear some land here, crops will grow themselves! I don't think we'll do better than this, Beta. Shall we land and see?"

A quarter-hour later the Pauillac had safely deposited them on a high, rocky plateau about half a mile back from the edge of the river canyon. Stern, in his eagerness, was all for cave-hunting that very evening, but the girl restrained him.

"Not so impatient, dear!" she cautioned. "'Too fast arrives as tardy as too slow!' Tomorrow's time enough."

"Ruling me with quotations from Shakespeare, eh?" he laughed, with a kiss. "All right, have your way—Mrs. Stern!"

She laughed, too, at this, the first time she had heard her new name. So they made camp and postponed further labors till daylight again.

Morning found them early astir and at work. Together they traversed the tropic-seeming woods, aflame with brilliant flowers, dank with ferns and laced with twining lianas.

In the treetops—strange trees, fruit laden—parrakeets and flashing green and crimson birds of paradise disturbed the little monkey-folk that chattered at the intruders. Once a coral-red snake whipped away, hissing, but not quick enough to dodge a ball from Stern's revolver.

Stern viewed the ugly, triangular head with apprehension. Well he knew that venom dwelt there, but he said nothing. The one and only chance of successfully transplanting the Folk must be to regions warm as these. All dangers must be braved a time till they could grow acclimated to the upper air. After that—but the vastness of the future deterred even speculation. Perils were inevitable. The more there were to overcome the greater the victory.

"On to the cliffs!" said he, clasping the girl's hand in his own and making a path for her.

Thus presently they reached the edge of the canyon.

"Magnificent!" cried Beatrice as they came out on the over-hang of the rock wall. "With these fruitful woods behind, that river in front, and these natural fortifications for our home, what more could we want?"

"Nothing except caves," Stern answered. "Let's call this New Hope River, eh? And the cliffs?"

"Settlement Cliffs!" she exclaimed.

"Done! Well, now let's see."

For the better part of the morning they explored the face of the palisade. Its height, they estimated, ranged from two to three hundred feet, shelving down in rough terraces to the rocky debris through and beyond which foamed the strong current of New Hope River, a stream averaging about two hundred yards in width.

Up-current a broader pool gave promise of excellent fishing. It overflowed into violent rapids, with swift, white waters noisily cascading.

"There, incidentally," Stern remarked, with the practical perception of the engineer, "there's power enough, when properly harnessed, to light a city and to turn machinery ad libitum. I don't see how we could better this site, do you?"

"Not if you think there are good chances for cave-dwellings," she made answer.

"From what we've seen already, it looks promising. Of course, there'll be a deal of work to do; but there are excellent possibilities here. First rate."

Fortune seemed bent on favoring them. The limestone cliff, fantastically eroded, offered a score of shelters, some shallow and needing to be walled up in front, others deep and tortuous. All was in utter confusion.

Stern saw that the terraces would have to be blasted and lev-eled, roads and stairs built along the face of the rock and down to the river, stalactites and stalagmites cut away, chambers fash-ioned, and a vast deal of labor done; but the rough framework of a cliff colony undeniably existed here. He doubted whether it would be possible to find a more favorable site without long and tedious travels.

"I guess we'll take the apartments and sign the lease," he decided toward noon, after they had clambered, pried, explored with improvised torches, and penetrated far into some of the grottoes. "The main thing to consider is that we can find darkness and humidity for the Folk by day. They mustn't be let out at first except in the night. It may be weeks or months before they can stand the direct sunlight. But that, too, will come. Patience, girl—patience and time—and all will yet be done."

Yet, even as he spoke, a strange anxiety, a prescience of tremendous difficulties, brooded in his soul. These were not cattle that he had to deal with, but men.

Could he and Beatrice, rulers of the Folk though they now were, could they—with their paltry knowledge of the people's language, superstitions, prejudices and inner life—really bring about this great migration?

Could they ravish a nation from its accustomed home, transplant it bodily, force new conditions on it, train, teach, civilize it? All this without rebellion, anarchy and failure?

"God!" thought the engineer. "The labors of Hercules were child's play beside this problem!"

His heart quaked at the thought of all that lay ahead; yet through everything, deep in the basic strata of his being, he knew that all should be and must be as he planned.

Barring death only, the seemingly impossible should come to pass.

"I swear it!" he murmured to himself. "For her sake, for theirs, and for the world's, I swear it shall be!"

At high noon they emerged once more from the caverns, climbed the steep cliff face, and again stood on the heights.

Facing northward, their gaze swept the lower river-bank opposite, and reached away, away, over the rolling hills and plains that lay, a virgin forest, to the dim horizon, brooding, mysterious, quivering with fertility and wild, strange life.

"Some time," he prophesied, sweeping his arm out toward the wilderness—"some time all that—and far beyond—shall be dotted with clearings and rich farms, with cottages, schools, towns, cities. Broad highways shall traverse it. The hum of motors, of machinery, of industry—of life itself—shall one day displace the cry of beast and bird.

"Some time the English tongue shall reign here again—here and beyond. Here strong men shall toil and build and reap and rest. Here love shall reign and women be called 'mother.' Here children shall play and learn and grow to manhood and to womanhood, secure and free.

"Some time all good things shall here come to realization.

Oppression and slavery, alone, shall be undreamed of. These, and poverty and pain, shall never enter into the new world that is to be.

"Some time, here, 'all shall be better than well.' Some time!"

He circled her with his arm, and for a while they stood surveying this cradle of the new race. Much moved, Beatrice drew very close to him. They made no speech.

For the dreams they two were dreaming, as the golden sun irradiated all that vast, magnificent wilderness, passed any power of words.

Only she whispered "Some time!" too, and Allan knew she shared with him the glory of his vast, tremendous vision!

CHAPTER X

SEPARATION

They spent the remainder of that day and all the next in hard work, making practical preparations for the arrival of the first settlers. Allan assured himself the waters of New Hope River were soft and pure and that an ample supply of fish dwelt in the pool as well as in the rapids—trout, salmon and pike of new varieties and great size, as well as other species.

Beatrice and he, working together, put the largest and darkest of the caves into habitable order. They also prepared, for their own use, a sunny grotto, which they thought could with reasonable labor be made into a comfortable temporary home.

"Though it isn't our own cozy bungalow, and never can be," she remarked rather mournfully, surveying the fireplace of roughly piled stones Allan had built. "Oh, dear, if we only could have had that to live in while—"

He stopped her yearning with a kiss.

"There, there, little girl," he cheered her, "don't be impatient. All in good time we'll have another, garden and sun-dial and everything. All in good time. The more we have to overcome, the more we'll appreciate results, eh? The only really serious matter to consider now is you!"

"Me, Allan? Why, what do you mean? What about me?"

He sat down on the rough-hewn bench of logs that he had fashioned and drew her to him.

"Listen, Beta. This is very serious."

"What, Allan? Has anything happened?"

"No, and nothing must, either. That's what's troubling me now. Our separation, I mean."

"Our—why, what—"

"Don't you see? Can't you understand? We've got to be apart a while. I must go alone—"

"Oh, no, no, Allan! You mustn't; I can't let you!"

"You've got to let me, darling! The machine will only carry, at most, three persons and a little freight. Now if you take the trip back into the Abyss I can only bring one, just one of the Folk back with me. And at that rate you can see for yourself how long it will take to make even a beginning at colonization. I figure three or four days for the round trip, at the inside. If you go we'll be all summer and more getting even twenty-five or thirty colonists here. Whereas, if you can manage to let me do this work alone, we'll have fifty in the caves by October. So you see—"

"You don't want to go and leave me, Allan?"

"God forbid! Shall I abandon the whole attempt and settle down with you here, all alone, and—"

"No, no, no! Not that, Allan!"

"I knew you'd say so. After all, the future of the race means more than our own welfare or comfort or anything. Even our safety has got to be risked for it. So you see—"

She thought a moment, clinging to him, somewhat pale and shaken, but with an indefinable courage in her eyes. Then asked she:

"Wouldn't it be possible in some way—for you can do anything, Allan—wouldn't it be possible for you to build another machine? Surely in the ruins of some city not too far away, in Nashville, Cincinnati, or Detroit, you could find materials! Couldn't you make another airplane and teach me how to fly, so I could help you? I'd learn, Allan! I'd dare, and be brave—awfully brave, for your sake, and theirs, and—"

He gravely shook his head in negation.

"I know you would, dearest, but you mustn't. Half my real reason for not wanting you to go with me is just this danger of flying. You'll be safer here. With plenty of supplies and your pistol you'll be all right. I know it seems heartless to talk of leaving you, even for three days, but, after all, it's far the wisest way. We'll build a barricade and make a regular fort for you and stock it with supplies. Then you can wait for me and the first two settlers. And after that you'll have company. Why, you'll have subjects—for, until they're educated, we've simply got to rule these people. It'll be only the first trip that will make you lonely, and it won't be long."

"I know; but suppose anything should happen to you!"

He laughed confidently.

"Nonsense!" he exclaimed. "You know nothing ever does happen to me! Everything will be all right, my best—beloved. Only a little patience and a little courage, that's all we need now. You'll see!"

Till late that night, sheltered in their cave, they talked of this momentous step. Redly their firelight glowed upon their walls and roof, where sparkled myriads of tiny rock-facets. Far below the rapids of New Hope River murmured a contra-bass to their voices.

And in the canyon the sighing of the night-wind, pierced now and then by some strange cry of beast-life from the forest beyond, heightened their pleasant sense of security. Only the knowledge of approaching separation weighed heavy on their souls.

From every possible standpoint they discussed the situation. Allan's plan, viewed with the eye of reason, was really the only sane one. Nothing could have been more absurdly wasteful of time and energy than the idea of carrying the girl down into the Abyss each time and bringing her up with every return.

Not only would it expose her needlessly to very grave perils, but it would bisect the efficiency of the Pauillac. Allan realized, moreover, that in the rebuilding of the world a time must inevitably come when he could not always stand by her side. She must learn self-reliance, harsh as that teaching might seem.

All this and much more he pointed out to her. And before midnight she, too, agreed. It was definitely decided that he was to undertake the transportation work alone.

Thus the matter was settled. But on that night there was little sleep for either of them. For, on the day after the morrow was to commence their first separation since the time they had awakened in the tower, more than a year ago.

Separation!

The thought weighed leaden on Allan's heart. As for Beatrice, though in the dark she hid her tears, she felt that grief could plumb no blacker depths save utter loss. Only the thought of the new world and all that it must mean steeled her to resignation.

Morning dawned, aflare with light and color, as only a June morning in that semitropic wilderness could glow. Allan and Beatrice, early at work, resolutely attacked their labor of preparation.

First of all they laid in adequate supplies of fruit and game, both of which, in that virgin wild, were to be had in a profusion undreamed of in the old days of civilization. With an improvised lance Ahan also speared three salmon in the rapids. The game and fish he dressed for her and packed among green leaves in the cool recesses at the extreme inner end of the cavern.

"No need whatever for you to leave the cave while I'm gone," he warned her. "I'm not forbidding you to, because I'm not your master. All I say is I'll be far happier if you stay close at home. Will you promise me that, whatever happens, you won't wander from the cave?"

"I needn't promise, dearest. All I need to know is your wish. That's enough for me!"

Together they set about fortifying the place. They built a rough but strong barricade of rocks across the mouth of the cavern, leaving only one small aperture, just sufficient to admit a single person on hands and knees.

Allan fetched a rounded stone that she could roll into this door by night and arranged a stout sapling to brace the stone immovably. He supplied her well with fire-wood and saw to it that her bandoliers were full of cartridges. In addition, he left her the extra gun and ammunition they had found in the crypt under the cathedral.

With a torch he carefully explored every crevice of the cave to make sure no noxious spiders, centipedes, or serpents were sheltered there.

From the Pauillac he brought his own cloak, which he insisted on her keeping. This, with hers, would add to the comfort of the bed they had made with fragrant ferns and grasses.

He fashioned, out of the tenacious clay of an earth-bank about half a mile down stream, two large water-jars, and baked them for some hours in a huge fire on the terrace in front of the cave.

When properly hardened he scoured them carefully with river-sand and filled them one at a time, struggling up the hard ascent with a stout heart—for all this toil meant safety for the girl; it was all another step on the hard pathway toward the goal.

In her sleep that night he bent above her, kissed her tenderly, and realized how inexpressibly dear she was to him.

The thought: "Tomorrow I must leave her!" weighed heavy on him. And for a long time he could not sleep, but lay listening to the night sounds of the forest and the brawling stream. Once a deep, booming roar echoed throughout the canyon, and thereto, hollow blows.

But Allan could not think their meaning. Only he knew the wild was full of perils; and in his mind he reviewed the precautions he had taken for her welfare. Bit by bit he analyzed them. He knew that he could do no more Now Fate must solve the rest.

He slept at length, not to waken till morning with its garish eye peeped in around the crevices of the rock doorway. Returning from his swim in the pool, he found Beatrice already making breakfast. They ate in silence, overborne with sad and bodeful thoughts.

But now the decision had been made, nothing remained save to execute it. Such a contingency as backing out of an undertaking once begun lay far outside their scheme of things.

The leave-taking was not delayed. They both realized that an early start was necessary if he were to reach the village of the Folk before sleep should assail him. Still more, they dreaded the departure less than the suspense.

Together they provisioned the Pauillac, back there on the rocky barren, and made sure everything was in order. Allan assured himself especially that he had fuel enough to last four or five hours.

"In that time," he told the girl, "I can easily reach the rim of the Abyss. You see, I needn't fly northward to the point where we emerged. That would be only an unnecessary waste of time and energy. I'm positive the chasm extends all the way up and down what was once the Mississippi Valley, and that the Great Central Sea is fed by that and other rivers. In that case, by striking almost due west, I can reach the rim. After that I can volplane easily till I sight the water."

"And then?"

"Then the power goes on again and I scout for the west shore and the village. The sustaining power of that lower-level air is simply miraculous. I realize perfectly well it's no child's play, but I can do it, Beta. I can find the place again. You see, I'm perfectly familiar with conditions down there now. The first time it was all new and strange. This time, after all those months in the Abyss, why, it will be almost like getting back home again. It'll be quite a triumphal return, won't it? The chief getting back to his tribe, eh?"

He tried to speak lightly, but his lips refused to smile. She frankly wept.

"There, there, little girl," he soothed her. "Now let's go back to the cave and see that you're all right and safe. Then I'll be going. Remember on the third night to kindle the big fire we've agreed on just outside your door on the terrace—the beacon-fire, you know. I'll have to reckon by the chronometer, so as to make the return by night. The risk of bringing any of the Folk into daylight is prohibitive. And the fire will be tremendously important. I can sight it a long way off. It will guide me home—to you!"

She nodded silently, for she did not trust herself to speak.. Hand in hand they returned along the path they had beaten through the rank half-tropic growth.

One last inspection he gave to all things necessary for her comfort. Then, standing in the warm, bright sunlight on the ledge before the new home, he took her in his arms.

A long embrace, a parting kiss that clung; then he was gone.

Not long after the girl, still standing there upon the wind-swept terrace overlooking New Hope River, heard the rapid chatter of the engine high in air and rapidly approaching.

A swift black shadow leaped the canyon and swept away across the plain. Far aloft she saw the skimming Pauillac, very small and black against the dazzling blue.

Did Allan wave a hand to her? Could she hear his farewell cry?

Impossible to tell. Her ears, confused by the roaring of the rapids, her eyes dazzled by the shimmer of the morning heavens and dimmed by burning tears, refused to serve her.

But bravely she waved her cloak on high. Bravely she strove to watch the arrow-flight of the swift bird-man till the tiny machine dwindled to a moving blur, a point, a mere speck on the far horizon, then vanished in the blue.

Choked with anguish, against which all her courage, all her philosophy could not make way, Beatrice sank down upon the rocky ledge and abandoned herself to grief.

Allan was gone at last! Gone—ever to return? At last she was alone in the unbroken wilderness!

CHAPTER XI

"HAIL TO THE MASTER!"

Eleven hours of incessant labor, care, watchfulness and fatigue, three hours of flight and eight of coasting into the terrific depths, brought Allan once more through the fogs, the dark, the heat, to sight of the vast sunken sea, five hundred miles below the surface.

Throughout the whole stupendous labor he thanked Heaven the girl was safely left behind, nor forced to share this travail and exhaustion. Myriad anxieties and fears assailed him—fears he had taken good care not to let her know or dream of.

Always existed the chance that something might go wrong about the machine and it be hurled, with him, into that black and steaming sea; the possibility of landing not among the Folk, but in some settlement of the Lanskaarn on the rumored islands he had never seen; the menace of the Great Vortex, of which he knew nothing save the little that the patriarch had told him.

All these and many other perils sought to force themselves upon his mind. But Allan put them resolutely back and, guided by his instruments, his reason, and that marvelous sixth sense of location which his long months of battling with the wilderness had brought to birth in him, swiftly yet carefully slid in vast spirals down the purple, then the black and terrifying void that yawned interminably below.

The beam of his underslung searchlight, shifting at his will, shot its white ray in a long, fading pencil downward as he coasted. And hour after hour it found nothing whereon to rest. It, too, seemed lost forever in the welter of uprushing, choking vapors from the pit.

"Ah! At last!"

The cry, dull in that compressed air, burst triumphantly from his lips as the light-ray, suddenly piercing a rift of cloud, sparkled dimly on a surface shiny-black as newly cleft anthracite.

Allan threw in the motor once more and quickly got the Pauillac under control. In a long downward slant he rushed, like some vast swallow skimming a pool, over the mysterious plain of steaming waters. And ever, peering eagerly ahead, he sought a twinkle of the fishermen's oil-flares wimpling across the sunken sea.

Moment by moment he consulted his instruments and the chart he had stretched before him under the gleam of the hooded bulbs.

"Inside of half an hour now," said he, "I ought to sight the first flash of the flares upon the parapet—the glow of the flaming well!"

And a singular eagerness all at once possessed him, a strange yearning to behold once more the strange, fog-shrouded, reeking City of the Lost People, almost as though it had been home, as though these white barbarians had been his own people.

Men! To see men once more! The idea leaped up and gripped him with a powerful fascination.

So it was that when in reality the first faint twinkle of the fishing-boats peeped through the mist—and beyond, a tiny necklace of gleaming points that he knew marked the walls of the town—his heart throbbed hotly and a cry of eager greeting welled from his soul.

Quickly the Pauillac swept him onward. Manoeuvering cautiously, jockeying the great machine with that consummate skill he had acquired from long practice, he soon beheld the dim outlines of the vast cliff, the long walls, the dull reflections of the fire-plume, the slanting slope of beach.

And with keen exultation, thrilled with his triumph and his greeting to the Folk he came to rescue, he landed with a whir upon the reeking slope.

To him, even before he had been able to free his cramped body from the saddle, came swarming the people, with loud cries of welcome and rejoicing. Powerfully the automatics he and Beatrice had used in the Battle of the Walls had impressed their simple minds with almost superstitious reverence. More powerfully still his terrible fight with Kamrou, ending with the death of that great chief in the boiling vat. And now, acknowledging him their overlord and ruler, whom they had feared to lose forever, they trooped in wild, disordered throngs to do him reverence.

In from the sea, summoned by waving flares, the fishing-boats came plowing mightily, driven by many paddles in the hands of the strange, white-haired men.

Along the beach the townsfolk thronged, and down the causeway, beneath the vast monolithic plinth of the fortified gate, jostled and pushed an ever-growing multitude.

Cries of "Kromno h'viat! Tai Kromno!" reechoed—"The chief has come back! The great master!"—and the confusion swelled to a mighty roar, close-pent under the heavy mists blued by the naphtha-torches.

But Stern noticed, and rejoiced to see it, that none prostrated themselves. None fell to earth or groveled in his presence. Disorderly and wild the greeting was, but it was the greeting of men, not slaves.

"Thank God, I've got a race of real men to deal with here!" thought he, surveying the pressing throng. "Hard they may be to rule, and even turbulent, but they're not servile. Rude, brave, bold—what better stock could I have hoped for in this great adventuring?"

For a while even thoughts of Beatrice were crowded back by the excitement of the arrival. In all his wonderful experience never before had he sensed a feeling such as this.

To be returning, master and lord of a race of long-buried people, his own people, after all—to be acknowledged chieftain—to hold their destinies within his hand for good or evil—the magnitude of the situation, the tremendous difficulties and responsibilities, almost overwhelmed him.

He felt a need to rest, and think, and plan, to recuperate from the long journey and to recover poise and strength.

And with relief, as he raised his hand for silence, he perceived the wrinkled face of one Vreenya, head councilor of Kamrou, his predecessor.

Him he summoned to come close, and to him gave his orders. With some degree of fluency—for in the months Beatrice and he had spent in the Abyss they had acquired much of the Merucaan tongue—he said:

"I greet you, Vreenya. I greet my people, all. Harken. I have made a long journey to return to you. I am tired and would rest. There be many things to tell you, but not now. I would sleep and eat. Is my house in readiness?"

"It is in readiness—the house of the Kromno. Your word is our law. It shall be as you have spoken."

"That is good. Now it is my will that this air-boat on which I ride should be carried close up to the walls and carefully covered with mantles, especially this part," and he gestured at the engines. "After that I rest."

"So it shall be," Vreenya made answer, while the Folk listened. "But, master, where is the woman? Where is the ancient man, J'hungaav, who sailed with you in the air-boat to those upper regions we know not of?"

"The woman is well. She awaits in a place we have prepared for you."

"It is well. And the ancient man?"

Stern thought quickly. To confess the patriarch's death would certainly be fatal to the undertaking. These simple minds would judge from it that certain destruction must be the portion of any who should dare venture into those mysterious upper regions which to them were but a myth, a strange tradition—almost a terror.

And though the truth was dear to him, yet under stress of the greater good he uttered falsehood by implication.

"The ancient man awaits you, too. He is resting in the far places. He would desire you to come to him."

"He is at peace? He found the upper world good?"

"He found it good, Vreenya. And he is at peace."

"It is well. Now the commands of Tai Kromno shall be done. His house is ready!"

While Stern clambered out of the machine and stretched his half-paralyzed limbs, the news ran, a murmur of many voices, through the massed Folk. Stern's heart swelled with pride at the success so far of his mission. If all should go as well from now on, his mighty object could and would be accomplished. But if not—

He shuddered slightly despite himself, for to his mind arose the ever-present possibility of the Folk's custom of trial by combat—the chance that some rebellious one might challenge him—that the outcome might another time turn against him.

He remembered still the scream of Kamrou as the deposed chieftain had plunged into the boiling pool. What if this fate should some time yet be his? And once more thoughts of Beatrice obtruded; and, despite himself, he felt the clutch of terror at his heart.

He put it resolutely away, however, for he realized that all depended now on maintaining good courage and a bold, commanding air. The slightest weakness might at any time prove fatal.

He understood enough of the barbarian psychology to know the value of dominance. And with a command to Vreenya: "Make way for me, your master!" he advanced through the lane which the crowding Folk made for him.

As, followed by the councilor and the elders, he climbed the slippery causeway and passed through the labyrinthine passes of the great gate, strange emotions stirred him.

The scene was still the same as when he first had witnessed it. Still flared the torches in the hands of the populace and along the walls, where, perched on the very ledge of the one-time battle with the Lanskaarn, the strange waterfowl still blinked their ghostly eyes.

No change was to be witnessed in the enclosure, the huts, the wide plaza, stretching away to the cliff, to the fire-pit, and the

Dungeon of Skeletons. But still how different was it all!

Only too clearly he remembered the first time he and Beatrice had been thrust into this weird community, bound and captive; with only too vivid distinctness he recalled the frightful indignities, perils and hardships inflicted on them.

The absence of the kindly patriarch saddened him; and, too, the fact that now no Beatrice was with him there.

Slowly, wearily, he moved along the slippery rock-floor toward his waiting house, unutterably lonesome even in this pushing throng that now acclaimed him, yet thanking God that the girl, at least, was far from the buried town of such hard ways and latent perils.

At the door of the round, conical stone hut that had been Kamrou's and now was his—so long as he could hold the chieftainship by sheer force of will and power—he paused a moment and faced the eager throng.

"Peace to you, my people!" he exclaimed, once more raising his hand on high. "Soon I shall tell you many wonders and things strange to hear—many things of great import and good tidings.

"When I have slept I shall speak with you. Now I go to rest. Await me, for the day of your deliverance is at hand!"

A face caught his attention, a sinister and, brutal face, doubly ominous in the flaring cresset-glare. He knew the man—H'yemba, the cunning ironsmith, one who in other days had before now crossed his will and, dog-like, snarled as much as he had dared. Now a peculiarly malevolent expression lay upon the evil countenance. The dead-white skin wrinkled evilly; the pink eyes gleamed with disconcerting malice.

But Stern, dead tired, only glanced at H'yemba for a second, then with Vreenya entered the hut and bade the door be closed.

All dressed as he was, he flung himself upon the rude bed of seaweed covered with the coarse brown stuff woven by the Folk.

"Sleep, master," Vreenya said. "I will sit here and watch. But before you sleep loosen the terrible fire-bow that shoots the bolts of lead and lay it near at hand."

"You mean—there may be trouble here?"

"Sleep!" was all the councilor would answer. "When you have rested there will be many things to ask and tell."

Spent beyond the power of any further effort, Stern laid his automatic handy and disposed himself to rest.

As his weary eyelids closed and the first outposts of consciousness began to fall before the attacking power of slumber, his thoughts, his love, his enduring passion, reverted to the girl, the wife, now so infinitely far away in the cavern beside the brawling canyon-stream. Yearning and tenderness unspeakable flooded his soul.

But once or twice her face faded from his mental vision and in its stead he seemed to see again the surly stare, the evil eyes, and venomously sinister expression of H'yemba, the resourceful man of fire and of steel.

CHAPTER XII
CHALLENGED!

After many hours of profound and dreamless sleep, Allan awoke filled with fresh vigor for the tasks that lay ahead. His splendid vitality, quickly recuperating, calmed his mind; and now the problems, the anxieties and fears of the day before—to call it such, though there was neither night nor day in this strange place—seemed negligible.

Only a certain haunting uneasiness about the girl still clung to him. But, sending her many a thought of love, he reflected that soon he should be back again with her; and so, resolutely grasping the labor that now awaited him, he felt fresh confidence and hope.

After a breakfast of the familiar sea-weeds, bulbs, fish and eggs, he bade Vreenya (who seemed devotion incarnate) summon the folk for a great charweg, or tribal council, at the Place of Skeletons.

Here they gathered, men, women and children, all of fifteen hundred, in close-packed, silent masses, leaving only the inner circle under the stone posts and iron rods clear for Allan and for Vreenya and some half-dozen elders.

The rocky plaza-floor sloping upward somewhat from the dungeon, formed a very shallow natural amphitheater, so that the majority could see as well as hear.

No platform was there for their Kromno to speak from. He had not even a block of stone. In the true native style he was expected to address them on their own level, pacing back and forth the while.

In his early days among them he had seen one or two such gatherings. His quick wit prompted a close imitation of their ceremonies and ancient customs.

First, Vreenya sprinkled the open space between the poles and the dungeon with a kind of sea-weed swab dipped in the waters of the boiling vat, then with a bit of the coarse brown cloth washed Allan's lips—a pledge of truth.

The councilor raised both hands toward the roaring flame back there by the cliff, and all inclined themselves thereto, the only trace of any religious ceremony still remaining among them.

Allan likewise saluted the flame; then he faced the multitude.

"O my people," he began, striving to speak clearly above the noise of the fire-jet, his voice sounding dull and heavy in that compressed atmosphere, "O Folk of the Merucaans, I greet you! There be many things to tell that you must know and believe. I have come back to you with great peril in my flying-boat to tell you of the upper world and all its goodness.

"Easily could I have stayed in those places of light and plenty, but my heart was warm for my people. I thought of my people night and day. The woman Beatrice thought of you. The ancient man thought of you. Alone, we could not enjoy those happy places. So I returned to tell you and to show you the way to liberty. Thus have we proved our love for you, my folk!"

He paused. Silence overhung the assemblage save for the fretful cry of children here and there, squeezed in the press or clinging to their mothers' backs after the fashion of the Merucaans.

Afar, on the walls, the faint and raucous quarreling of the sea-birds drifted through the fog. Allan drew breath and began again:

"In those places, my people, those far places whence your forefathers came, are many wonders. Betimes it is dark, as always here. Betimes a great fire mounts into the upper air and make the whole world brighter than around your flaming well. In the dark time lesser fires travel in the air. Of birds there are many kinds, strangely colored. Of beasts, many kinds—I cannot make you understand because none of you have ever seen any animal but fish and bird. But I speak truth. There be many other creatures with good flesh to eat, and the skins of them are proper for soft clothing.

"Here you have only weeds of the sea. There we have tall growing things, many hundred spedi high, and rich fruit, delicious to the taste, grows on some kinds. In a few words, it is a place of wondrous plenty, where you can all live more easily than here, and with more pleasure—far—"

Again he ceased his discourse, but still continued to pace up and down the open space under the swaying skeletons on the poles above.

Through the dense press of the Folk murmurs were wandering. Man spoke to man, and many a new thought was coming now to birth among those white barbarians.

The elders, too, were whispering together: "So runs the ancient tradition. So said the ancient man! Can it be true, indeed?"

Stern continued, more and more earnestly, with the sweat now beginning to dot his brow:

"It were too long, my people, to tell you everything about that land of ours above. Only remember it is richer far and far more beautiful than this, your place of darkness and of clouds. It is the ancient home of your fathers in the very long ago. It is waiting for you once again, more fertile and more beautiful than ever.

"My errand is to carry you thither—two or three at a time. At last I shall be able to take you all.

"Then the world will begin to be as it once was, before the great explosion destroyed all but a few of your people, who were my people once. Will any of you—any two bold men—believe my words and go with me? Will any be as brave as—the patriarch?"

He flung the veiled taunt loudly at them, with a raising of both arms.

"I have spoken truth! Now answer!"

He ceased, and for a short minute there was silence. Then spoke Vreenya:

"O Kromno, master! We would question you!"

"I will answer and say only the thing that is."

"First, can our people live in that other, lighter air?"

"They can live. We have prepared caves for you. At first you shall not see the light. Only little by little you shall see it, and you and your children will change, till at last you shall be as I am and as your people were in the old days!"

Vreenya pondered, while tense interest held the elders and the Folk. Then he nodded, for his understanding—like that of all—was keen in spite of his savagery.

"And we can eat, O Kromno? This flesh off beasts you speak of may be good. This strange fruit may be good. I know not. It may also be as the poison weeds of our sea to us. But, if so, there are fish in those waters of the upper world?"

"There are fish, Vreenya, and of the best, and many! Near the caves runs a river—"

"A what, master?"

"A going of the waters. In those waters live fish without number. At the dark times you can catch them with nets, even as here. The dark times are half of each day. You shall have many hours for the fishing. Even that will suffice to live; but the flesh and fruits will not hurt you. They are good. There will be food for all, and far more than enough for all!"

Vreenya pondered again.

"We would talk together, we elders," he said, simply.

"It meets my pleasure," answered Allan. "And when ye have talked, I desire your answer!"

He crossed his arms, faced the multitude, and waited, while

the elders gathered in a little group by the dungeon and for some minutes conferred in low and earnest tones.

Outwardly, the man seemed calm, but his soul burned within him and his heart was racing violently.

For on this moment, he well knew, hung the world's destiny. Should they decide to venture forth into the outer world all would be well. If not, the long labor, the plans, the hopes were lost forever.

Well he knew the stubborn nature of the Folk. Once their minds set, nothing on earth could ever stir them.

"Thank God I managed that lie about the patriarch!" thought Allen quickly. "If I'd slipped up on that, and told them he died at the very minute the sunlight struck him, it would have been all off, world without end. Hope it doesn't make a row later. But if it does, I'll face it. The main and only thing now is to get 'em started. They've got to go, that's all there is about it.

"Gad! After all, it's a terrific proposition I'm putting up to these simple fishers of the Abyss. I'm asking them, just on my say-so, to root up the life, the habits, the traditions of more than a thousand years and make a leap into the dark—into the light, I mean.

"I'm asking them to leave everything they've ever known for thirty generations and take a chance on what to them must be the wildest and most hare-brained adventure possible to imagine. To risk homes, families, lives, everything, just on my unsupported word. Jove! Columbus's proposal to his men was a mere afternoon jaunt compared with this! If they refuse, how can I blame them? But if they accept—God! what stuff I'll know they're made of! With material like that to work with, the conquest of the world's in sight already."

His eyes, wandering nervously along the front ranks of the waiting Folk, dimly illumined by the dull blue glow of the fire-well that shone through the mist, suddenly stopped with apprehension. His brows contracted, and on his heart it seemed as though a gripping hand had suddenly laid hold.

"H'yemba, the smith, again! Damn him! H'yemba!" he muttered, in sudden anger strongly tinged with fear.

The smith, in fact, was standing there a little to the left of him, huge and sinewed hands loosely clasped in front of him, face sinister, eyes glowing like two malevolent evil fires.

Allan noted the defiant poise of the body, the vast breadth of the shoulders, the heavy hang of the arms, biceped like a gorilla's.

For a minute the two men looked each other steadfastly in the eye, each measuring the other. Then suddenly the voice of Vreenya broke the tension.

"O Kromno, we have spoken. Will you hear us?"

Stern faced him, a strange sinking at his heart, almost as though the foreman of a jury stood before him to announce either freedom or sentence of death.

But, holding himself in check, lest any sign of fear or nervousness betray him, he made answer:

"I will hear you. Speak!"

"We have listened to your words. We believe you speak truth. Yet—"

"Yet what? Out with it, man!"

"Yet will we not compel any man to go. All shall be free—"

"Thank God!" breathed Allan, with a mighty sigh.

"—Free to stay or go, as they will. Our village is too full, even now. We have many children. It were well that some should make room for others. Those who dare, have our consent. Now, speak you to the people, your people, O Kromno, and see who chooses the upper world with you!"

Once more Allan turned toward the assemblage. But before he had found time to frame the first question in this unfamiliar speech, a disturbance somewhat to the left interrupted him.

There came a jostling, a pushing, a sound of voices in amazement, anger, approbation, doubt.

Into the clear space stepped H'yemba, the smith. His powerful right hand he raised on high. And boldly, in a loud voice, he cried:

"Folk of the Merucaans, this cannot be!"

CHAPTER XIII

THE RAVISHED NEST

"It cannot be? Who says it cannot be? *Who dares stand out and challenge me?*"

"I, H'yemba, the man of iron and of flame!"

Stern faced him, every nerve and fiber quivering with sudden passion. At realization that in the exact psychological moment when success lay almost in his hand, this surly brute might baffle him, he felt a wave of murderous hate.

He realized that the dreaded catastrophe had indeed come to pass. Now his sole claim to chieftainship lay in his power to defend the title. Failure meant—death.

"You?" he shouted, advancing on the smith.

His opponent only leered and grimaced offensively. Then without even having vouchsafed an answer, he swung toward the elders.

"I challenge!" he exclaimed. "I have the right of words!"

Vreenya nodded, fingering his long white beard.

"Speak on!" he answered. "Such is our ancient custom."

"Oh, people," cried the smith, suddenly facing the throng, "will ye follow one who breaks the tribal manners of our folk? One who disdains our law? Who has neglected to obey it? Will ye trust yourselves into hands stained with law-breaking of our blood?"

A murmur, doubtful, wondering, obscure, spread through the people. By the greenish flare-light Stern could see looks of wonder and dismay. Some frowned, others stared at him or at the smith, and many muttered.

"What the devil and all have I broken now?" wondered Allan. "Plague take these barbarous customs! Jove, they're worse than the taboos of the old Maoris, in the ancient days! What's up?"

He had not long to wonder, for of a sudden H'yemba wheeled on him, pointed him out with vibrant hands, and in a voice of terrible anger cried:

"The law, the law of old! No man shall be chief who does not take a wife from out our people! None who weds one of the Lanskaarn, the island folk, or the yellow-haired Skeri beyond the Vortex, none such shall ever rule us. Yet this man, this stranger who speaks such great things very hard to be believed, scorns our custom. No woman from among us he has taken, but instead, that vuedma of his own kind! What? Will ye—"

He spoke no further, for Allan was upon him with one leap. At sound of that word, the most injurious in their tongue, the fires of Hell burst loose in Stern.

Reckoning no consequences, staying for no parley or diplomacy, he sprang; and as he sprang, he struck.

The blow went home on the smith's jaw with a smash like a pile-driver. H'yemba, reeling, swung at him—no skill, no science, just a wild, barbaric, sledge-hammer sweep.

It would have killed had it landed, but Allan was not there. In point of tactics, the twentieth century met the tenth.

And as the smith whirled to recover, a terrible left-hander met him just below the short ribs.

With a grunt the man doubled, sprawled and fell. By some strange atavism, which he never afterward could understand, Allan counted, in the Folk's tongue: "Hathi, ko, zem, baku" and so up to "lamnu"—ten.

Still the smith did not rise, but only lay and groaned and sought to catch the breath that would not come.

"I have won!" cried Allan in a loud voice. "Here, you people, take this greun, this child, away! And let there be no further idle talk of a dead law—for surely, in your custom, a law dies when its champion is beaten! Come, quick, away with him!"

Two stout men came forward, bowed to Allan with hands clasped upon their breasts in signal of fresh allegiance, and without ceremony took the insensible smith, neck-and-heels, and lugged him off as though he had only been a net heavily laden with fish.

The crowd opened in awed silence to let them pass. By the glare Allan noticed that the man's jaw hung oddly awry, even as the obeah's had hung, in Madison Forest.

"Jove, what a wallop that must have been!" thought he, now perceiving for the first time that his knuckles were cut and bleeding. "Old Monahan himself taught me that in the Harvard gym a thousand odd years ago—and it still works. One question settled, mighty quick; and H'yemba won't have much to say for a few weeks at least. Not till his jawbone knits again, anyhow!"

Upon his arm he felt a hand. Turning, he saw Vreenya, the aged counselor.

"Surely, O master, he shall not live, now you have conquered him? The boiling pit awaits. It is our custom—if you will!"

Allan only shook his head.

"All customs change, these times," he answered. "I am your law! This man's life is needed, for he has good skill with metals. He shall live, but never shall he speak before the Folk again. I have said it!"

To the waiting throng he turned again.

"Ye have witnessed!" he cried, in a loud voice. "Now, have fear of me, your master! Once in the Battle of the Walls ye beheld death raining from my fire-bow. Once ye watched me vanquish your ruler, even the great Kamrou himself, and fling him far into the pit that boils. And now, for the third time, ye have seen. Remember well!"

A stir ran through the multitude. He felt its potent meaning, and he understood.

"I am the law!" he flung at them once more. "Declare it, all! Repeat!"

The thousand-throated chorus: "Thou art the law!" boomed upward through the fog, rolled mightily against the towering cliff, and echoed thunderlike across the hot, black sea.

"It is well!" he cried. "One more sleep, and then—then I choose from among ye two for the journey, two of your boldest and best. And that shall be the first journey of many, up to the better places that await ye, far beyond the pit!"

Straining his eyes in the night, pierced only by the electric beam that ran and quavered rapidly over the broken forest-tops far below, Allan peered down and far ahead. The fire, the signal-fire he had told Beatrice to build upon the ledge—would he never sight it?

Eagerly he scanned the dark horizon only just visible in the star-shine. Warmly the rushing night wind fanned his cheek; the roar of the motor and propellers, pulsating mightily, made music to his ears. For it sang: "Home again! Beatrice, and love once more!"

Many long hours had passed since, his fuel-tanks replenished from the apparatus for distilling the crude naphtha, which he had installed during his first stay in the Abyss, he had risen a second time into that heavy, humid, purple-vapored air.

With him he now bore Bremilu, the strong, and Zangamon, most expert of all the fishermen. Slung in the baggage-crate aft lay a large seine, certain supplies of fish, weed and eggs, and—from time to time noisily squawking—some half-dozen of the strange sea-birds, in a metal basket.

The pioneers had insisted on taking these impedimenta with them, to bridge the gap of changed conditions, a precaution Stern had recognized as eminently sensible.

"Gad!" thought he, as the Pauillac swept its long, flat-arc'd trajectory through the night, "under any circumstances this must be a terrific wrench for them. Talk about nerve! If they haven't got it, who has? This trip of these subterranean barbarians, thus flung suddenly into midair, out into a world of which they know absolutely nothing, must be exactly what a journey to Mars would mean to me. More, far more, to their simple minds. I wonder myself at their courage in taking such a tremendous step."

And in his heart a new and keener admiration for the basic stamina of the Merucaans took root.

"They'll do!" he murmured, as he scanned his lighted chart once more, and cast up reckonings from the dials of his delicately adjusted instruments.

Half an hour more of rapid flight and he deemed New Hope River could not now be far.

"No use to try and hear it, though, with this racket of the propellers in my ears," thought he. "The searchlight might possibly pick up a gleam of water, if we fly over it. But even that's a small index to go by. The signal-fire must be my only real guide—and where is it, now, that fire?"

A vague uneasiness began to oppress him. The fire, he reckoned, should have shown ere now in the far distance. Without it, how find his way? And what of Beatrice?

His uneasy reflections were suddenly interrupted by a word from Zangamon, at his right.

"O Kromno, master, see?"

"What is it, now?"

"A fire, very distant, master!"

"Where?" queried Stern eagerly, his heart leaping with joy. "I see no fire. Your eyes, used to the dark places and the fogs, now far surpass mine, even as mine will yours when the time of light shall come. Where is the fire, Zangamon?"

The fisher pointed, a dim huge figure in the star-lit gloom. "There, master. On thy left hand, thus."

Stern shifted his course to southwest by west, and for some minutes held it true, so that the needle hardly trembled on the compass dial.

Then all at once he, too, saw the welcome signal, a tiniest pin-prick of light far on the edge of the world, no different from the sixth-magnitude stars that hung just above it on the horizon, save for its redness.

A gush of gratitude and love welled in the fountains of his heart.

"Home!" he whispered. "Home—for where you are that's

home to me! Oh, Beatrice, I'm coming—coming home to you!"

Slowly at first, then with greater and ever greater swiftness, the signal star crept nearer; and now even the flames were visible, and now behind them he caught dim sight of the rock-wall.

On and on, a very vulture of the upper air, planed the Pauillac. Stern shouted with all his strength. The girl might possibly hear him and might come out of their cave. She might even signal—and the nearness of her presence mounted upon him like a heady wine.

He swung the searchlight on the canyon, as they swept above it. He flung the pencil of radiance in a wide sweep up the cliff and down along the terrace.

It gave no sight, no sign of Beatrice.

"Sleeping, of course," he reflected.

And now, Hope River past, and the canyon swallowed by the dense forest, he flung his light once more ahead. With it he felt out the rocky barrens for a landing-place.

Not more than twenty minutes later, followed by Bremilu and Zangamon, Stern was making way through the thick-laced wood and jungle.

Awed, terrified by their first sight of trees and by the upper world which to them was naught but marvel and danger, the two Merucaans followed close behind their guide. Even so would you or I cling to the Martian who should land us on that ruddy planet and pilot us through some huge, inchoate and grotesque growth of things to us perfectly unimaginable.

"Oh, master, we shall see the patriarch soon?" asked Bremilu, in a strange voice—a voice to him astonishingly loud, in the clear air of night upon the surface of the world. "Soon shall we speak with him and—"

"Hark! What's that?" interrupted Stern, pausing, the while he gripped his pistol tighter.

From afar, though in which direction he could not say, a vague, dull roar made itself heard through the forest.

Sonorous, vibrant, menacing, it echoed and died; and then again, as once before, Stern heard that strange, hollow booming, as of some mighty drum struck by a muffled fist.

A cry? Was that a cry, so distant and so faint? Beast-cry, or call of night-bird, shrill and far?

Stern shuddered, and with redoubled haste once more pushed through the vague path he and Beatrice had made from the barrens to Settlement Miffs.

Presently, followed by the two colonists who dared not let him for a moment out of their sight, he reached the brow of the canyon. His hand flash-lamp showed him the rough path to the terrace.

With fast-beating heart he ran down it, unmindful of the unprotected edge or the sheer drop to the rocks of New Hope River, far below.

Bremilu and Zangamon, seeing perfectly in the gloom, hurried close behind, with words of awe, wonder and admiration in their own tongue.

"Beta! Oh, Beatrice! Home again!" Stern shouted triumphantly. "Where are you, Beta? Come! I'm home again!"

Quickly he scrambled along the broken terrace, stumbling in his haste over loose rocks and debris. Now he had reached the turn. The fire was in sight.

"Beta!" again he hailed. "O-he! Beatrice!"

Still no answer, nor any sign from her. As he came to the fire he noted, despite his strong emotions, that it had for the most part burned down to glowing embers.

Only one or two resinous knots still flamed. It could not have been replenished for some time, perhaps two hours or more.

Again, his quick eye caught the fact that cinders, ashes and half-burned sticks lay scattered about in strange disorder.

"Why, Beatrice never makes a fire like that!" the thought pierced through his mind.

And—though as yet on no very definite grounds—a quick prescience of catastrophe battered at his heart.

"What's this?"

Something lying on the rock-ledge, near the fire, caught his eye. He snatched it up.

"What—what can this mean?"

The colonists stood, frightened and confused, peering at him in the dark. His face, in the ruddy fire-glow, as he studied the thing he now held in his hand, must have been very terrible.

"Cloth! Torn! But—but then—"

He flung from him the bit of the girl's cloak which, ripped and shredded as though by a powerful hand, cried disaster.

"Beatrice!" he shouted. "Where are you? Beatrice!"

To the doorway in the cliff he ran, shaken and trembling.

The stone had been pushed away; it lay inside the cave. Ominously the black entrance seemed staring at him in the dull gleam of the firelight.

On hands and knees he fell, and hastily crawled through. As he went, he flashed his lamp here, there, everywhere.

"Beatrice! Beatrice!"

No answer.

In the far corner still flickered some remainder of the cooking-fire. But there, too, ashes and half-burned sticks lay scattered all about.

To the bed he ran. It was empty and cold.

"Beatrice! Oh, my God!"

A glint of something metallic on the floor drew his bewildered, terror-smitten gaze.

He sprang, seized the object, and for a moment stood staring, while all about him the very universe seemed thundering and crashing down.

The object in his hand was the girl's gun. One cartridge, and only one, had been exploded.

The barrel had been twisted almost off, as though by the wrenching clutch of a hand inhuman in its ghastly power.

On the stock, distinctly nicked into the hard rubber as Stern held the flash-lamp to it, were the unmistakable imprints of teeth.

With a groan, Allan started backward. The revolver fell with a clatter to the cave floor.

His foot slid in something wet, something sticky.

"Blood!" he gasped.

Half-crazed, he reeled toward the door.

The flash-lamp in his hand flung its white brush of radiance along the wall.

With a chattering cry he recoiled.

There, roughly yet unmistakably imprinted on the white limestone surface, he saw the print, in crimson, of a huge, a horrible, a brutally distorted hand.

CHAPTER XIV

ON THE TRAIL OF THE MONSTER

Stern's cry of horror as he scrambled from the ravaged, desecrated cave, and the ghastly horror of his face, seen by the firelight, brought Zangamon and Bremilu to him, in terror.

"Master! Master! What—"

"My God! The girl—she's gone!" he stammered, leaning against the cliff in mortal anguish.

"Gone, master? Where?"

"Gone! Dead, perhaps! Find her for me! Find her! You can see—in the dark! I—I am as though blind! Quick, on the trail!"

"But tell us—"

"Something has taken her! Some savage thing! Some wild man! Even now he may be killing her! Quick—after them!"

Bremilu stood staring for a moment, unable to grasp this catastrophe on the very moment of arrival. But Zangamon, of swifter wit, had already fallen on his knees, there by the mouth of the cave, and now—seeing clearly by the dim light which more than sufficed for him—was studying the traces of the struggle.

Stern, meanwhile, clutching his head between both hands, dumb-mad with agony, was choking with dry sobs.

"Master! See!"

Zangamon held up a piece of splintered wood, with the bark deeply scarred by teeth.

Stern snatched it.

"Part of the pole I gave her to brace the rock with," he realized. "Even that was of no avail."

"Master—this way they went!"

Zangamon pointed up along the rock-terrace. Stern's eyes could distinguish no slightest trace on the stone, but the Merucaan spoke with certainty. He added:

"There was fighting, all the way along here, master. And then, here, the girl was dragged."

Stern stumbled blindly after him as he led the way.

"There was fighting here? She struggled?"

"Yes, master."

"Thank God! She was alive here, anyhow! She wasn't killed in the cave. Maybe, in the open, she might—"

"Now there is no more fighting, master. The wild thing carried her here."

He pointed at the rock. Stern, trembling and very sick, flashed his electric-lamp upon it. With eyes of dread and horror he looked for blood-stains.

What? A drop! With a dull, shuddering groan, he pressed forward again.

Out he jerked his pistol and fired, straight up, their prearranged signal: One shot, then a pause, then two. Some bare possibility existed and that she still might live and hear and know that rescue came—if it could come before it were eternally too late!

"On, on!" cried Allan. "Go on, Zangamon! Quick! Lead me on the trail!"

The Merucaan, now aided by Bremilu, who had recovered his wits, scouted ahead like a blood-hound on the spoor of a fugitive. One gripped his stone ax, the other a javelin.

Bent half double, scrutinizing in the dark the stony path which Allan followed behind them only by the aid of his flash, they proceeded cautiously up toward the brow of the cliff again.

But ere they reached the top they branched off onto another lateral path, still rougher and more tortuous, that led along the breast of the canyon.

"This way, master. It was here, most surely, the thing carried her."

"What kind of marks? Do you see signs of claws?"

"Claws? What are claws?"

"Sharp, long nails, like our nails, only much larger and longer. Do you see any such marks?"

Zangamon paused a second to peer.

"I seem to see marks as of hands, master, but—"

"No matter! On! We must find her! Quick—lead the way!"

Five minutes of agonizing suspense for Allan brought him, still following the guides, without whom all would have been utterly lost, to a kind of thickly wooded dell that descended sharply to the edge of the canyon. Into this the trail led.

Even he himself could now here and there make out, by the aid of his light, a broken twig, trampled ferns and down-crushed grass. Once he distinguished a blood-stain on a limb—fresh blood, not coagulated. A groan burst from between his chattering teeth.

He turned his light on the grass beneath. All at once a blade moved.

"Oh, thank God!" he wheezed. "They passed here only a few minutes ago. They can't be far now!"

Something drew his attention. He snatched at a sapling.

"Hair!"

Caught in a roughness of the bark a few short, stiff, wiry hairs, reddish-brown, were twisted.

"One of the Horde?" he stammered.

A lightning-flash of memory carried him back to Madison Forest, more than a year ago. He seemed to see again the obeah, as that monster advanced upon the girl, clutching, supremely hideous.

"The hair! The same kind of hair! In the power of the Horde!" he gasped.

A mental picture of extermination flashed before his mind's eye. Whether the girl lived or died, he knew now that his life work was to include a total slaughter of the Anthropoids. The destruction he had already wrought among them was but child's play to what would be.

And in his soul flamed the foreknowledge of a hunt a l'outrance, to the bitter end. So long as one, a single one of that foul breed should live, he would not rest from killing.

"Master! This way! Here, master!"

The voice of Zangamon sent him once more crashing through the jungle, after his questing guides. Again he fired the signal-shot, and now with the full power of his lungs he yelled.

His voice rang, echoing, through the black and tangled growths, startling the night-life of the depths. Something chippered overhead. Near-by a serpent slid away, hissing venomously. Death lurked on every hand.

Stern took no thought of it, but pressed forward, shouting the girl's name, hallooing, beating down the undergrowth with mad fury. And here, there, all about he flung the light-beam.

Perhaps she might yet hear his hails; perhaps she might even catch some distant glimmer of his light, and know that help was coming, that rescuers were fighting onward to her.

Silent, lithe, confident even among these new and terribly strange conditions, the two men of the Folk slid through the jungle.

No hounds ever trailed fugitive more surely and with greater skill than these strange, white barbarians from the underworld. Through all his fear and agony, Stern blessed their courage and their skill.

"Men, by God! They're men!" he muttered, as he thrashed his painful way behind them in the night.

Of a sudden, there somewhere ahead, far ahead in the wilderness—a cry?

Allan stopped short, his heart leaping.

Again he fired, and his voice set all the echoes ringing.

A cry! He knew it now. There could be no mistake—a cry!

"Beatrice!" he shouted in a terrible voice, leaping forward. The guides broke into a crouching run. All three crashed through the thickets, split the fern-masses, struggled through the tall saber-grass that here and there rose higher than their heads.

Allan cursed himself for a fool. That other cry he had heard while on his way from the Pauillac to Settlement Cliffs—that had been her cry for help—and he had neither known nor heeded.

"Fool that I was! Oh, damnable idiot that I was!" he panted as he ran.

From moment to moment he fired. He paused a few seconds to jack a fresh cartridge-clip into the automatic.

"Thank God I've got a belt full of ammunition!" thought he, and again smashed along with the two Merucaans.

All at once a formidable roar gave them pause.

Hollow, booming, deep, yet rising to a wild shriek of rage and horrid brutality, the beast-cry flung itself through the jungle.

And, following it, they heard again that muffled drumming, as though gigantic fists were flailing a tremendous tambour in the darkness.

"Master!" whispered Zangamon, recoiling a step. "Oh, Kromno, what is that?"

"Never have we heard such in our place!" added Bremilu, gripping his ax the tighter. "Is that a man-cry, or the cry of a beast—one of the beasts you told us of, that we have never seen?"

"Both! A man-beast! Kill! Kill!"

Now, Allan, sure of his direction, took the lead. No longer he flashed the light, and only once more he called:

"Beatrice! O Beatrice! We're coming!"

Again he heard her cry, but suddenly it died as though swiftly choked in her very throat. Allan spat a blasphemy and surged on.

The two white barbarians followed, peering with those strange, pinkish eyes of theirs, courageous still, yet utterly at a loss to know what manner of thing they were now drawing near.

They burst through a thicket, waded a marshy swale and went splashing, staggering and slipping among tufts of coarse and knife-edged grasses, the haunt of unknown venomous reptiles.

Up a slope they won; and now, all at once the roar burst forth again close at hand, a rending tumult, wild, earthshaking, inexpressibly terrible.

All three stopped.

"Beatrice! Are you there? Answer!" shouted Stern.

Silence, save for a peculiar mumbling snuffle off ahead, among the deeper shadows of a fern-tree thicket.

"Beatrice!"

No answer. With a groan Allan shot his light toward the thicket. He seemed to distinguish something moving. To his ears now came a sound of twigs and brushwood snapping.

Absolutely void of fear he pressed forward, and the two colonists with him, their weapons ready. Stern held his revolver poised for instant action. His heart was hammering, and his breath surged pantingly; but within him his consciousness and soul lay calm.

For he knew one of two things were now to happen. Either that beast ahead there in the gloom, or he, must die.

CHAPTER XV

IN THE GRIP OF TERROR

As the three pursuers steadily advanced, the thing roared once more, and again they heard the hammering, drumming boom. Zangamon whispered some unintelligible phrase.

Allan projected the light forward again, and at sight of a moving mass, vague and intangible, among the gigantic fronds, leveled his automatic.

But on the instant Bremilu seized his arm.

"O master! Do not throw the fire of death!" he warned. "You cannot see, but we can! Do not throw the fire!"

"Why not? What is that thing?"

"It seems a man, yet it is different, master. It is all hair, and very thick and strong, and hideous! Do not shoot, O Kromno!"

"Why not?"

"Behold! That strange man-thing holds the woman, Beatrice, in his left arm. Of a truth, you may kill her, and not the enemy."

Allan steadied himself against a palm. His brain seemed whirling, and for a moment all grew vague and like a dream.

She was there—Beatrice was there, and they could see her. There, in the clutches of some monster, horrible and foul! Living yet? Dead?

"Tell me! Does she live?"

"We cannot say, O Kromno. But do not shoot. We will creep close—we, ourselves, will slay, and never touch the woman."

"No, no! If you do he'll strangle her—provided she still lives! Don't go! Wait! Let me think a second."

With a tremendous effort Allan mastered himself. The situation far surpassed, in horror, any he had ever known.

There not a hundred yards distant in the dense blackness was Beatrice, in the grip of some unknown and hideous creature. Advance, Allan dared not, lest the creature rend her to tatters. Shoot, he dared not.

Yet something must be done, and quickly, for every second, every fraction of a second, was golden. The merest accident might now mean death or life—life, if the girl still lived!

"Zangamon!"

"Yea, master?"

"Be very bold! Do my bidding!"

"Speak only the word, Kromno, and I obey!"

"Go you, then, very quietly, very swiftly, to the other side of these great growing things—these trees, we call them. Then call, so that this thing shall turn toward you. Thus, I may shoot, and perhaps not kill the woman. It is the only way!"

"I hear, master. I go!"

Allan and Bremilu waited, while from the thicket came, at intervals, the savage snuffling, with now and then a grumbling mutter.

All at once a call sounded from far ahead.

"Come!" commanded Allan. Together he and Bremilu crept through the jungle toward the thicket.

Wide-eyed, yet seeing almost nothing, Allan crawled noiselessly, automatic in hand. The Merucaan slid along, silent as an Apache.

"Tell me if you see the thing again—if you see it turn!" whispered Stern. "Tell me, for you can see."

Now the distance was cut in half; now only a third of it remained. Before Stern it seemed a fathomless pit of black was opening. Under the close-woven arches of the giant fern-trees the night was impenetrable.

And as yet he dared not dart the light-beam into that pit of darkness, for fear of precipitating an unthinkable tragedy—if, indeed, the horror had not already been cons summated.

But now Bremilu gripped his arm. Afar, on the other side of the thicket, they heard a singular commotion, cries, shouts, and the vigorous beating of the fern-trees.

"The thing has turned, master!" the Merucaan exclaimed, at Allan's side. "Now throw the fire-death! Etvur! Quickly, throw!"

Stern swept the thicket with his beam.

"Ah! There—there!"

The light caught a moving, hairy mass of brown—a huge, squat, terrible creature, its back now toward them. At one side Stern saw a vague blackness—the long, unbound hair of Beatrice!

He glimpsed a white arm dangling limp; and in his breast the heart flamed at white-heat of rage and passion.

But his hand was steel. Never in his life had he drawn so fine a bead.

"Hold the light for me!" he whispered, passing it to his companion. "I want both hands for this!"

Bremilu held the beam true, blinking strangely with his pink eyes. Stern, resting his pistol hand in the hollow of his left elbow, sighted true.

A fraction of a hair to the left, and the bullet might crash through the brain of Beatrice!

"Oh, God—if there be any God—speed the shot true—" he prayed, and fired.

A hideous yell, ripping the night to shreds, burst in a raw and rising discord through the forest—a scream as of a damned soul flung upon the brimstone.

Then, as he glimpsed the white arm falling and knew the thing had loosed its grip, the light died. Bremilu, starting at the sudden discharge close to his ear, had pressed the ivory button.

Stern snatched for the flash-lamp, fumbled it, and dropped it there among the lush growths underfoot.

Before he could more than stoop to feel for it a heavy crash through the wood told that the thing was charging.

With bubbling yells it came, trampling the undergrowth, drumming on its huge breast, gibbeting with demoniac rage and pain—came swiftly, like the terrific things that people nightmares.

Behind it, shouts echoed. Stern heard the voice of Zangamon as, spear in hand, the Merucaan pursued.

He raised his revolver once more, but dared not fire.

Yet only an instant he hesitated, in the fear of killing Zangamon.

For, quick-looming through the darkness, a huge bulk, panting, snarling, chattering, sprang—an avalanche of muscle, bone, fur, mad with murder—rage.

Crack! spoke the automatic, point-blank at this rushing horror, this blacker shadow in the blackness.

The fire-stab revealed a grinning white-fanged face close to his own, and clutching hands, and terrible, thick, hairy arms.

Then something hurled itself on Stern; something bore him backward—something beside which his strength was as a baby's—something vast, irresistible, hideous beyond all telling.

Stern felt the flesh of his left arm ripped up. Crushed, doubled, impotent, he fell.

And at his throat long fingers clutched. A fetid, stinking breath gushed hot upon his face. He heard the raving chatter of ivories, snapping to rend him.

Up sprang another shadow. High it swung a weapon. The blow thudded hollow, smashing, annihilating.

Hot liquid gushed over Allan's hand as he sought to beat the monster back.

Then, fair upon him, fell a crushing weight.

Swooning, he knew no more.

CHAPTER XVI

A RESPITE FROM TOIL

The bright beam of the flash-lamp in his face roused Allan to a consciousness that he was bruised and suffering, and that his left arm ached with dull insistence. Dazed, he brought it up and saw his sleeve of dull brown stuff was dripping red.

Beside him, in the trampled grass, he vaguely made out a hairy bulk, motionless and huge. Bremilu was kneeling beside his master, with words of cheer.

"It is dead, O Kromno! The man-beast is dead! My stone ax broke its skull. See, now it lies here harmless!"

The currents of thought began to flow once more. Allan struggled up, unmindful of his wounds.

"Beatrice! Where is the girl?" he gasped.

As though by way of answer, the tall growths swayed and crackled, and through them a dim figure loomed—a man with something in his arms.

"Zangamon!" panted Allan, springing toward him. "Have you got her? The girl—is she alive?"

"She lives, master!" replied a voice. "But as yet she remains without knowledge of aught."

"Wounded? Is she wounded?"

Already he had reached Zangamon, and, injured though he was, had taken the beloved form in his arms.

"Beatrice! Beatrice!" he called, pressing kisses to her brow, her eyes, her mouth—still warm, thank God!

He sank down among the underbrush and gathered her to his breast, cradling her, cherishing her to him as though to bring back life and consciousness.

To her heart he laid his ear. It beat! She breathed!

"The light, here! Quick!"

By its clear ray he saw her hair disheveled; her coarse mantle of brown stuff ripped and torn, and on her throat long scratches.

Bruises showed on her hands and arms, as from a terrible fight she had put up against the monster. And his heart bled; and to his lips rose execrations, mingled with the tenderest words of pity and love.

"We must get her back to the cave at once!" he exclaimed. "Quick! Break branches. Make a litter—a bed—to carry her on! Everything depends on getting her to shelter now!"

But the two Merucaans did not understand. All this was beyond their knowledge. Ignoring his hurts, Allan laid the girl down very gently, and with them set to work, directing the making of the litter.

They obeyed eagerly. In a few minutes the litter was ready-made of fern-tree branches thickly covered with leaves and odorous grasses.

On this he placed the girl.

"You, Zangamon, take these boughs here. Bremilu, those others. Now I will hold the light. Back to the cave, now—quick!"

"We need not the light, master. We see better without it. It dazzles our eyes. Use it for yourself. We need it not!" exclaimed Bremilu, stooping above the body of the dead monster to recover his ax.

Involuntarily Allan turned the beam upon the horrible creature. There stood Bremilu, his foot upon the hairy shoulder, tugging hard at the ax-handle. Thrice he had to pull with all his might to loosen the blade which had buried itself deep in the shattered skull.

"A giant gorilla, so help me!" he cried, shuddering. "My God, Beatrice—what a ghastly terror you've been through!"

Still grinning ferociously, in death, with blood-smeared face and glazed, staring eyes, the creature shocked and horrified even Allan's steady nerves. He gazed upon it only a moment, then turned away.

"Enough!" said he. "To the cave!"

A quarter-hour had passed before they reached shelter again. Allan bade the Merucaans heap dry wood on the embers in the cavern, while he himself laid Beatrice upon the bed.

With a piece of their brown cloth dipped in one of the water-jars he bathed her face and bruised throat.

"Fresh water! Fetch a jar of fresh water from the river below!" he commanded Zangamon.

But even as the white barbarian started to obey, the girl stirred, raised a hand, and feebly spoke.

"Allan—oh—are you here again? Allan—my love!"

He strained her to his breast and kissed her; and his eyes grew hot with tears.

"Beatrice!"

Her arms were round his neck, and their lips clung.

"Hurt? Are you hurt?" he cried. "Tell me—how—"

"Allen! The monster—is he dead?" she shivered, sitting up and staring wildly round at the cave walls on which the fresh-built fire was beginning to throw dancing lights.

"Dead, yes. But hush, Beta! Don't think of that now. Everything's all right—you're safe! I'm here!"

"Those men—"

"Two of our own Folk. I brought them back with me—just in time, darling. Without them—"

He broke short off. Not for worlds would he have told her how near the borderland she had been.

"You heard my shouts? You heard our signal?"

"Oh—I don't know Allan. I can't think, yet—it's all so terrible—so confused—"

"There, there, sweetheart; don't think about it any more. Just lie down and rest. Go to sleep. I'll watch here beside you. You're safe. Nothing can hurt you now!"

She lay back with a sigh, and for a while kept silence while he sat beside her, his uninjured arm beneath her head.

His one ambition, now that he found she was not seriously hurt in body, was to keep her from talking of the horrible affair—from exciting herself and rehearsing her terrors. Above all, she must be quieted and kept calm.

At last, in her own natural voice, she spoke again.

"Allan?"

"What is it, sweetheart?"

"I owe you my life once more! If I was yours before, I'm ten times more yours now!"

He bent and kissed her, and presently her deepened breathing told him she had drifted over the borderline into the sleep of exhaustion.

He blessed her strength and courage.

"No futility here," thought he. "No useless questions or hysterics; no scene. Strong! Gad, but she's strong! She realized she was safe and I was with her again; that sufficed. Was there ever another woman like her since the world began?"

Only now that the girl slept did he pay attention to the two Merucaans who, sitting by the cave door, were regarding him with troubled looks.

"Master!" said Zangamon, arising and coming toward him.

"Well, what is it now?"

"You are wounded, O Kromno! Your arm still bleeds. Let us bind it."

"It is nothing—only a scratch!"

But Zangamon insisted.

"Master," said he, "in this we cannot obey you. See? While you and the woman talked I fetched water, as you commanded. Now I must wash your hurts and bind them."

Allan had to accede. Together the two Merucaans examined the injuries with words of commiseration. The "scratch" turned out to be three severe lacerations of the forearm. The gorilla's teeth had missed the radial artery only by a fluke of fortune.

They bathed away the clotted blood and bandaged the arm not unskilfully. Allan pressed the hand of Zangamon, then that of his companion.

"No thanks of mine can tell you what I feel!" he exclaimed straight from the heart. "Only for you to guide me, to drive the man-brute, to strike it down when it was just about to throttle me—only for you, both she and I—"

He could not finish. The words choked him. He felt, as never before, a sudden, warm, human touch of kinship with the Merucaans—a strong, nascent affection. Till now they had been savages to him—inferiors.

Now he perceived their inner worth—the strong and manly stamina of soul and body; and through him thrilled a love for these strange men, his saviors and the girl's.

Once more he seemed to see a vision of the future—a world peopled by the descendants of this hardy and resourceful folk, "without disease of flesh or brain, shapely and fair, the married harmony of form and function"—and, as with a gesture, he dismissed them wondering, not understanding in the least why he should thank them, he knew the world already had begun once more to come back under the hand, under the strong control of man.

"Sleep now, master," Bremilu entreated. "We who are new to this strange world will sit outside the door upon the rock and watch those fires so far above that you call stars. And the big sun-fire that is coming, too—we would see that!"

"No, not yet!" Stern commanded. "You cannot bear it for a while. Stay within and roll the rock against the door and sleep. The great fire might injure you or even kill you, as it did the—"

He checked himself just in time, for "the patriarch" had all but escaped him. Zangamon, with sudden understanding, once more advanced toward him as he sat there by the girl.

"O master! You mean the ancient man? He is dead?"

Stern nodded.

"Yes," he answered. "He was so old and weak, the touch of the fire in the sky—he could not bear it. But his death was happy, for at least he felt its warmth upon his brow!"

The Merucaans kept silence for a moment, then Stern heard them murmuring together, and a vague uneasiness crept over him.

He strove, however, to put it away; though in his heart the shame of the lie he had been forced to tell would not be quieted.

The colonists, however, made no further speech, but presently rolled the rock in front of the cave entrance, then wrapped themselves in their long cloaks and lay down by the fire.

Soon, like the healthy savages they were, they were fast asleep, with vigorous snorings.

Thus the night passed, while Stern kept watch over the girl; and another day crept slowly up the sky, and in the cave now rested four human beings—the vanguard of the coming nation.

CHAPTER XVII

THE DISTANT MENACE

Stern never knew when he, too, drifted off to sleep; but he awoke to find Zangamon sitting beside him, with his cloak drawn over his head, while Beatrice and Bremilu still slept.

"The light, master—it is like knives to me! Like spears to my eyes, master! I cannot bear it!" whispered the Merucaan, pointing to where, around the interstices of the doorway, bright white gleams were streaming in.

Allan considered with perplexity.

"It hurts, you say?"

"Yes, Kromno! Once or twice I have tried to watch that strange fire, but I cannot. The pain is very great!"

"Humph!" thought Allan. "This may be a more serious factor than I've reckoned on. These people are albinos. White hair and pink eyes—not a particle of protecting pigmentation. For thirty or so generations they've been subjected to nothing but torchlight. The actinic rays of the sun are infinitely more penetrating than anything they've ever known. It may take months, years even, to accustom them to sunlight!"

And disquieting situations presented themselves to his mind. True, if it were necessary, the Folk could work and take the air only at night.

They could fish, hunt and till the soil by star and moonlight, and sleep by day; but this was by no means the veritable reestablishment of a real, human civilization.

Then an idea struck him.

"The very thing!" cried he. "Once I can put it into effect, it will solve the question. And the second generation, at the outside, will be normal. They'll 'throw back' to remote ancestry under changed conditions. In time, even if only a long time, all will yet be well!"

But now immediate labors and difficult problems were pressing. The future would have to look out for itself.

Stern felt positive that to let the Merucaans out of the cave would not only blind them, but might also kill them outright as well.

Their unprotected skins would inevitably burn to a blister under the rays of the sun, and they would in all probability die. So said he:

"Listen, Zangamon! You must stay here till the dark comes again, which will not be very long. The woman and I will prepare another cave for your dwelling. When it is dark you can fish in the flowing water beneath. In the mean time we will bring you your accustomed food and your nets from the flying boat.

"You must be patient. In a short time all things shall be as you wish, and you shall see the wonderful and beautiful world up into which I have brought you!"

The man nodded, yet Stern clearly saw his face betrayed uneasiness, distrust and pain. In all fairness, the Merucaans' first experience of the upper world had been enough to shake the faith even of a philosopher—how much more so that of simple and untaught barbarians!

Terror, violence, slaughter and insecurity—these all had greeted the colonists; and now, in addition, they found the patriarch was dead. Above all, they were virtually prisoners in this gloomy cavern of the rock.

But Stern was very wise. He by no means thought of commiserating or excusing. His only course was to make light of trials and hardships, and, if need were, to command.

He arose, carefully stopped up the chinks around the rock at the doorway, and bade Zangamon replenish the fire with dry sticks. Then, Bremilu awakening, they prepared food.

Now Beatrice, too, awoke. Allan took her in his arms, unmindful of the newcomers, and there were words of love and joy, and self-reproaches, and a new faith plighted between them once again.

She was unharmed, except for a few bruises and scratches. Her nerves had already recovered something of their usual strength. But at sight of Allan's bandaged arni she turned pale, and not even his assurances could comfort her.

They talked of the terrible adventure.

"It was all my fault, Allan—every bit my fault!" she exclaimed remorsefully. "It all came from my not obeying orders. You see, I was expecting you last night. Instead of staying in the cave, with the door barricaded, I lingered on the terrace, after having piled the signal-fire high with wood.

"I sat down and watched the sky, and listened to the river down below, and thought of you. I must have dozed a little, for all of a sudden I came wide-awake, shuddering with a terror I couldn't understand. Then I heard something moving down the path—something that grunted and snuffled savagely.

"I started up, ran for the cave, and just got inside when the brute reached it. I rolled the stone in place, Allan, but before I could brace it with the pole it was hurled back, and in crawled the gorilla, roaring and snapping like a demon!"

She hid her face in both hands, shuddering at the terrible memory. But, forcing herself to be calm, she went on again:

"I snatched up the pistol and fired. Then—"

"You hit him?"

"I must have, for he screeched most horribly and pawed at his breast—"

"So, then, that explains the blood-marks on the floor and the great hand-print on the wall?"

"Hand-print? Was there one?"

"Yes; but no matter now. Go on!"

"After that—oh, it was too ghastly! He seized me and I fought—I struggled against that huge, hairy chest; he gripped me like iron. My blows were no more than so many pats to him.

"I tried to fire again, but he wrenched the pistol away, and bent it in his huge teeth and flung it down. But, though he was raging, he didn't wound me—didn't try to kill me, or anything. He seemed to want to capture me alive—"

Allan shuddered. Only too well he understood. Gorilla nature had not changed in fifteen hundred years.

"After that?" he questioned eagerly.

"Oh, after that I don't remember much. I must have fainted. Next thing I knew, everything was dark and the forest was all about. I screamed and then again I knew nothing. Once more I seemed to sense things, and once more all grew black. And after that—"

"Well?"

"Why—I was here on the bed, and you were beside me, Allan—and these men of our Folk were here! But how it all happened, God knows!"

"I'll tell you some time. You shall have the story from our side some day, but not now. Only one thing—if it hadn't been for Zangamon here and Bremilu—well—"

"You mean they helped rescue me?"

He nodded.

"Without them I'd have been helpless as a child. They traced you in the dark, for they could see as plainly as we see by day. It was a blow from Bremilu's stone ax that killed the brute. They saved you, Beatrice! Not I!"

She kept a little silence, then said thoughtfully:

"How can I ever thank them, Allan? How can I thank them

best?"

"You can't thank them. There's no way. I tried it, but they didn't understand. They only did what seemed natural to them. They're savages, remember; not civilized men. It's impossible to thank them! The only thing you can do, or I can do, is work for them now. The greatest efforts and sacrifices for these men will be small payment for their deed. And if—as I believe—the whole race is dowered with the same spirit and indomitable courage—the courage we certainly did see in the Battle of the Wall—then we need have no fear of our transplanted nation dying out!"

Much more there might have been to say, but now the meal was ready, and hunger spoke in no uncertain tones. All four of the adventurers ate in silence, thoughtful and grave, cross-legged, about the meat and drink, which lay on palm-leaves or in clay bowls hard-burned and red.

A kind of embarrassment seemed to rest on all, for this was the first time they had eaten together—these barbarians with the two folk of the upper world.

But the meal was soon at an end, and the prospect of labors to be undertaken cheered Allan's spirit. Despite his stiff and painful arm, he felt courage and energy throbbing in his veins, and longed to be at work.

"The very first thing we must do," said he, "is fix up a place for our guests. They've got to stay here, out of the light, till nightfall. That will give us plenty of time. I want to get them settled in their own quarters, and bring them into some regular routine of life and labor, before they have a chance to get homesick and dejected."

He warned the Merucaans to cover their heads with their cloaks while Beatrice and he opened the doorway.

He closed it then, with other rocks outside, and covered it with his own outer cloak; then, wearing only his belted tunic, he rejoined Beatrice half-way up the path to the cliff-top. Both were armed; he with his own automatic, she with the one they had found in the crypt.

"Our first move," said he, "will be to transport the various things from the airplane. It will be something of a task, but I don't dare leave them out there on the barrens till night, when the men themselves could bring them in. The sooner we get things to rights the better."

She agreed, and together they took the path toward the landing-place, which they had christened Newport Heights. Stern felt grateful that his right arm, his gun arm, was uninjured.

The other mattered little for the present.

An idea crossed his mind to seek out the dead gorilla and make a trophy of the pelt; but he dismissed it at once. The beast was so repellent that the very thought of it fair sickened him.

They reached the plane in some few minutes, found everything uninjured, and loaded themselves with the Merucaans' goods and chattels. Stern took the bags of edible seaweed and the metal crate of fowl; she draped the big net over her shoulders, and together, not without difficulty, they returned to Settlement Cliffs.

Pass, now, all the minute details of the installation. By noon they had prepared a habitation for the newcomers, deep in a far recess of a winding gallery which thoroughly excluded all direct sunlight.

Only the dimmest glow penetrated even at high noon. Here they stowed the freight, built a rock fireplace, and threw down quantities of the long, fragrant grass for bedding.

They returned to their own cave, bade the colonists once more cover their heads, and entered, carefully closing the doorway after them. All four dined together, in true Merucaan style, on the familiar food of the Abyss. The colonists seemed a little more reassured, but talk languished none the less.

The afternoon was spent in preparing a second cave; for, in spite of all the girl's entreaties, Allan was determined to make another visit to the village of the Lost Folk as soon as his arm should permit.

"Nothing can happen this time, dear girl," he assured her as they sat resting by the mouth of the newly prepared dwelling. "You'll have two absolutely faithful and efficient guards always within call by night. By day you can barricade yourself with them, if there's any sign of danger."

"I know, Allan, but—"

"There's no other way! Our work is just begun!"

She nodded silently, then said in a low tone:

"Yours the labor; mine the waiting, the watching, and the fear!"

"The fear? Since when have you grown timid?"

"Only for you, Allan! Only for you! Suppose, some time, you should not come back!"

He laughed.

"We thrashed that all out the first time. It's old straw, Beta. My end of the task is getting these people here. Yours is waiting, watching—and being strong!"

Her hand tightened on his, and for a little while they sat quite still and without speech, watching the day draw to its close.

Far below, New Hope River chattered its incessant gossip to the vexing boulders. Above, in the sky, lazy June clouds, wool-white, drifted to westward, as though seeking the glory that there promised to transmute them into gold and crimson.

A pleasant wind swayed the forest, wherein the scarlet birds flitted like flashes of flame. The beauty of the outlook thrilled their hearts, leaving no room for words.

But suddenly Allan's eyes narrowed, and with a singular hardening of expression, a tightening of the jaw, he peered away at the dim, haze-shrouded line of far horizon to northeastward.

He cast a sidelong glance at Beatrice. She had noticed nothing.

One moment he made as though to speak, then repressed the words, and once more gazed at the horizon.

There, so vague as almost to leave a doubt in mind, yet, after all, only too terribly real, his keen sight had detected something which caused his heart to throb the quicker and his eye to gleam with hate.

For, at the very rim of the world, dim, pale, ominous, three tiny threads of smoke were hanging in the evening air.

CHAPTER XVIII

THE ANNUNCIATION

A week later all was ready for Allan's second trip into the Abyss.

His arm had recovered its usual strength and suppleness, for his flesh, healthy as any savage's, now had the power of healing with a rapidity unknown to civilized men in the old days.

And his abounding vigor dictated action—always action, progress, and accomplishment. Only one thing depressed him—idleness.

It was on the second day of July, according to the rude calendar they were keeping, that he once more bade farewell to Beatrice and, borne by the Pauillac, headed for the village of the Lost Folk.

He left behind him all matters in a state of much improvement. Zangamon and Bremilu were now well installed in the new environment and seemingly content. By night they fished in New Hope Pool, making hauls such as their steaming sea had never yielded.

They wandered—not too far, however—in the forest, gradually making the acquaintance of the wondrous upper world, and with their strangely acute instincts finding fruits, bulbs and plants that well agreed with them for food.

Allan had carefully instructed them in the use of the wonderful "fire-bow"—the revolver—warning them, however, not to waste ammunition. They learned quickly, and now Beatrice found her larder supplied each night with game, which they dressed and brought her in the evening gloom, eager to serve their mistress in all possible ways.

They fished for her as well, and all the choicest fruits were her portion. She, in turn, cooked for them in their own cave. And for an hour or two each night she instructed them in English.

Short are the annals of peace—and peace reigned at Settlement Cliffs those few days at least. Progress!

She could feel it, see it, every hour. And her thoughts of Allan, now abandoning their melancholy hue, began to thrill with a new and even greater pride.

"Only he, only he could have brought these things to pass!" she murmured sometimes. "Only he could have planned all this, dreamed this dream, and brought it to reality; only he could labor for the future so strongly and so well!"

And in her heart the love that had been that of a girl became that of a woman. It broadened, deepened and grew calmer.

Its fever cooled into a finer, purer glow. It strengthened day by day, transmuting to a perfect trust and confidence and peace.

Allan returned safely inside the week with two more of the Folk—warriors and fishers both. Beatrice would have welcomed the arrival of even one woman to bear her some kind of company, but she realized the wisdom of his plan.

"The main thing at first," he explained, as they sat again on the terrace the evening of his return, "the very most essential thing is to build up even a small force of fighting men to hold the colony and protect it—a stalwart advance-guard, as if this were a military expedition. After that the women and children can come. But for the present there's no place for them."

Now that there were four Merucaans, all seemed more contented. The little group settled down into some real semblance of a community.

Work became systematized. Life was beginning to take firm root in the world again, and already the outlines of the future colony were commencing to be sketched in.

So far as Stern could discover, no disaffection as yet existed. The Folk, in any event, were singularly stolid, here as in their own home. If the colonists sometimes muttered together against conditions or concerning the lie Allan had told about the patriarch, he could never discover the fact.

He derived a singular sense of power and exaltation from watching his settlers at their work.

Strange figures they made in the upper world, descending the cliff at night, their torches flaring on their pure-white hair bound with gold ornaments, their nets slung over their brown-clad shoulders.

Strange, too, were the sensations of Beta and Allan as they beheld the flambeaux gleaming silently along the pool or over the surface when the Folk put forth on the rude rafts Allan had helped them build.

And as, with the same weird song they had used in the under world, the heavy-laden Merucaans clambered again up the terraces to their dwelling in the rock, something drew very powerfully at Allan's heart.

He analyzed it not, being a man of deeds rather than of introspection; yet it was "the strong man yearning toward his kind," the very love of his own race within him—the thrill, the inspiration of the master builder laying the foundations for better things to be.

Allan and the girl had long talks about the character of the future civilization they meant to raise.

"We must begin right this time at all hazards," he told her. "The world we used to know just happened; it just grew up, hit-or-miss, without scientific planning or thought or care. It was partly the result of chance, partly of ignorance and greed. The kind of human nature it developed was in essence a beast nature, with 'Grab!' for its creed.

"We must do better than that! From the very start, now, we must nip off the evil bud that might later blossom into private property and wealth, exploitation and misery. There shall be no rich men in our world now and no slaves. No idlers and no oppressed. 'Service' must be our watchword, and our motto 'Each for all and all for each!'

"While there are fish within the river and fruit upon the palm, none shall starve and none shall hoard. Superstition and dogma, fear and cruelty, shall have no place with us. We understand—you and I; and what we know we shall teach. And nothing shall survive of the world that was, save such things as were good. For the old order has passed away—and the new day shall be a better one."

Thus for hours at a time, by starlight and moonlight on the rock-terrace or by fire-glow in their cave—now homelike with rough-hewn furniture and mats of plaited grass—they talked and dreamed and planned.

And executed, too; for they drew up a few basic, simple laws, and these they taught their little colony even now, for from the very beginning they meant the germs of the new society should root in the hearts of the rescued race.

The third trip was delayed by a tremendous rain that poured with tropic suddenness and fury over the face of the world, driven on the breath of a wild-shouting tempest.

For the space of two days heaven and earth were blotted out by the gray, hurling sheets of wind-driven water, while down the canyon New Hope River roared and foamed in thunder cadences.

Beta and Allan, warmly and snugly sheltered in their cave, cared nothing for the storm. It only served to remind them of that other torrential downpour, soon after they had reached the village of the Folk; but now how altered the situation! Captives then, they were masters now; and the dread chasms of the Abyss were now exchanged for the beauties and the freedom of the upper world.

No wind could shake, no deluge invade, their house among the everlasting rock-ribs. Bright crackled their fire, and on the broad divan of cedar he had hewn and covered thick with furs, they two could lie and talk and dream, and let the storm rage, careless of its impotent fury.

"There's only one sorrow in my heart," whispered Beta, drawing his head down on her breast and smoothing his hair with that familiar, well-loved caress. "Just one, dear—can you guess it?"

"No millinery shops to visit, you mean?" he rallied her.

"Oh, Allan, when I'm so much in earnest, how can you?"

"Well, what's the trouble, sweetheart?"

"When the storm ends you're going to leave me again! I wish—I almost wish it would rain forever!"

He made no answer, and she, as one who sees strange and sad visions, gazed into the leaping flames, and in her deep gray eyes lay tears unshed.

"Sing to me!" he murmured presently.

Stroking his head and brow, she sang as aforetime at the bungalow upon the Hudson:

Stark wie der Fels, Tief wie das Meer, Muss deine Liebe, Muss deine Liebe sein! ...

The third trip was made in safety, and others after it, and steadily the colony took shape and growth.

More and more the caves came to be occupied. Stern set the Merucaans to work excavating the limestone, piercing tunnels and chimneys, making passageways and preparing for the ever-increasing number of settlers.

Their native arts and crafts began to flourish. In the gloomy recesses fires glowed hot. Ores began to be smelted, with primitive bellows and technique as in the Under-world, and through the night—stillness sounded the ring and clangor of anvils mightily smitten.

Palm-fibers yielded cordage for more nets or finer thread for the looms that now began to clack—for at last some few women had arrived, and even a couple of the strong, pale children, who had traveled stowed in crates like the water-fowl.

By night the pool and river gleamed more and more brightly. Boats navigated even the rapids, for these were hardy water-people, whose whole life had been semi-aquatic.

The strange fowl nested in the cliff below the settlement, hiding by day, flying abroad by night, swimming and diving in the river, even rearing their broods of squawking, naked little monsters in rough nests of twigs and mud.

Some of the hardier of the first-arrived colonists had already—far sooner than Allan had hoped—begun to tolerate a little daylight.

Following his original idea, he prepared some sets of brown mica eye-shields, and by the aid of these a number of the Merucaans were able to endure an hour or two of early dawn and late evening in the open air.

The children, he found, were far less sensitive to light than the adults—a natural sequence of the atavistic principle well known to all biologists.

He hoped that in a year or so many of the Folk might even bear the noon-day sun. Once he could get them to working with him by daylight his progress would leap forward mightily in many lines of activity that he had planned.

An occasional short raid with the Pauillac had stocked the colony with firearms, chemicals and necessary drugs, cutlery, ammunition and some glassware, from the dismantled cities of Nashville, Cincinnati, Indianapolis and other places unidentified.

Allan foresaw almost infinite possibilities in these raids. Civilization he felt, would surge onward with amazing rapidity fostered by this detritus of the distant past.

He also unearthed and brought back to Settlement Cliffs the phonographs and records, sealed in their oiled canvas and hidden in the rock-cleft near the patriarch's grave.

Thereafter of an evening the voices of other days sang in the cave. Around the entrance, now protected by stout and ample timber doors, gathered an eager, wondering, fascinated group, understanding the universal appeal of harmony, softened and humanized by the music of the world that was. And thus, too, was the education of the Folk making giant strides.

Progress, tremendous progress, toward the goal!

Autumn came down the world, and the sun paled a little as it sank to southward in the heavens. Warmth and luxuriant fertility, fecundity without parallel, still pervaded the earth, but a certain change had even so become well marked. Slowly the year was dying, that another might be born.

It was of a glorious purple evening late in October that Allan made the great discovery.

He had come in from working with two or three of the hardier Folk on the temporary hangar he was building for the Pauillac on Newport Heights, to which a broad and well-graded roadway now extended through the jungle.

Entering the home-cave suddenly—and it was home now indeed, with its broad stone fireplace, its comfortable furnishings, its furs, its mats of clean, sweet-smelling rushes—he stopped, toil-worn and weary, to view the well-loved place.

"Well, little wife! Busy, as usual? Always busy, sweetheart?"

At his greeting Beatrice looked up as though startled. She was sitting in a low easy-chair he had made for her of split bamboos cleverly lashed and softly cushioned.

At her left hand, on the palm-wood table, stood a heavy bronze lamp from some forgotten millionaire's palace in Atlanta. Its soft radiance illumined her face in profile, making a wondrous aureole of her clustered hair, as in old paintings of the Madonna at the Annunciation.

A presage gripped the man's heart, drawing powerfully at its strings with pain, yet with delicious hope and joy as she turned toward him.

For something in her face, some new, beatified, maternal loveliness, not to be analyzed or understood, betrayed her wondrous secret.

With a little gasp, she dropped into her lap the bit of needlework and sought to hide it with her hands—a gesture wholly girlish yet—to hide and guard it with those hands, so useful and beautiful, so precious and so dearly loved.

But Allan, breathing hard and deep, strode to her, his face aflame with hope and adoration. He caught them up together in the gentle strength of his rough hands and pressed them to his heart.

Beside her he knelt silently; he encircled her with his right arm. Then he took up the tiny garment, smiling.

For a long minute their eyes met.

His brimmed with sudden tears. Hers fell, and her head drooped down upon his breast, and—as once before, at the cathedral—an eloquent tide of crimson mounted from breast to throat, from cheek to tendrilled hair.

About his neck her arms slid, trembled, tightened.

No word was uttered there under the golden lamp-glow; but the strong kiss he pressed, reverently, proudly, upon her brow, renewed with ten-time depth their eternal sacrament of love.

CHAPTER XIX

THE MASTER OF HIS RACE

Days, busy days, lengthened into weeks, and these to months happy and full of labor; and in the ever-growing colony progress and change came steadily forward.

All along the cliff-face and the terraces the cave-dwellings now extended, and the smoke from a score of chimneys fashioned among the clefts rose on the temperate air of that sub-tropic winter.

At the doors, nets hung drying. On the pool, boats were anchored at several well-built stone wharfs. The terraces had been walled with palisades on their outer edge and smooth roadways fashioned, leading to all the dwellings as well as to the river below.

On top of the cliff and about three hundred yards back from the edge another palisade had been built of stout timbers set firmly in the earth, interlaced with cordage and propped with strong braces.

The enclosed space, bounded to east and west by the barrier which swung toward and touched the canyon, had all been cleared, save for a few palms and fern-trees left for shade.

Beside drying-frames for fish and game and a well-smoothed plaza for public assemblies and the giving of the Law, it now contained Stern's permanent hangar. The Pauillac had been brought along the road from Newport Heights and housed there.

This road passed through strong gates of hewn planks hinged with well-wrought ironwork forged by some of the Folk under the direction of H'yemba, the smith. For H'yemba, be it known, had been brought up by Stern early in December.

The man was essential to progress, for none knew so well as he the arts of smelting and of metal-work. Stern still felt suspicious of him, but by no word or act did the smith now betray any rebellious spirit, any animosity, or aught but faithful service.

Allan, however, could not trust him yet. No telling what fires might still be smoldering under the peaceful and industrious exterior. And the master's eye often rested keenly on the powerful figure of the blacksmith.

Across the canyon, from a point about fifty yards to eastward of Cliff Villa—as Beta and Allan had christened their home—a light bridge had been flung, connecting the northern with the southern bank and saving laborious toil in crossing via the river-bed.

This bridge, of simple construction, was merely temporary. Allan counted on eventually putting up a first-class cantilever; but for now he was content with two stout fiber cables anchored to palm-trunks, floored with rough boards lashed in place with cordage, and railed with strong rope.

This bridge opened up a whole new tract of country to northward and vastly widened the fruit and game supply. Plenty reigned at Settlement Cliffs; and a prosperity such as the Folk had never known in the Abyss, a well-being, a luxurious variety of foodstuffs—fruits, meats, wild vegetables—as well as a profusion of furs for clothing, banished discontent.

Barring a little temporary depression and lassitude due to the great alteration of environment, the Folk experienced but slight ill effects from the change.

And, once they grew acclimated, their health and vigor rapidly improved. Strangest of all, a phenomenon most marked in the children, Allan noticed that after a few weeks under the altered conditions of food and exposure to the actinic rays of the sun as reflected by the moonlight, pigmentation began to develop. A certain clouding of the iris began to show, premonitory of color-deposit. The skin lost something of its chalky hue, while at the roots of the hair, as it grew, a distinct infiltration of pigment-cells was visible. And at this sight Allan rejoiced exceedingly.

Beatrice did not now go much abroad with him, on account of her condition. She hardly ventured farther than the top of the cliff, and many days she sat in her low chair on the terrace, resting, watching the river and the forest, thinking, dreaming, sewing for the little new colonist soon to arrive. Some of their most happy hours were spent thus, as Allan sat beside her in the sun, talking of their future. The bond between them had grown closer and more intimate. They two, linked by another still unseen, were one.

"Will you be very angry with me, dear, if it's a girl?" she asked one day, smiling a little wistfully.

"Angry? Have I ever been angry with you, darling? Could I ever be?"

She shook her head.

"No; but you might if I disappointed you now."

"Impossible! Of course, the world's work demands a chief, a head, a leader, to come after me and take up the reins when they fall from my hands, but—"

"Even if it's a girl—only a girl—you'll love me just the same?"

His answer was a pressure of her hand, which he brought to

his lips and held there a long minute. She smiled again and in the following silence their souls spoke together though their lips were mute.

But Beta had her work to do those days as well as Allan.

While he planned the public works of the colony and directed their construction at night, or made his routine weekly trip into the Abyss for more and ever more of the Folk—a greatly shortened trip, now that he knew the way so well and needed stop below ground only long enough to rest a bit and take on oil and fuel—she was busy with her teaching of the people.

They had carefully discussed this matter, and had decided to impose English bodily and arbitrarily upon the colonists. Every evening Beatrice gathered a class of the younger men and women, always including the children, and for an hour or two drilled them in simple words and sentences.

She used their familiar occupations, and taught them to speak of fishing, metal-working, weaving, dyeing, and the preparation of food.

And always after they had learned a certain thing, in speaking to them she used English for that thing. The Folk, keen-witted and retentive of memory as barbarians often are, made astonishing strides in this new language.

They realized fully now that it was the speech of their remote and superior ancestors, and that it far surpassed their own crude and limited tongue.

Thus they learned with enthusiasm; and before long, among them in their own daily lives and labors, you could hear words, phrases, and bits of song in English. And at sound of this both Allan and the girl thrilled with pride and joy.

Allan felt confident of ultimate success along this line.

"We must teach the children, above all," he said to her one day. "English must come to be a secondary tongue to them, familiar as Merucaan. The next generation will speak English from birth and gradually the other language will decay and perish—save as we record it for the sake of history.

"It can't be otherwise, Beatrice. The superior tongue is always bound to replace the inferior. All the science and technical work I teach these people must be explained in English.

"They have no words for all these things. Bridges, flying-machines, engines, water-pipes for the new aqueduct we're putting in to supply the colony from the big spring up back there, tools, processes, everything of importance, will enforce English. The very trend of their whole evolution will drive them to it, even if they were unwilling, which they aren't."

"Yes, of course," she answered. "Yet, after all, we're only two—"

"We'll be three soon."

She blushed.

"Three, then, if you say so. So few among so many—it will be a hard fight, after all."

"I know, but we shall win. Old man Adams and one or two others, at the time of the mutiny of the 'Bounty' taught English to all their one or two score wives and numerous children on Pitcairn.

"The Tahitan was soon forgotten, and the brown half-breeds all spoke good English right up to the time of the catastrophe, when, of course, they were all wiped out. So you see, history proves the thing can be done—and will be."

Came an evening toward the beginning of spring again—an evening of surpassing loveliness, soft, warm, perfumed with the first crimson blossoms of the season—when Bremilu ran swiftly up the path to the cliff-top and sought Allan in the palisaded enclosure, working with his men on the new aqueduct.

"Come, master, for they seek you now!" he panted.

"Who?"

"The mistress and old Gesafam, the aged woman, skilled in all maladies! Come swiftly, O Kromno!"

Allan started, dropped his lantern, and turned very white.

"You mean—"

"Yea, master! Come!"

He found Beatrice in bed, the bronze lamp shining on her face, pale as his own.

"Come, boy!" she whispered. "Let me kiss you just once before—before—"

He knelt, and on her brow his lips seemed to burn. She kissed him, then with a smile of happiness in all her pain said:

"Go, dearest! You must go now!"

And, as he lingered, old Gesafam, chattering shrilly, seized him by the arm and pushed him toward the doorway.

Dazed and in silence he submitted. But when the door had closed behind him, and he stood alone there in the moonlight above the rushing river, a sudden exaltation thrilled him.

He knelt again by the rough sill and kissed the doorway of the house of pain, the house of life; and his soul flamed into prayer to whatsoever Principle or Power wrought the mysteries of the ever-changing universe.

And for hours, keeping all far away, he held his vigil; and the stars watched above him, too, mysterious and far.

But with the coming of the dawn, hark! a cry within! The cry—the thrilling, never-to-be-forgotten, heart-wringing cry of the first-born!

"Oh, God!" breathed Allan, while down his cheeks hot tears gushed unrestrained.

The door opened. Gesafam beckoned.

Trembling, weak as a child, the man faltered in. Still burned the lamp upon the table. He saw the heavy masses of Beta's hair upon the pillow of deerskin, and something in his heart yearned toward her as never until now.

"Allan!"

Choking, unable to formulate a word, shaking, he sank beside the bed, buried his face upon it, and with his hand sought hers.

"Allan, behold your son!"

Into his quivering arms she laid a tiny bundle wrapped in the finest cloth the Folk could weave of soft palm-fibers.

His son!

Against his face he held the child, sobbing. One hand sheltered it; the other pressed the weak and trembling hand of Beatrice.

And as the knowledge and the joy and pain of realization, of full achievement, of fatherhood, surged through him, the strong man's tears baptized the future master of the race!

CHAPTER XX

DISASTER!

That evening, the evening of the same day, Allan presented the man-child to his assembled Folk.

Eager, silent, awed, the white barbarians gathered on the terrace, all up and down the slope of it, before the door of their Kromno's house, waiting to behold the son of him they all obeyed, of him who was their law.

Allan took the child and bore it to the doorway; and in the presence of all he held it up, and in the yellow moonlight dedicated it to their service and the service of the world.

"Listen, O folk of the Merucaans!" he cried. "I show you and I give you, now, into your keeping and protection forever, this first-born child of ours!

"This is the first American, the first of the ancient race that once was, the same race whence you, too, have descended, to be born in the upper world! His name shall be my name—Allan. To him shall be taught all good and useful things of body and of mind. He shall be your master, but more than master; he shall be your friend, your teacher, your strength, your guide in the days yet to come! To you his life is given. Not for himself shall he live, not for power or oppression, but for service in the good of all!

"To you and your children is he given, to those who shall come after, to the new and better time. When we, his parents, and when you, too, shall all be gone from here, this man-child shall carry on the work with your descendants. His race shall be your race, his love and care all for your welfare, his every thought and labor for the common good!

"Thus do I consecrate and give him to you, O my Folk! And from this hour of his naming I give you, too, a name. No longer shall you be Merucaans, but now Americans again. The ancient name shall live once more. He, an American, salutes you, Americans! You are his elder brothers, and between you the bond shall never loosen till the end.

"I have spoken unto you. This is the Law!"

In silence they received it, in silence made obeisance; and, as Allan once more carried the child back to its mother, silently they all departed to their homes and labors.

From that moment Allan believed his rule established now by stronger bonds of love than any force could be. And through all the intoxication of success and consummated power he felt a love for Beatrice, who had rendered all this possible, such as no human words could ever say.

Allan, Junior, grew lustily, waxed strong, and filled the colony with joy. A new spirit pervaded Settlement Cliffs. The vital fact of new life born there, an augury of strength and increase and world-dominance once more, cemented all the social bonds.

An esprit de corps, an admirable and powerful cooperative sense developed, and the work of reconstruction, of learning, of progress went on more rapidly than ever.

Beatrice, seated at the door of Cliff Villa with the child upon her knee, made a veritable heart and center for all thought and labor. She and Allan, Junior, became objects almost of worship for the simple Folk.

It was heart-touching to see the eager interest, the love and veneration of the people, the hesitant yet fascinated way in which they contemplated this strange boy, blue-eyed and with yellow hair beginning to grow already; this, the first child they had ever seen to show them what the children of their one-time ancestors had been.

The hunters, now growing very expert in the use of firearms, fairly overloaded the larder of the villa with rare game-birds and venison. The fishers outdid themselves to catch choice fish for their master's family. And every morning fruits and flowers were piled at the doorway for their rulers' pleasure.

Even then, when so much still remained to do, it seemed as though the Golden Age of Allan's dreams already was beginning to take form. These were by far the happiest days Beta and he had ever lived. Love, work, hopes and plans filled their waking hours.

Put far away were all discouragements and fears. All dangers seemed forever to have vanished. Even the portent of the signal-fires, from time to time seen on the northern or eastern horizons, were ignored. And for a while all was peace and joy.

How little they foresaw the future; how little realized the terrible, the inevitable events now already closing down about them!

Allan made no further trips into the Abyss for about two months and a half. Before bringing any more of the people to the surface, he preferred to put all things in readiness for their reception.

He now had a working force of fifty-four men and twelve women. Including his own son, there were some seven children at Settlement Cliffs. The labor of civilization waxed apace.

With large plans in view, he dammed the rapids and set up a

small mill and power-plant, the precursor of a far larger one in the future. Various short flights to the ruins of neighboring towns put him in possession, bit by bit, of machinery which he could adapt into needful forms.

In a year or two he knew he would have to clear land and make preparations for agriculture. A grist-mill would soon be essential. He could not always depend upon the woods and streams for food for the colony.

There must be cultivation of fruits and grains; the taming of wild fowl, cattle, horses, sheep and goats—but no swine; and a regular evolution up through the stages again by which the society of the past had reached its climax.

And to his ears the whirring of his turbine as the waters of New Hope River swirled through the penstocks, the spinning of the wheels, the slapping of the deerskin belting, made music only second to the voices of Beatrice and his son.

Allan brought piecemeal and fitted up a small dynamo from some extensive ruins to southeastward. He brought wiring and several still intact incandescent lights. Before long Cliff Villa shone resplendent, to the awe and marvel of the Folk.

But Allan made no mystery of it. He explained it all to Zangamon, Bremilu and H'yemba, the smith; and when they seemed to understand, bade them tell the rest.

Thus every day some new improvement was installed, or some fresh knowledge spread among the colonists.

June had drawn on again, and the hot weather had become oppressive, before Allan thought once more of still further trips into the Abyss. Beatrice tried to dissuade him. Her heart shrank from further separation, risk and fear.

"Listen, dearest," she entreated as they sat by young Allan's bedside, one sultry, breathless night. "I think you've risked enough; really I do. You've got a boy now to keep you here, even if I can't! Please don't go! Follow out the plan you spoke to me about yesterday, but don't go yourself!"

"The plan?"

"Yes, you know. Your idea of training three or four of the most intelligent men to fly, and perhaps building one or two more planes—that is, establishing a regular service to and from the Abyss. That would be so much wiser, Allan! Think how deadly imprudent it is for you, you personally, to take this risk every time! Why, if anything should happen—"

"But it won't! It can't!"

"—What would become of the colony? We haven't got anything like enough of a start to go ahead with, lacking you! I speak now without sentiment or foolish, womanly fears, but just on a common-sense, practical basis. Viewed at that angle, ought you to take the risk again?"

"There's no time now, darling, to build more planes! No time to teach flying! We've got to recruit the colony as fast as possible, in case of emergencies. Why, I haven't made a trip since—since God knows when! It's time I was off now!"

"Allan!"

"Well?"

"Suppose you never went again? With the population we now have, and the natural increase, wouldn't civilization reestablish itself in time?"

"Undoubtedly. But think how long it would take! Every additional person imported puts us ahead tremendously. I may never be able to bring all the Folk, all the Lanskaarn, and those other mysterious yellow-haired people they talk about from beyond the Great Vortex. But I can do my share, anyhow. Our boy here may have to complete the process. It may take a lifetime to accomplish the rescue, but it must be done!"

"So you're determined to go again?"

"I am! I must!"

She seized his hand imploringly.

"And leave us? Leave your boy? Leave me?"

"Only to return soon, darling! Very soon!"

"But after this one trip, will you promise to train somebody else to go in your place?"

"I'll see, dearest!"

"No, no! Not that! Promise!"

She had drawn his head down, and now her face close to his, was trembling in her eagerness.

"Promise! Promise me, Allan! You must!"

Suddenly moved by her entreaty, he yielded.

"I promise, Beta!" he exclaimed. "Gad, I didn't know you were so deadly afraid of my little expeditions! If I'd understood, I might have been arranging otherwise already. But I certainly will change matters when I get back. Only let me go once more, darling—that'll be the last time, I swear it to you!"

She gave a great sigh of relief unspeakable and kept silence. But in her eyes he saw the shine of sudden tears.

Allan had been gone more than four days and a half before Beatrice allowed herself to realize or to acknowledge the sick terror that for some hours had been growing in her soul.

His usual time of return had hitherto been just a little over three days. Sometimes, with favorable winds to the brink of the Abyss, and unusually strong rising currents of vapors from the sunken sea—from the Vortex, perhaps?—he had been able to make the round trip in sixty hours.

But now over a hundred and eight hours had lagged by since Beatrice, carrying the boy, had accompanied him up the steep path to the hangar in the palisaded clearing.

How light-hearted, confident, strong he had been, filled with great dreams and hopes and visions! No thought of peril, accident, or possible failure had clouded his mind.

She recalled his farewell kiss given to the child and to herself, his careful inspection of the machine, his short and vigorous orders, and the supreme skill with which he had leaped aloft upon its back and gone whirring up the sky till distance far to the northwestward had swallowed him.

And since that hour no sign of return. No speck against the blue. No welcome chatter of the engine far aloft, no hum of huge blades beating the summer air! Nothing!

Nothing save ever-growing fear and anguish, vain hopes, fruitless peerings toward the dim horizon, agonizing expectations always frustrated, a vast and swiftly growing terror.

Beatrice cringed from her own thoughts. She dared not face the truth.

For that way, she felt instinctively, lay madness.

CHAPTER XXI
ALLAN RETURNS NOT

Five days dragged past, then six, then seven, and still no sign of Allan came to lighten the terrible and growing anguish of the woman.

All day long now she would watch for him—save at such times as the care and nursing of her child mercifully distracted her attention a little while from the intolerable grief and woe consuming her.

She would stand for hours on the rock terrace, peering into the northwest; she would climb the steep path a dozen times a day, and in distraction pace the cliff-top inside the palisaded area, where now some few wild sheep and goats were penned in process of domestication.

Here she would walk, calling in vain his name to the uncaring winds of heaven. With the telescope she would untiringly sweep the far reaches of the horizon, hoping, ever hoping, that at each moment a vague and distant speck might spring to view, wing its swift way southeastward, resolve itself into that one and only blessed sight her whole soul craved and burned for—the Pauillac and her husband!

And so, till night fell, and her strained eyes could no longer distinguish anything but swimming mists and vapors, she would watch, her every thought a prayer, her every hope a torment—for each hope was destined only to end in disappointment bitterer far than death.

And when the shrouding dark had robbed her of all possibility for further watching she would descend with slow and halting steps, grief-broken, dazed, half-maddened, to the home-cavern—empty now, in spite of her child's presence there—empty, and terrible, and drear!

Then would begin the long night vigil. Daylight gave some simulacrum of relief in action, some slight deadening of pain in the very searching of the sky, the strong, determined hope against what had now become an inner conviction of defeat and utter loss. But night—

Night! Nothing, then, but to sit and think, and think, and think, to madness! Sleep was impossible. At most, exhausted nature snatched only a few brief spells of semi-consciousness.

Even the sight of the boy, lying there sunk in his deep and

healthy slumber, only kindled fresh fires of woe. For he was Allan's child—he spoke to her by his mere presence of the absent, the lost, perhaps the dead man.

And at thought that now she might be already widowed and her boy fatherless, she would pace the rock-floor in terrible, writhen crises of agony, hands clenched till the nails pierced the delicate flesh, eyes staring, face waxen, only for the sake of the child suppressing the sobs and heart-torn cries that sought to burst from her overburdened soul.

"Oh, Allan! Allan!" she would entreat, as though he could know and hear. "Oh, come back to me! What has happened? Where are you? Come back, come back to your boy—to me!"

Then, betimes, she would catch up the child and strain it to her breast, even though it awakened. Its cries would mingle with her anguished weeping; and in the firelit gloom of the cave they two—she who knew, and he who knew not—would in some measure comfort one another.

On the eighth day she sustained a terrible shock, a sudden joy followed by so poignant a despair that for a moment it seemed to her human nature could endure no more and she must die.

For, eagerly watching the cloud-patched sky with the telescope, from the cliff-top—while on the terrace old Gesafam tended the child—she thought suddenly to behold a distant vision of the airplane!

A tiny spot in the heavens, truly, was moving across the field of vision!

With a cry, a sudden flushing of her face, now so wan and colorless, she seemed to throw all her senses into one sense, the power of sight. And though her hand began to shake so terribly that she could only with a great effort hold the glass, she steadied it against a fern-tree and thus managed to find again and hold the moving speck.

The Pauillac! Was it indeed the Pauillac and Allan?

"Merciful Heaven!" she stammered. "Bring him back—to me!"

Again she watched, her whole soul aflame with hope and eagerness and tremulous joy, ready to burst into a blaze of happiness—and then came disillusion and despair, blacker than ever and more terrible.

For suddenly the moving speck turned, wheeled and rose. One second she caught sight of wings. She knew now it was only some huge, tropic bird, afar on the horizon—some condor, vulture, or other creature of the air.

Then, as with a quick swoop, the vulture slid away and vanished behind a blue hill-shoulder, the woman dropped her glass, sank to earth, and—half-fainting—burst into a terrible, dry, sobbing plaint. Her tears, long since exhausted, would not flow. Grief could pass no further limits.

After a time she grew calmer, arose and thought of her child once more. Slowly she returned down the via dolorosa of the terrace-path, the walk where she and Allan had so often and so gaily trodden; the path now so barren, so hateful, so solitary.

To her little son she returned, and in her arms she cherished him—in her trembling arms—and the tears came at last, welcome and heart-stilling.

Old Gesafam, gazing compassionately with troubled eyes that blinked behind their mica shields, laid a comforting hand on the girl's shoulder.

"Do not weep, O Yulcia, mistress!" she exclaimed in her own tongue. "Weep not, for there is still hope. See, all things are going on, as before, in the colony!" She gestured toward the lower caves, whence the sounds of smithy-work and other toil drifted upward. "All is yet well with us. Only our Kromno is away. And he will yet come! He will come back to us—to the child, to you, to all who love and obey him!"

Beatrice seized the old woman's hand and kissed it in a burst of gratitude.

"Oh—if I could only believe you!" she sobbed.

"It will be so! What could happen to him, so strong, so brave? He must come back! He will!"

"What could happen? A hundred things, Gesafam! One tiny break in the flying boat and he might be hurled to earth or down the Abyss, to death! Or, among your Folk, he may have been defeated, for many of the Folk are still savage and very cruel! Or, the Horde—"

"The Horde? But the Horde, of which you have so often spoken, is now afar."

"No, Gesafam. Even today I saw their signal-fires on the horizon."

The old woman drew an arm about the girl. All barbarian that she was, the eternal, universal spirit of the feminine, pervading her, made her akin with the sorrowing wife.

"Go rest," she whispered. "I understand. I, too have wept and mourned, though that was very long ago in the Abyss. My man, my Nausaak, a very brave and strong catcher of fish, fought with the Lanskaarn—and he died. I understand, Yulcia! You must think no more of this now. The child needs your strength. You must rest. Go!"

Gently, yet with firmness that was not to be disputed, she forced Beatrice into the cave, made her lie down, and prepared a drink for her.

Though Beta knew it not, the wise old woman had steeped therein a few leaves of the ronyilu weed, brought from the Abyss, a powerful soporific. And presently a certain calm and peace began to win possession of her soul.

For a time, however, distressing visions still continued to float before her disordered mind. Now she seemed to behold the Pauillac, flaming and shattered, whirling down, over and over, meteor-swift, into the purple mists and vapors of the Abyss.

Now the scene changed; and she saw it, crushed and broken, lying on some far rock-ledge, amid impenetrable forests, while from beneath a formless tangle of wreckage protruded a hand—his hand—and a thin, dripping stream of red.

Gasping, she sought to struggle up and stare about her; but the drugged draft was too potent, and she could not move. Yet still the visions came again—and now it seemed that Allan lay there, in the woods, somewhere afar, transfixed with an envenomed spear, while in a crowding, hideous, jabbering swarm the distorted, beast-like anthropoids jostled triumphantly all about him, hacked at him with flints and knives, flayed and dismembered him, inflicted unimaginable mutilations—

She knew no more. Thanks to the wondrous beneficence of the ronyilu, she slept a deep and dreamless slumber. Even the child being laid on her breast by the old woman—who smiled, though in her eyes stood tears—even this did not arouse her.

She slept. And for a few blessed hours she had respite from woe and pain unspeakable.

At last her dreams grew troubled. She seemed caught in a thunder-storm, an earthquake. She heard the smashing of the lightning bolts, the roaring shock of the reverberation, then the crash of shattered buildings.

A sudden shock awoke her. She thought a falling block of stone had struck her arm. But it was only old Gesafam shaking her in terror.

"Oh, Yulcia, noa!" the nurse was crying in terror. "Up! Waken! The cliff falls! Awake, awake!"

Beatrice sat up in bed, conscious through all the daze of dreams quick broken, that some calamity—some vast and unknown peril—had smitten the colony at Settlement Cliffs.

CHAPTER XXII

THE TREASON OF H'YEMBA

Not yet even fully awake, Beatrice was conscious of a sudden, vast responsibility laid on her shoulders. She felt the thrill of leadership and command, for in her hands alone now rested the fate of the community.

Out of bed she sprang, her grief for the moment crushed aside, aquiver now with the spirit of defense against all ills that might menace the colony and her child.

"The cliff falls?" she cried, starting for the doorway.

"Yea, mistress! Hark!"

Both women heard a grating, crushing sound. The whole fabric of the cavern trembled again, as though shuddering; then, far below, a grinding crash reechoed—and now rose shouts, cries, wails of pain.

Already Beatrice was out of the door and running down the terrace.

"Yulcia! Yulcia!" the old woman stood screaming after her. "You must not go!"

She answered nothing, but ran the faster. Already she could see dust rising from the river-brink; and louder now the cries blended in an anguished chorus as she sped down the terrace.

What could have happened? How great was the catastrophe? What might the death-roll be?

Her terrors about Allan had at last been thrown into the background of her mind. She forgot the boy, herself, everything save the crushing fact of some stupendous calamity.

All at once she stopped with a gasp of terror.

She had reached the turn in the path whence now all the further reach of the cliff was visible. But, where the crag had towered, now appeared only a great and jagged rent in the limestone, through which the sky peered down.

An indescribable chaos of fragments, blocks, debris, detritus of all kinds half choked the river below; and the swift current, suddenly blocked, now foamed and chafed with lathering fury through the newly fallen obstacle.

Broken short off, the path stopped not a hundred yards in front of her.

As she stood there, dazed and dumb, harkening the terrible cries that rose from those still not dead in the ruins, she perceived some of the Folk gathered along the brink of the new chasm. More and more kept coming from the scant half of the caves still left. And all, dazed and numbed like herself, stood there peering down with vacant looks.

Beatrice first recovered wit. Dimly she understood the truth. The cavern digging of the Folk, the burrowing and honeycombing through the cliff, must have sprung some keystone, started some "fault," or broken down some vital rib of the structure.

With irresistible might it had torn loose, slid, crashed, leaped into the canyon, carrying with it how many lives she knew not.

All she knew now was that rescues must be made of such as still lived, and that the bodies of the dead must be recovered.

So with fresh strength, utterly forgetful of self, she ran once more down the steep terrace, calling to her folk:

"Men! My people! Down to the river, quickly! Take hammers, bars, tools—go swiftly! Save the wounded! Go!"

There was no sleep for any in the colony that day, that night, or the next day. The vast pile of debris rang with the sledge blows, louder than ever anvil rang, and the torches flared and sparkled over the jumble of broken rock, beneath which now lay buried many dead—none knew how many—nevermore to be seen of man. Great iron bars bent double with the prying of strong arms.

Beatrice herself, flambeau in hand, directed the labor. And as, one by one, the wounded and the broken were released, she ordered them borne to the great cave of Bremilu, the Strong.

Bremilu had been in the house of one Jukkos at the time of the catastrophe. His body was one of the first to be found. Beta transformed his cave into a hospital.

And there, working with the help of three or four women, hampered in every way for lack of proper materials, she labored hour after hour dressing wounds, setting broken bones, watching no few die, even despite the best that she could do.

Old Gesafam came to seek her there with news that the child cried of hunger. Dazed, Beta went to nurse it; and then returned, in spite of the old woman's pleadings; and so a long time passed—how long she never knew.

Disaster! This was her one clear realization through all those hours of dark and labor, anguish and despair. For the first time the girl felt beaten.

Till now, through every peril, exposure and hardship, she had kept hope and courage. Allan had always been beside her—wise, and very strong to counsel and to act.

But now, alone there—all alone in face of this sudden devastation—she felt at the end of her resources. She had to struggle to hold her reason, to use her native judgment, common sense and skill.

The work of rescue came to an end at last. All were saved who could be. All the bodies that could be reached had been carried into still another cave, not far from the path of the disaster. All the wounds and injuries had been dressed, and now Beatrice knew her force was at an end. She could do no more.

Drained of energy, spent, broken, she dragged herself up the path again. In front of the cave of H'yemba, the smith, a group of survivors had gathered.

Dimly she sensed that the ugly fellow was haranguing them with loud and bitter words. As she came past, the speech died; but many lowering and evil looks were cast on her, and a low murmur—sullen and ominous—followed her on up the terrace.

Too exhausted even to note it or to care, she staggered back to Cliff Villa, flung herself on the bed, and slept.

How long? She could not tell when she awoke again. Only she knew that a dim light, as of evening, was glimmering in at the doorway, and that her child was in the bed beside her.

"Gesafam!" she called, for she heard some one moving in the cave. "Bring me water!"

There came no answer. Beta repeated the command. A curious, sneering mockery startled her. Still clad in her loose brown cloak, belted at the waist—for she had thrown herself upon the bed fully clad—she sat up, peering by the light of the fireplace into the half dark of the room.

A third time she called the old woman.

"It is useless!" cried a voice. "She will not come to help you. See, I have bound her—and now she lies in that further chamber of the cave, helpless. For it is not with her I would speak, but with you. And you shall hear me."

"H'yemba!" cried Beatrice, startled, suddenly recognizing the squat and brutal figure that now, a threat in every gesture, approached the bed. "Out! Out of here, I say! How dare you enter my house? You shall pay heavily for this great insult when the master comes. Out and away!"

The ugly fellow only laughed menacingly.

"No, I shall not go, and there will be no payment," he retorted in his own speech. "And you must hear me, for now I, and not he, shall be the master here."

Beta sprang from the bed and faced him.

"Go, or I shoot you down like a dog!" she threatened.

He sneered.

"There will be no shooting," he answered coolly. "But there will be speech for you to hear. Now listen! This is what ye brought us here to? The man and you? This? To death and woe? To accidents and perishings?

"Ye brought us to hardship and to battle, not to peace! With lies, deceptions and false promises ye enticed us! We were safe and happy in our homes in the Abyss beside the sunless sea, till ye fell thither in your air-boat from these cursed regions. We—"

"For this speech ye shall surely die when the master comes!" cried she. "This is treason, and the penalty of it is death!"

He continued, paying no heed:

"We had no need of you, your ways, or your place. But the man Allan would rule or he would ruin. He overthrew and killed our chief, the great Kamrou himself—Kamrou the Terrible! To us he brought dissensions. From us he bore the patriarch away and slew him, and then made us a great falsehood in that matter.

"So he enticed us all. And ye behold the great disaster and the death! The man Allan has deserted us all to perish here. Coward in his heart, he has abandoned you as well! Gone once more to safety and ease, below in the Abyss, there to rule the rest of the Folk, there to take wives according to our law, while we die here!"

Menacingly he advanced toward the dumb-stricken woman, his face ablaze with evil passion.

"Gremnya!" (coward) he shouted. "Weakling at heart. Great boaster, doer of little deeds! Even you, who would be our mistress, he has abandoned—even his own son he has forsaken. A rotten breed, truly! And we die!

"But listen now. This shall not be! I, H'yemba, the smith, the strongest of all, will not permit it. I will be ruler here, if any live to be ruled! And you shall be my serving-maid—your son my slave!"

Aghast, struck dumb by this wild tempest of rebellion, Beatrice recoiled. His face showed like a white blur in the gloom.

"Allan!" she gasped. "My Allan—"

The huge smith laughed a venomous laugh that echoed through the cave.

"Ha! Ye call on the coward?" he mocked, advancing on her. "On the coward who cannot hear, and would not save you if he could? Behold now ye shall kneel to me and call me master! And my words from now ye shall obey!"

She snatched for her pistol. It was not there. In the excitement of the past hours she had forgotten to buckle it on. She was unarmed.

H'yemba already grasped for her, to force her down upon the floor, kneeling to him—to make her call him master.

Already his strong and hairy fingers had all but seized her robe.

But she, lithe and agile, evaded the grip. To the fire she sprang. She caught up a flaming stick that lay upon the hearth. With a cry she dashed it full into his glaring eyes.

So sudden was the attack that H'yemba had no time even to ward it off with his hands. Fair in the face the scorching flame struck home.

Howling, blinded, stricken, he staggered back; beat the air with vain blows and retreated toward the door.

As he went he poured upon her a torrent of the most hideous imprecations known to their speech—and they were many.

But she, undaunted now, feeling her power and her strength again, followed close. And like blows of a flail, the sputtering, flaring flame beat down upon his head, neck, shoulders.

His hair was blazing now; a smell of scorched flesh diffused itself through the cavern.

"Go! Go, dog!" she shouted, maddened and furious, in consuming rage and hate. "Coward! Slanderer and liar! Go, ere I kill you now!"

In panic-stricken fright, unable to see, trying in vain to ward off the devastating, torturing whip of flame and to extinguish the fire ravaging his hair, the brute half ran, half fell out of the cave.

Down the steep path he staggered, yelling curses; down, away, anywhere—away from this pursuing fury.

But the woman, outraged in all her inmost sacred tendernesses, her love for child and husband, still drove him with the blazing scourge—drove, till the torch was beaten to extinction—drove, till the smith took refuge in his own cave.

There, being spent and weary, she let him lie and howl. Exhausted, terribly shaken in body and soul, yet her eyes triumphant, she once more climbed the precipitous path to her own dwelling. The torch she flung away, down the canyon into the river.

She ran to the far recess of the cave, found Gesafam indeed bound and helpless, and quickly freed her.

The old woman was shaking like a leaf, and could give no coherent account of what had happened. Beta made her lie down on the couch, and herself prepared a bowl of hot broth for the faithful nurse.

Then she bethought herself of the pistol Allan had given her.

"I must never take that off again, whatever happens," said she. "But—where is it now?"

In vain she hunted for it on the table, the floor, the shelves, and in the closets Allan had built. In vain she ransacked the whole cave.

The pistol, belt, and cartridges—all were gone.

CHAPTER XXIII

THE RETURN OF THE MASTER

Suddenly finding herself very much alarmed and shaken, Beatrice sat down in the low chair beside her bed, and covering her face with both hands tried to think.

The old woman, somewhat recovered, moved about with words of pity and indignation, and sought to make speech with her, but she paid no heed. Now, if ever, she had need of self-searching—of courage and enterprise. And all at once she found that, despite everything, she was only a woman.

Her passion spent, she felt a desperate need of a man's strength, advice, support. In disarray she sat there, striving to collect her reason.

Her robe was torn, and her loosened hair, escaping from its golden pins, cascaded all about her shoulders. Loudly her heart throbbed; a certain shivering had taken possession of her, and all at once she noticed that her brow was burning.

Resolutely she tried to put her weakness from her, and marshalled her thoughts. In the bed her son still slept quietly, his fat fist protruding from the clothes, his ruddy, healthy little face half buried in the pillow.

A great, overpowering wave of mother-love swept her heart. She leaned forward, and through lids now tear-dimmed, with eyes no longer angry, peered at the child—her child and Allan's.

"For your sake—for yours if not for mine," she whispered, "I must be strong!"

She thought.

"Evidently some great conspiracy is going on here. Beyond and apart from the calamity of the landslide, some other and even greater peril menaces the colony!"

She reflected on the incident of her pistol and ammunition being stolen.

"There can be no doubt that H'yemba did that," she decided. "In the confusion of the catastrophe he has disarmed me. That means well-planned rebellion—and at this time it will be fatal! Now, above all else, we must work in harmony, stand fast, close up the ranks! This must not be!"

Yet she could see no way clear to crush the danger. What could she do against so many—nearly all provided with firearms? Why had H'yemba even taken the trouble to steal her weapon?

"Coward!" she exclaimed. "Afraid for his own life—afraid even to face me, so long as I had a pistol! As I live, and heaven is above me, in case of civil war he shall be the first to die!"

She summoned Gesafam.

"Go, now!" she commanded; "go among the remaining Folk and secretly find me a pistol, with ammunition. Steal them if you must. Say nothing, and return as quickly as you can. There be many guns among the Folk. I must have one. Go!"

"O, Yulcia, will there be fighting again?"

"I know not. Ask no questions, but obey!"

Trembling—shaking her head and muttering strange things, the old woman departed.

She returned in a quarter-hour with not only one, but two pistols and several ammunition-belts cleverly concealed beneath her robe. Beta seized them gladly with a sudden return of confidence.

But the old woman, though she said no word, eyed her mistress in a strange, disquieting manner. What had she heard, or seen, down in the caves? Beatrice had now neither time nor inclination to ask.

"Listen, old mother," she commanded. "I am now going to leave you and my son here together. After I am gone lock the door. Let no one in. I alone shall enter. My signal shall be two knocks on the door, then a pause, then three. Do not open till you hear that signal. You understand me?"

"I understand and I obey, O Yulcia noa!"

"It is well. Guard my son as your life. Now I go to see the wounded and the sick again!"

The old woman let her out and carefully barred the door behind her. Beatrice, unafraid, with both her weapons lying loose in their holsters, belted under her robe, advanced alone down the terrace path.

Her hair had once more been bound up. She had recovered something of her poise and strength. The realization of her mission inspired her to any sacrifice.

"It's all for your sake, Allan," she whispered as she went. "All for yours—and our boy's!"

Far beneath her New Hope River purled and sparkled in the morning sun. Beyond, the far and vivid tropic forest stretched in wild beauty to the hills that marked the world's end—those hills beyond which—

She put away the thought, refusing to admit even the possibility of Allan's failure, or accident, or death.

"He will come back to me!" she said bravely and proudly, for a moment stopping to face the sun. "He will come back from beyond those hills and trackless woods! He will come back—to us!"

Again she turned, and descending some dozen steps in the terrace path, once more reached the doorway of the hospital cave.

Pausing not, hesitating not, she lifted the rude latch and pushed.

The door refused to give.

Again she tried more forcibly.

It still resisted.

Throwing all her strength against the barrier, she fought to thrust it inward. It would not budge.

"Barred!" she exclaimed, aghast.

Only too true. During her absence, though how or by whom she could not know, the door had been impassably closed to keep her out!

Who, now, was working against her will? Could it be that H'yemba, all burned and blinded as he was, could have returned so soon and once more set himself to thwart her? And if not the smith, then who?

"Rebellion!" she exclaimed. "It's spreading—growing—now, at the very minute when I should have help, faith and cooperation!"

"Open! Open, in the name of the law that has been given you—our law!" she cried loudly in the Merucaan tongue.

No answer.

She snatched out a pistol, and with the butt loudly smote the planks of palm-wood. Within, the echoes rumbled dully, but no human voice replied.

"Traitors! Cowards!" she defied the opposing power. "I, a woman, your mistress, am come to save you, and you bar me out! Woe on you! Woe!"

Waiting not, but now with greater haste, she ran down along the pathway toward the next door.

That, too, was sealed. And the next, and the fourth, and all, every one, both on the upper and the lower terrace, all—all were barricaded, even to the great gap made by the landslide.

From within no sound, no reply, no slightest sign that any heard or noticed her. Dumb, mute, passive, invincible rebellion!

In vain she called, commanded, pleaded, explained, entreated. No answer. The white barbarians, all banded against her now, had shut themselves up with their wounded and their dying, to wait their destiny alone.

How many were already dead? How many might yet be saved,

who would die without her help? She could not tell. The uncertainty maddened her.

"If they den up, that way," she said, "pestilence may break out among them and all may die! And then what? If I'm left all alone in the wilderness with Gesafam and the boy—what then?"

The thought was too horrible for contemplation. So many blows had crashed home to her soul the past week—even the past few hours—that the girl felt numbed and dazed as in a nightmare.

It was, it must be, all some frightful unreality—Allan's absence, the avalanche, H'yemba's attack, and this widespread, silent defiance of her power.

Only a few days before Allan had been there with her—strong, vigorous, confident.

Authority had been supreme. Labor, content, prosperity had reigned. Health and life and vigor had been everywhere. On the horizon of existence no cloud; none over the sun of progress.

And now, suddenly—annihilation!

With a groan that was a sob, her face drawn and pale, eyes fixed and unseeing, Beatrice turned back up the terrace path, back up the steep, toward the only door still at her command—Hope Villa.

Back toward the only one of these strange Folk still loyal; back toward her child.

Her head felt strangely giddy. The depths at her left hand, below the parapet of stone, seemed to be calling—calling insistently. Before her sight something like a veil was drawn; and yet it was not a veil, but a peculiar haze, now and then intershot with sparkles of pale light.

Through her mind flittered for the first time something like an adequate realization of the vast, abysmal gulf in culture-status still yawning between these barbarians and Allan and herself.

"Civilization," she stammered in an odd voice; "why that means—generations!"

All at once she wondered if she were going to faint. A sudden pain had stabbed her temples; a humming had attacked her ears.

She put out her hand against the rock wall of the cliff at the right to steady herself. Her mouth felt hot and very dry.

"I—I must get back home," she said weakly. "I'm not at all well—this morning. Overexertion—"

Painfully she began to climb the stepped path toward the upper level and Cliff Villa. And again it seemed to her the depths were calling; but now she felt positive she heard a voice—a voice she knew but could not exactly place—a hail very far away yet near—all very strange, unreal and terrifying.

"Oh—am I going to be ill?" she panted. "No, no! I mustn't! For the boy's sake, I mustn't! I can't!"

With a tremendous effort, now crawling rather than walking—for her knees were as water—the girl dragged herself up the path almost to her doorway.

Again she heard the call, this time no hallucination, but reality.

"Beatrice! Beatrice!" the voice was shouting. "O-he! Beatrice!"

His hail! Allan's!

Her heart stopped, a long minute, and then, leaping with joy, a very anguish of revulsion from long pain, thrashed terribly in her breast.

Gasping with emotion, burned with the first sudden onset of a consuming fever, half-blind, shivering, parched and in agony, the girl made a tremendous effort to hear, to see, to understand.

"Allan! Allan!" she shouted wildly. "Where are you? Where?"

"Beatrice! Here! On the bridge! I'm coming!"

She turned her dimming eyes toward the suspension bridge hung high above the swift and lashing rapids of New Hope River—the bridge, a cobweb-strand in space, across the chasm.

There it seemed to her, though now she could be sure of nothing, so strangely did the earth and sky and cliffs, the bridge, the jungle, all dance and interplay—there, it seemed, she saw a moving figure.

Disheveled, torn, almost naked, lame and slow, yet with something still of power and command in its bearing, this figure was advancing over the swaying path of bamboo-rods lashed to the cables of twisted fiber.

Now it halted as in exhaustion and great pain; now, once more, it struggled forward, limping, foot by foot; crawling, hanging fast to the ropes like some great insect meshed in the wind-swung filaments.

She saw it, and she knew the truth at last.

"Allan! Allan—come quick! Help me—help!"

Then she collapsed. At her door she fell. All things blent and swirled, faded, darkened.

She knew no more.

CHAPTER XXIV

THE BOY IS GONE!

The man, weak, wounded, racked with exhaustion from the terrible ordeal of the past days, felt fresh vigor leap through his spent veins at sight of her distress, afar.

He broke into a strange, limping run across the slight and shaking bridge; and as he ran he called to her, words of cheer and greeting, words of encouragement and love.

But when, having penetrated the palisaded area and stumbled down the terraces, he reached her side, he stopped short, shaking, speechless, with wide and terror-stricken eyes.

"Beatrice! Beta! My God, what's—what's happened here?" he stammered, kneeling beside her, raising her in his weakened arms, covering her pallid face with kisses, chafing her throat, her temples, her hands.

The girl gave no sign of returning consciousness. Allan stared about him, sensing a great and devastating change since his departure, but as yet unable to comprehend its nature.

Giddy himself with loss of blood and terrible fatigues, he hardly more than half saw what lay before him; yet he knew catastrophe had befallen Settlement Cliffs.

The river now foamed through strange new obstructions. A whole section of the cliff was gone. No sign of life at all was to be seen anywhere down the terraces or paths.

None of the Folk, their blinking eyes shielded by their mica glasses from the morning sun, were drying fish or fruit at the frames.

The nets hung brown, and stiff, and dry; they should, at this hour, have been limp and wet, from the night's fishing. The life of the colony, he knew, had suddenly and for some incomprehensible reason stopped, as a watch stops when the spring is broken.

And, worse than all, here Beatrice now lay in his arms, stricken by some strange malady. He could not know the cause—the sleepless nights, the terrible toil, the shattering nervous strain of catastrophe, of nursing, of the swift rebellion.

But he saw plainly now, the girl was burning with fever. And, raising his face to heaven, he uttered a cry, half a groan, half a sob—the cry of a soul racked too long upon the torture-wheel of fate.

"But—but where's the boy?" he asked himself, striving to

recover his self-control; trying to understand, to act, to save. "What's happened here? God knows! An earthquake? Disaster, at any rate! Beatrice! Oh, my Beta! Speak to me!"

Unable to solve any of the terrible problems now beating in upon him, he raised her still higher in his arms.

Loudly he shouted for help down the terrace, calling on his Folk to show themselves; to come to him and to obey.

But though the shattered cliff rang with his commands, no one appeared. In all seeming as deserted and as void of human life as on the first day he and Beta had set foot there, the canyon brooded under the morning sun, and for all answer rose only the foaming tumult of the rapids far below.

"Merciful Heavens, I've got to do something!" cried Allan, forgetting his own lacerations and his pain, in this supreme crisis. "She—she's sick! She's got a fever! I've got to put her to bed anyhow! After that we'll see!"

With a strength he knew not lay now in his wasted arms, he lifted her bodily and carried her to the door of Cliff Villa, their home among the massive buttresses of rock.

But, to his vast astonishment and terror, he found the door refused to open. It was fast barred inside.

Even from his own house he found himself shut out, an exile and a stranger!

Loudly he shouted for admission, savagely beat upon the planks, all to no purpose. There came no sound from within, no answering word or sign.

Eagerly listening for perhaps the cry of his child, he heard nothing. A tomblike silence brooded there, as in all the stricken colony.

Then Allan, fired with a burning fury, laid the girl down again, and seizing a great boulder from the top of the parapet that guarded the terraced walk, dashed it against the door. The planks groaned and quivered, but held.

Recoiling, exhausted by even this single effort, the disheveled, wounded man stared with haggard eyes at the barrier.

The very strength he had put into that door to guard his treasures, his wife and his son, now defied him. And a curse, bitter as death, burst from his trembling lips.

But now he heard a sound, a word, a phrase or two of incoherent speech.

Whirling, he saw the girl's mouth move. In her delirium she was speaking.

He knelt again beside her, cradled her in his arms, kissed and cherished her—and he heard broken, disjointed words—words that filled him with passionate rage and overpowering woe.

"So many dead—so many!—And so many dying.—You, H'yemba! You beast! Let me go!—Oh, when the master comes!"

Allan understood at last. His mind, now clear, despite the maddening torments of the past week, grasped the situation in a kind of supersensitive clairvoyance.

As by a lightning-flash on a dark night, so now the blackness of his wonder, of this mystery, all stood instantly illumined. He understood.

"What incredible fiendishness!" he exclaimed, quite slowly, as though unable to imagine it in human bounds. "At a time of disaster and of death, such as has smitten the colony—what hellish villainy!"

He said no more, but in his eyes burned the fire that meant death, instant and without reprieve.

First he looked to his automatic; but, alas, not one cartridge remained either in its magazine or in the pouches of his belt. The fouled and blackened barrel told something of the terrible story of the past few days.

"Gone, all gone," he muttered; but, with sudden inspiration, bent over the girl.

"Ah! Ammunition again!"

Quickly he reloaded from her belts. One belt he buckled round his waist. Then, pistol in hand, he thought swiftly.

Thus his mind ran: "The first thing to do is look out for Beatrice, and make her comfortable—find out what the matter is with her, and give treatment. I need fresh water, but I daren't go down to the river for it and leave her here. At any minute H'yemba may appear. And when he does, I must see him first.

"Evidently the thing most necessary is to gain access to our home. How can it be locked, inside, when Beatrice is here? Heaven only knows! There may be enemies in there at this minute. H'yemba may be there—"

Anguish pierced his soul at thought of his son now possibly in the smith's power.

"By God!" he cried, "something has got to be done, and quick!"

His rage was growing by leaps and bounds.

He advanced to the door, and putting the muzzle of his automatic almost on the lock, shattered it with six heavy bullets.

Again he dashed the boulder against the door. It groaned and gave.

Reloading ere he ventured in, he now set his shoulder to the door and forced it slowly open, with the pistol always ready in his right hand.

Keenly his eyes sought out the darkened corners of the room. Here, there they pierced, striving to determine whether any ambushed foe were lying there in wait for him.

"Surrender!" he cried loudly in the Merucaan tongue. "If there be any here who war with me, surrender! *At the first sign of fight, you die!*"

No answer.

Still leaving the girl beside the broken door till he should feel positive there was no peril—and always filled with a vast wonder how the door could have been locked from within—Allan advanced slowly, cautiously, into their home.

He was cool now—cool and strong again. The frightful perils and exposures of the week past seemed to have fallen from him like an outworn mantle.

He ignored his pain and weakness as though such things were not. And, with index on trigger, eyes watchful and keen, he scouted down the cave-dwelling.

Suddenly he stopped.

"Who's there?" he challenged loudly.

At the left of the room, not far from the big fireplace, he had perceived a dim, vague figure, prone upon the floor.

"Answer, or I shoot!"

But the figure remained motionless. Allan realized there was no fight in it. Still cautiously, however, he advanced.

Now he touched the figure with his foot, now bent above it and peered down.

"Old Gesafam! Heaven above! Wounded! What does this mean?"

Starting back, he stared in horror at the old woman, stunned and motionless, with the blood coagulating along an ugly cut on her forehead.

Then, as though a prescience had swept his being, he sprang to the bed.

"My son! My boy! Where are you?" he shouted hoarsely.

With a shaking hand he flung down the bedclothes of finely woven palm fiber.

"My boy! My boy!"

The bed was empty. His son had disappeared.

CHAPTER XXV

THE FALL OF H'YEMBA

Blinded with staggering grief and terror, stunned, stricken, all but annihilated, the man recoiled.

Then, with a cry, he sprang to the bed again, and now in a very passion of eagerness explored it. His trembling hands dragged all the bedding off and threw it broadcast. By the dim light he peered with wide and terror-smitten eyes.

"My boy!" he choked. "My boy!"

But beyond all manner of doubt the boy had been stolen.

Unable to understand, or think, or plan, Allan stood there, his face ghastly, his heart quivering within him.

What could have happened? How and why? If the door had been securely locked and the old nurse been with the child, how could the kidnapper have borne him away?

What? How? Why?

More, ever more, questions crowded the man's brain, all equally without answer.

But now, he dimly realized, was no time for solving problems. The minute demanded swift and drastic action. He must find, must save, his son! After that other riddles could he unraveled.

"H'yemba!" he cried hoarsely. "This is H'yemba's work! Revenge and hate have driven him to rebel again. To try to seize Beatrice! To steal my son! At this time of peril and affliction, above all others! H'yemba! The smith must die!"

But first he realized he must get Beatrice into safety.

In haste he ran to the door, picked up the girl and carried her to the bed. Here he disposed her at ease, covered her with the bedding, and bathed her face and hands with water from the cooling-jar.

The old nurse he laid upon the broad couch by the fire and likewise tended. He saw now she had been struck with a stone ax, a glancing blow, severe, but not necessarily fatal.

"Probably trying to defend the boy!" thought he. "Brave heart! Faithful even unto death—if death be your reward!"

Leaving her, he returned to his wife.

Now, he well understood, he had no time for emotion. There must be no false move. Even at the expense of a little time, he must plan the campaign with skill and execute it with relentless energy.

He alone now stood for power, rule, order, law, in this disintegrated community—this colony racked with disaster, anarchy and death.

Upon him alone now depended its whole fate and future, and, with it, the fate and future of the world.

"Merciful Lord, what a situation!" he whispered. "At home, disruption and savagery. Outside, the Horde—the Horde now pressing onward after me!"

He sat down beside the bed and forced himself to think. Weak as he was and wounded with a spear-thrust in the lower leg as well as a jagged cut across the breast, he felt that he might still keep strength enough for a few hours more of toil.

Of a sudden he realized an over-powering thirst. Till now he had not felt it. He arose, drank deeply from the jar, then—something cooler and more calm—once more returned to Beatrice.

"The first thing is to help her," he said. "No use in losing my wits and rushing out unprepared to find the boy. If H'yemba has stolen him it's certain the boy is hidden beyond my present power in some far recess of the inter-communicating rabbit-warren of caves below there in the cliff.

"I feel positive no bodily harm will be done the child. H'yemba will hold him for power over me. He will try to exact terms—even to leadership in the colony, even to possession of Beatrice. And the penalty of refusal may be the boy's death—"

He shuddered profoundly, and with both wasted hands covered his face. For a moment madness sought to possess him.

He felt a wild desire to shout imprecations, to rush out, fling himself against the cave-door of H'yemba and riddle it with bullets—but presently calm returned again. For in Stern's nature lay nothing of hysteria. Reason and calm judgment dominated. And before he acted he always reckoned every pro and con.

"It must be a battle of wits as well as force," thought he. "A little time will decide all that. For now Beatrice demands my first care and thought!"

Now he examined the girl once more. Closing the door and lighting the bronze lamp, he carefully studied the sick woman, noting her symptoms, pulse and respiration.

"What to do?" he asked himself. "What means to tale?"

He arose and rummaged the stores for drugs. Above all, he must break the fever. He therefore prepared and administered a powerful febrifuge, covered the girl with all the available bedding, and determined, if possible, to make her sweat. This done, he found no further means at hand and now turned his attention once more to Gesafam.

Her wound he bathed and bandaged and, having given her a stiff drink of brandy, poured between resisting teeth which he had to separate with his knife-blade, he presently perceived some signs of returning consciousness.

But, though he questioned the old woman and tried desperately to make her answer, he could get no coherent information.

Only the name of H'yemba and some few disconnected mutterings of terror rewarded him. He knew now, however, with positive certainty that the smith was responsible for the kidnapping of his son.

"And that," said he, "means I must seek him out at once. All I ask is just one sight of him. One sight, one bullet—and the score is paid!"

He arose and, again making sure his automatic was in complete readiness, stood for a second in thought. Whatever he was now to do must be done quickly.

In a few hours, at the outside, he knew the vanguard of the pursuing Horde would enter the last valley on the other side of the canyon. By afternoon another battle might be on.

"Whatever happens, I must get my grip on the colony again at once!" he realized. "Such of the Folk as are still sound must be rallied. Otherwise nothing but annihilation awaits us all!"

But, even as he faced the exit of Cliff Villa, all at once the door was hurled violently open and a harsh, discordant cry of hatred and defiance burst into the cave.

Stern saw the detested figure of H'yemba standing there, loose-hung, powerful, barbaric, his eyes blinking evilly behind the mica screens that Allan himself had made for him.

With a cry Allan started forward.

"My son!" he gasped.

There, clutched in the smith's left arm, lay the boy!

Allan heard his child crying as in pain, and rage swept every caution to the winds.

He sprang toward H'yemba, cursing; but the smith, with a beast-laugh, raised his right hand.

"Master!" he mocked. "No nearer or ye die!"

Allan, aghast, saw the flicker of sunlight on a pistol-barrel. With only too true an aim, H'yemba had him covered.

Came a little pause, tense as steel wire. Somewhere down the terrace sounded a murmur of voices. Allan seemed to sense that the rebel had now gathered his forces and that a general attack was imminent.

Time! At all hazards he must gain a moment's time!

"H'yemba!" cried he. "What is your speech with me, your master?"

"Master?" sneered the smith again. "My slave! Power has passed from you to me. From you, who speak the false, who entrap us here to suffer and die, who slay and ruin us, to me, who will yet lead the people back to their far home, to safety and to life!"

"You lie, hound!"

The smith laughed bitterly.

"That shall be seen—who lies!" he gibed. "But now power is mine. I have your son in my hand. Move only and I fling him from the cliff!"

Allan felt his brain whirl; all things seemed to turn about him. But he fought off his faintness, and in a shaken voice once more demanded:

"What terms, H'yemba?"

"Slavery for you and yours! Your son shall be my serf; your woman my chattel! Ha, that woman! She has already fought me, like one of these strange woods-beasts you have made us kill! See! My hair is burned and my flesh blistered with her fire-beating! But when I hold her in these hands then she shall pay for all, the vuedma!"

Stern's hand twitched, with the automatic gripped in the fingers, but the blacksmith cried a warning.

"Raise not that hand, slave!" he ordered. "You cannot shoot without the danger of killing this vile spawn of yours! And remember, too, the river lies far below, and very sharp are the waiting rocks!

"Fool that you are, that think yourself so wise! To leave this place with me! With me, skilled in all labors of metal and stone, strong to cut passage-ways—"

"You devil! You hewed a way into my house?"

H'yemba laughed brutally.

"Silently, steadily, I labored!" he boasted. "And behold the reward! Power for me; eternal slavery for you and all your blood—if any live!"

Insane with rage and hate, Allan nevertheless realized that now all depended on keeping his thought and nerve.

One single premature move and his son would inevitably be hurled over the parapet, down two hundred and fifty feet to the river-bed below. At all hazards, he must keep cool!

The smith, after all only a barbarian and of limited intelligence, had not even thought of the obvious command to make Stern drop his pistol on the floor.

Upon this oversight now hung all Allan's hopes.

Even though the man's retainers might rush the cave and slaughter all, yet in Allan's heart burned a clear and steady flame of hot desire to compass H'yemba's death.

And as the smith now loudly boasted, insulted, vilified, in the true manner of the savage, imperceptibly, inch by inch, Allan was turning his pistol-barrel upward.

Higher, higher, bit by bit it crept toward the horizontal. Unaccustomed to shoot from the hip, Allan realized that right before him lay a supreme test of nerve and marksmanship and skill.

To shoot and kill his boy—the thought was too hideous even to be considered. His father-heart yearned toward the frightened, crying child there in the traitor's grip.

The unconscious form of Beatrice fever-burned and panting on the bed, seemed calling aloud to him: "Aim true, Allan! Aim true!"

For one false shot inevitably sealed the child's death. To wound H'yemba and not kill him meant the catastrophe. If the bullet failed to enter brain or heart, H'yemba—though mortally hurt—would of a surety, with his last quiver of strength, sling the boy outward over the dizzying parapet.

Allan prayed; yet his prayer was wordless, formless and unconscious.

He dared not glance down at the automatic. His eyes must hold the smith's. And he must speak, must parley, at all hazards must still gain another moment's respite.

What Allan said in those last terrible, eternal seconds he could never afterward recall.

He only knew he was treating with the enemy, making terms, listening, answering—all with mechanical sub-consciousness.

His real personality, his true ego, was absolutely absorbed in the one vital, all-deciding problem of that stiffening pistol-hand.

Suddenly something seemed to cry in his ear:

"You have it now! Fire!"

His hand leaped back with the crashing discharge, loud-echoing in the cave.

H'yemba did not even yell. But at the second when he seemed to crumple all together, falling as an empty sack falls, some involuntary jerk of his finger sent a bullet zooming into the cave.

It shattered beyond Allan in a little shower of steel and lead fragments, mingled with rock-dust.

Before these had even fallen Allan was upon him.

Neglecting for an instant the bruised and screaming child,

who lay there struggling on the terrace-path, Allan seized the still-twitching body of the monstrous traitor.

With passionate strength he dragged it to the parapet.

Below, down the path, he caught a swift glimpse of grouped Folk, wondering, staring, aghast.

To them he gave no heed.

He lifted the body, dripping bright blood.

Silent, indomitable, disheveled, he raised it on high.

Then, with a cry: "See, ye people, how I answer traitors!" he whirled it outward into the void.

Over and over it gyrated through vacant space. Then, with an echoing splash, the river took it, and the swift current, white-foaming, boisterous, wild, rolled it and tumbled it away, away forever, into the unknown.

With harsh cries and a wild spatter of bullets aimed high above them, Allan drove the cowed and beaten partizans of H'yemba jostling, fleeing, howling for mercy, down the terrace-path between the cliff and parapet.

Only then, when he knew victory was secure and his own dominance once more sealed on them, did he run swiftly back to his boy.

Snatching up the child, he retreated into the home cave again; and now for the first time he realized his wan and sunken cheeks were wet with tears.

CHAPTER XXVI

THE COMING OF THE HORDE

Now that, for an hour or two at least, he felt himself free and master of the situation, Allan devoted himself with energy to the immediate situation in Cliff Villa.

Though still weak and dazed, old Gesafam had now recovered strength and wit enough to soothe and care for the child.

Allan heard from her, in a few disjointed words, all she knew of the kidnapping. H'yemba, she said, had suddenly appeared to her, from the remote end of the cave, and had tried to snatch the child.

She had fought, but one blow of his ax had stunned her. Beyond this, she remembered nothing.

Allan sought and quickly found the aperture made by the smith through the limestone.

"Evidently he'd been planning this coup for a long time," thought he. "The great catastrophe of the land-slide broke the last bonds of order and restraint, and gave him his opportunity. Well, it's his last villainy! I'll have this passageway cemented up. That's all the monument he'll ever get. It's more than he deserves!"

He returned to Beatrice. The girl still lay there, moaning a little in her fevered sleep. Allan watched her in anguish.

"Oh, if she should die—if she should die!" thought he, and felt the sweat start on his forehead. "She must not! She can't! I won't let her!"

A touch on his arm aroused him from his vigil. Turning, he saw Gesafam.

"The child, O Kromno, hungers. It is crying for food!" Allan thought. He saw at once the impossibility of letting the boy come near its mother. Some other arrangement must be made.

"Ah!" thought he. "I have it!"

He gestured toward the door.

"Go," he commanded. "Go up the path, to the palisaded place. Take this rope. Bring back, with you a she-goat. Thus shall the child be fed!"

The old woman obeyed. In a quarter-hour she had returned, dragging a wild goat that bleated in terror.

Then, while she watched with amazement, Allan succeeded in milking the creature; though he had to lash securely all four feet and throw it to the cave-floor before it would submit.

He modified the milk with water and bade the old woman administer it by means of a bit of soft cloth. Allan, Junior, protested with yells, but had to make the best of hard necessity; and, after a long and painful process, was surfeited and dozed off. Gesafam put him to bed on the divan by the fire.

"A poor substitute," thought Allan, "but it will sustain life. He's healthy; he can stand it—he's got to. Thank God for that goat! Without it he might easily have starved."

He tied the animal at the rear of the cave, and had Gesafam fetch a good supply of grass. Thus for the present one problem at least was solved.

Beatrice's condition remained unchanged. Now and then she called for water, which he gave her plentifully. Once he thought she recognized him, but he could not be certain.

And day wore on; and now the hour of noon was at hand. Allan knew that other duties called him. He must go down among the Folk and save them, too, if possible.

Eating a little at random and making sure as always that his pistols were well loaded, he consigned Beatrice and the child into the old woman's keeping and left the cave.

On the terrace he stopped a moment, gazing triumphantly at the bloodmarks now thickly coagulated down the rocks.

Then, out over the canyon and the forest to northward he peered. His eyes caught the signal-fires he knew must be there now, not ten miles away; and with a nod he smiled.

"They've certainly trailed me close, the devils!" sneered he. "Since the minute they first attacked my two men and me, trying to repair the disabled Pauillac in that infernal valley so far to northward, they haven't given me an hour's respite! Before night there'll be war! Well, let them come. The quicker now the better!"

Then he turned, and with a determined step, still clad in his grotesque rags, descended toward the caves of the Folk, such as still were left.

Where all had been resistance and defiant surliness before, now all had become obedience and worship. He understood enough of the barbarian psychology to know that power, strength and dominance—and these alone—commanded respect with the Folk.

And among them all, those who had not seen as well as those that had, the sudden, dramatic, annihilating downfall of H'yemba had again cemented the bonds of solidarity more closely than ever.

The sight of that arch-rebel's body hurled from the parapet

had effectually tamed them, every one. No longer was there any murmur in their caves, no thought save of obedience and worship.

"It's not what I want," reflected Allan. "I want intelligent cooperation, not adulation. I want democracy! But, damn it! if they can't understand, then I must rule a while. And rule I will—and they shall obey or die!"

Quickly he got in touch with the situation. From cave to cave he went, estimating the damage. At the great gap in the terrace he stood and carefully observed the wreckage in the river-bed below.

He visited the hospital-cave, administered medicines, changed dressings and labored for his Folk as though no shadow of rebellion ever had come 'twixt them and him. The news of Bremilu's death moved him profoundly. Bremilu had been one of his two most competent and trusted followers, and Allan, too, felt a strong personal affection for the man who had saved his life that first night at the cliffs.

Beside the body he stood, in the morgue-cave whither it had been borne. With bowed head the master looked upon the man; and from his eyes fell tears; and in his heart he felt a vacant place not soon to be made whole.

With profound emotion he took Bremilu's cold hand in his—the hand that had so deftly and so powerfully stricken down the gorilla—and for a while held it, gazing on the dead man's face.

"Good-by," said he at length. "You were a brave heart and a true. Never shall you be forgotten. Good-by!"

He summoned a huge fellow named Frumuos, now the most intelligent of the Folk remaining, and together they directed the work of carrying the bodies up to the cliff-top and there burying them.

By the middle of the afternoon some semblance of order and control had become organized in the colony. He returned to Cliff Villa, leaving strict orders for Frumuos to call him in case of need.

Very beautiful the world was that afternoon. In the soft south wind the fronded palms across the river were bowing and nodding gracefully. Overhead, dazzling clouds drifted northward.

It seemed to him he could almost hear the rustle of the dry undergrowth, parched by the past fortnight of exceptionally hot weather; but, above all, rose the eternal babble of the rapids. High in air, a vulture wheeled its untiring spirals. At sight of it he frowned. It reminded him of the Pauillac, now wrecked far beyond the horizon, where the Horde had trapped him. He shuddered, for the memories of the past week were infinitely horrible, and he longed only to forget.

With a last glance at the scene, over which the ominous threads of smoke now drifted in considerable numbers, he frowned. He reentered the villa.

"No matter what happens now," he muttered, "I've got to snatch a few minutes rest. Otherwise, I'm liable to drop in my tracks. And, above all, I must try to pull through. For on me, and me alone, now everything depends!"

He sat down by the bed again, too stupefied by the toxins of fatigue and exhaustion to do more than note that Beatrice was, at any rate, no worse.

Human effort and emotion had, in fact, reached their extreme climax in him. He felt numb all over, in body, mind and soul. A weaker man would have succumbed long ago to but half the hardships he had struggled through. Now he must rest a bit.

"Bring water, Gesafam!" he commanded. When she had obeyed, he let her wash his wounds and dress them with leaves and ointment. Then he himself bandaged them, his head nodding, eyes already drooping shut from moment to moment.

His head sank on the bed, and one hand sought the girl's. Despite his wonderful vitality and strength, Allan was on the verge of collapse.

Vague and confused thoughts wandered through his unsettled brain.

What was the destiny of the colony to be, now that the Pauillac was lost and so many of the Folk wiped out? Were there any hopes of ultimate success? And the Horde, what of that? How long a respite might be counted on before the inevitable, decisive battle?

A score, a hundred questions, more and more illusory, blent and faded and reformed in his overtaxed mind.

Then, blessed as a balm, sleep took him.

A violent shaking roused him from dead slumber. Old Gesafam stood there beside him. She had him by the arm.

"Waken, O master!" she was crying. "O Kromno, rouse! For now there is great need!"

Dazed, he started up.

"What—what is it now? More trouble?"

She pointed toward the door.

"Beyond there, master! Beyond the river there be many moving creatures! Darts and arrows have begun to fall against the cliff. See, one has even come into the cave! What shall be done, master?"

Broad awake now, Allan ran to the door and peered out.

Daylight was fading. He must have slept an hour or two; it had seemed but a second. In the west the sun was burning its way toward the horizon, through a thick set of haze that cloaked the rim of the earth.

"Here, master! See!"

Stooping, she picked up a long, slight object and handed it to him.

"One of their poisoned darts, so help me!" he exclaimed. "Cast that into the fire, Gesafam. And have a care lest it wound you, for the slightest scratch is death!"

While she, wondering, obeyed, he hastily reconnoitered the situation.

He had felt positive the Horde, after his escape from it by devious and terrible ways, would track him down.

He had known the army of the hideous little beast-folk, that for a year now had been slowly gathering from north and east for one final assault, would eventually find Settlement Cliffs and there make still another attempt to crush him and his.

But, knowing all this, knowing even that the whole region beyond the river now swarmed with these ghastly monstrosities, the actuality appalled him.

Now that the attack was really at hand, he felt a strange and sudden sense of helplessness.

And with a bitter curse he shook his fist at the dark forest across the canyon where—even as he looked—he saw a movement of crouching, furtive things; he heard a dull thump-thump as of clubs beating hollow logs.

"You devils!" he execrated. "Oh, for a ton of Pulverite to drop among you!"

"Look, master, look! The bridge! The bridge!"

He turned quickly as old Gesafam pointed up-stream.

There, clearly outlined against the sky, he saw a dozen—a score of little, crouching figures emerge from the forest on the north bank, and at a clumsy run defile along the swaying footpath high above the rapids.

CHAPTER XXVII

WAR!

At sight of the advance-guard of the Horde now already loping, crouched and ugly, over the narrow bridge to Settlement Cliffs Allan's first impulse was one of absolute despair.

He had expected an attack ere night, but at least he had hoped an hour's respite to recover a little of his strength and to muster all the still valid men of the Folk for resistance. Now, however, he saw even this was to be denied him. For already the leaders of the Horde scouts had passed the center of the bridge.

Three or four minutes more and they would be inside the palisade, upon the cliff!

"God! If they once get in there, we're gone!" cried Allan. "We're cut off from everything. Our animals will be slaughtered. The boy will die! They can bombard us with rocks from aloft. It means annihilation!"

Already he was running up the path toward the palisade. Not one second was to be lost. There was no time even to call a single man of the Folk to reenforce him. Single-handed and alone he must meet the invaders' first attack.

Panting, sweating, stumbling, he scrambled up the steep terrace. And as he ran his thoughts outdistanced him.

"Fool that I was to have left the bridge!" choked he. "My first act when I set foot on solid land should have been to cut the ropes and drop the whole thing into the rapids! I might have known this would happen—fool that I was!"

The safety, the life, of the whole colony, including his wife and son, now depended solely on his reaching the southern end of the bridge before the vanguard of the Horde.

With a heart-racking burst of energy he sprang to the defence, and as he ran he drew his hunting-knife.

Reeling with exhaustion, spent, winded, yet still in desperation struggling onward, he won the top of the cliff, swung to the left along the path that led to the bridge, and—more dead than alive—rushed onward in a last, supreme effort.

Already he saw the Anthropoids were within a hundred feet of the abutment. He could plainly see their squat, hideous bodies, their hairy and pendent arms, and the ugly shuffle of their preposterous legs, as at their best speed they made for the cliff.

Three or four poisoned darts fell clicking on the stones about him. Howls and yells of rage burst from the file of beast-men.

One of the horrible creatures even—with apelike agility—sprang up into the guy ropes of the bridge, clung there, and discharged an arrow from its bamboo blow-gun, chattering with rage.

Stern, running but the faster, plugged him with a forty-four. The Anthropoid, still clinging, yowled hideously, then all at once dropped off and vanished in the depths.

Full drive, Allan hurled himself toward the entrance of the bridge. It seemed to him the beasts were almost on him now.

Plainly he could hear the slavering click of their tushes and see the red, bleared winking of their deep-set eyes.

Now he was at the rope-anchorage, where the cables were lashed to two stout palms.

He emptied his automatic point-blank into the pack.

Pausing not to note effects, he slashed furiously at the left-hand rope.

One strand gave. It sprang apart and began untwisting. Again he hewed with mad rage.

"Crack!"

The cable parted with a report like a pistol-shot. From the bridge a wild, hideous tumult of yells and shrieks arose. The whole fabric, now unsupported on one side, dropped awry. Covered from end to end with Anthropoids, it swayed heavily.

Had men been on it, all must have been flung into the rapids by the shock. But these beast-things, used to arboreal work, to scaling cliffs, to every kind of dangerous adventuring, nearly all succeeded in clinging.

Only three or four were shaken off, to catapult over and over down into the foaming lash of the river.

And still, now creeping with hideous agility along the racked and swinging bridge that hung by but a single rope, they continued to make way, howling and screaming like damned souls.

One gained the shore! At Allan it bounded, crouching, ferocious, deadly. He saw the tiny, venomous lance raised for the throw.

"Flick!"

He felt a twitch on his arm. Was he wounded? He knew not. Only he knew that with blind rage he had flung himself on the second rope, and now with demon-rage was hacking at it desperately.

The snapping whirl of the cable as it parted flung him backward.

He had an instant's vision of the whole bridge-structure crumpling. Then it vanished. From the depths rose the most awful scream, quickly smothered, that he had ever heard.

And as the bestial bodies went tumbling, rolling, fighting, down the rapids, he suddenly beheld the bridge footway hanging limp and swaying against the further cliff.

"Thank God! In time, in time!" he panted, staggering like a drunken man.

But all at once he beheld two of the Horde still there in front of him—the one that had flung the dart and another. They were advancing at a lope.

Allan turned and fled.

His ammunition was all spent, he knew that to face them was madness.

"I must load up again," thought he. "Then I'll make short work of them!"

Fortunately he could far outstrip them in flight. That, and that alone, had already saved him in the past week of horrible pursuit through the forests to northward. And quickly now he ran down the terrace again—down to the caves below. As he ran he shouted in Merucaan:

"Out, my people! Out with you! Out to battle! Out to war!"

Half way upward down to Cliff Villa he met Frumuos toiling upward. Him he greeted and quickly informed of the situation.

"The bridge is down!" he panted. "I cut it! The further shore is swarming with enemies. Two have reached this side!"

"What is this, O Kromno?" asked the man anxiously, pointing at Allan's shoulder. "Have they wounded you?"

Allan looked and saw a poisoned dart hanging loosely in his left sleeve. As he moved he could feel the point rubbing against his naked skin.

"Merciful Heaven!" he exclaimed. "Has it scratched me?"

With infinite precautions he loosened and threw off his outer garment. He flung it, with the dart still adhering, down over the cliff.

"Look, Frumuos!" he commanded. "Search carefully and see if there be any scratch on the skin!"

The man obeyed, making a minute inspection through his mica eye-shields. Then he shook his head.

"No, Kromno," he answered. "I see nothing. But the arrow came near, near!"

Stern, tremendously relieved, gestured toward the caves.

"Go swiftly!" he commanded. "Bring up every man who still

can fight. All must have full burdens of cartridges. Even though the bridge be down, the enemy will still attack!"

"But how, since the great river lies between?"

"They can climb down those cliffs and swim the river and scramble up this side as easily as we can walk on level ground. Go swiftly! There is no time to lose!"

"I go, master. But tell me, the two who have already reached this side—shall we not first slay them?"

Allan thought. For the first time he now realized clearly the terrible peril that lay in these two Anthropoids already inside the limits of the colony.

He peered up the pathway. No sign of them above. Their animal cunning had warned them not to descend to certain death.

Now Allan knew they were at liberty inside the palisades, waiting, watching, constituting a deadly menace at every turn.

In any one of a thousand places they could lie ambushed, behind trees or bushes, or in the limbs aloft, and thence, unseen, they could discharge an indefinite number of darts.

It was now perilous in the extreme even to venture back to the palisade. Any moment might bring a flicking, stinging messenger of death. Those two, alone, might easily decimate the remaining men of the colony—and now each man was incalculably precious.

"Go, Frumuos," Allan again commanded. "For the moment we must leave those two up there. Go, muster all the fighting men and bring them up here along the terrace. I must think! Go!"

Suddenly, before the messenger had even had time to disappear round the first bend in the path, Allan found his inspiration.

"Regular warfare will never do it!" he exclaimed decisively. "They have thousands where we have tens. Before we could pick them off with our firearms they'd have exhausted all our ammunition and have rushed us—and everything would be all over.

"No; there must be some quicker and more drastic way! Even dynamite or Pulverite could never reach them all, swarming over there through miles of forest. Only one thing can stand against them—fire!

"With fire we must sweep and purge the world, even though we destroy it! With fire we must sweep the world!"

CHAPTER XXVIII

THE BESOM OF FLAME

Stern was not long in carrying out his plan.

Even before Frumnos had returned, with the seventeen men still able to bear arms, he was at work.

In Cliff Villa he hastily lashed up half a dozen fireballs, of coarse cloth, thoroughly soaked them in oil, and, with a blazing torch, brought them out to the terrace. Old Gesafam, at his command, bolted the door behind him. At all hazards, Beta and the child must be protected from any possibility of peril.

"Here, Frumnos!" cried Stern.

"Yes, master?"

"Run quickly! Fetch the strongest bow in the colony and many arrows!"

"I go, master!"

Once more the man departed, running.

"Gad! If I only had my oxygen-containing bullets ready!" thought Stern, his mind reverting to an unfinished experiment down there in his laboratory in the Rapids power-house. "They would turn the trick, sure enough! They'd burst and rain fire everywhere. But they aren't ready yet; and even if they were, nobody could venture down there now!"

For already, plainly visible on the farther edge of the canyon, scores and hundreds of the hideous little beast-men were beginning to swarm. Their cries, despite the contrary stiff wind, carried across the river; and here and there a dart broke against the cliff.

Already a few of the Anthropoids were beginning to scramble down the opposite wall of stone.

"Men!" cried Allan commandingly, "not one of those creatures must ever reach this terrace! Take good aim. Waste no single shot. Every bullet must do its work!"

Choosing six of the best marksmen, he stationed them along the parapet with rifles. The firing began at once.

Irregularly the shots barked from the line of sharpshooters; and the little stabs of smoke, drifting out across the river, blent in a thin blue haze. Every moment or two, one of the Horde would writhe, scream, fall—or hang there twitching, to the cliff, with terrible, wild yells.

Stern greeted the return of Frumuos with eagerness.

"Here!" he exclaimed, scattering the arrows among half a

dozen men. "Bind these fireballs fast to the arrowheads!"

He dealt out cord. In a moment the task was done.

"Sivad!" he called a man by name. "You, the best bowman of all! Here quickly!"

Even as Sivad fitted the first arrow to the string, and Stern was about to apply the torch, a rattling crash from above caused all to cringe and leap aside.

Down, leaping, ricochetting, thundering, hurtled a great boulder, spurning the cliff-face with a tremendous uproar.

It struck the parapet like a thirteen-inch shell, smashed out two yards of wall, and vanished in the depths. And after it, sliding, rattling and bouncing down, followed a rain of pebbles, fragments and detritus.

"Those two above—they're attacking!" shouted Stern. "Quick—after them! You, you, you!"

He told off half a dozen men with rifles and revolvers.

"Quick, before they can hide! Look out for their darts! Kill! Kill!"

The detachment started up the path at a run, eager for the hunt.

Stern set the flaring torch to the first fireball. It burst into bright flame.

"Shoot, Sivad! Shoot!" he commanded. "Shoot high, shoot far. Plant your arrow there in the dry undergrowth where the wind whips the jungle! Shoot and fail not!"

The stout bowman drew his arrow to the head, back, back till the flame licked his left hand.

"Zing-g-g-g-g!"

The humming bowspring sang in harmony with the zooning arrow. A swift blue streak split the air, high above the river. In a quick trajectory it leaped.

It vanished in the wind-swept forest. Almost before it had disappeared, Sivad had snatched another flaming arrow and had planted it farther down stream.

One by one, till all were gone, the marksman sowed the seed of conflagration. And all the while, from the rifles along the parapet, death went spitting at the forefront of invasion.

Another boulder fell from aloft, this time working havoc; for as one of the riflemen sprang to dodge, it struck a shoulder of limestone, bounded, and took him fair on the back.

His cry was smashed clean out; he and the stone, together, plumbed the depths.

But, as though to echo it, shots began to clatter up above.

Then all at once they ceased; and a cheer floated away across the canyon.

"They're done, those two up there, damn them!" shouted Stern. "And look, men, look! The fire takes! The woods begin to burn!"

True! Already in three places, coils of greasy smoke were beginning to writhe upward, as the resinous, dry undergrowth blossomed into red bouquets of flame.

Now another fire burst out; then the two remaining ones. From six centers the conflagration was already swiftly spreading.

Smoke-clouds began to drift downwind; and from the forest depths arose not only harsh cries from the panic-stricken Horde, but also beast and bird-calls as the startled fauna sought to flee this new, red terror.

Shouts and cheers of triumph burst from the little band of defenders on the terrace as the sweeping wind, flailing the flame through the sun-dried underbrush, whirled it crackling aloft in a quick-leaping storm of fire.

But Stern was silent as he watched the fierce and sudden onset of the conflagration. Between narrowed lids, as though calculating a grave problem, he observed the crazed birds taking sudden flight, launching into air and whirling drunkenly hither and yon with harsh cries for their last brief bit of life.

He listened to the animal calls in the forest and to the strange crashings of the underwood as the creatures broke cover and in vain sought safety.

Mingled with these sounds were others—yells, shrieks, and gibberings—the tumult of the perishing Horde.

Swiftly the fire spread to right and left, even as it ate northward from the river.

The mass of Anthropoids inevitably found themselves trapped; their slouching, awkward figures could here or there be seen in some clear space, running wildly. Then, with a gust of flame, that space, too, vanished, and all was one red glare.

The riflemen, meanwhile, were steadily potting such of the little demons as still were crawling up or down the cliffside opposite. Surely, relentlessly, they shot the invaders down. And, even as Stern watched, the enemy melted and vanished before his eyes.

Allan was thinking.

"What may this not result in?" he wondered as he observed the swift and angry leap of the forest-fire to northward. "It may ravage thousands of square miles before rain puts an end to it. It may devastate the whole country. A change in the wind may even drive it back on us, across the river, sweeping all before it. This may mean ruin!"

He paused a moment, then said aloud:

"Ruin, perhaps. Yes; but the alternative was death! There was no other way!"

Now none of the attackers remained save a few feebly twitching, writhing bodies caught on some protuberance of rock. Here, there, one of these fell, and like the rest was borne away down stream.

Through the heated air already verberated a strange roar as the forest-fire leaped up the opposite hillside in one clear lick of incandescence. This roar hummed through the heavens and trembled over the long reaches of the river.

The fire jumped a little valley and took the second hill, burning as clear as any furnace, with a swift onward, upward slant as the wind fanned it forward through the dry brush and among the crowded palms.

Now and then, with a muffled explosion, a sap-filled palm burst. Here, or yonder, some brighter flare showed where the fire had run at one clear leap right to the fronded top of a fern-tree.

Fire-brands and dry-kye, caught up by the swirl, spiralled through the thick air and fell far in advance of the main fire-army, each outpost colonizing into swift destruction.

Already the nearer portion of the opposite cliff-edge was barren and smoking, swept clean of life as a broom might sweep an ant-hill. Tourbillons of dense smoke obscured the sky.

The air flew thick with brands, live coals and flaring bits of bark, all whirling aloft on the breath of the fire-demon. Showers of burning jewels were sown broadcast by the resistless wind.

Stern, unspeakably saddened in spite of victory by this whole-sale destruction of forest, fruit and game, turned away from the magnificent, the terrifying spectacle.

He left his riflemen staring at it, amazed and awed to silence by the splendor of the flame-tempest, which they watched through their eye-shields in absolute astonishment.

Back to Cliff Villa he returned, his step heavy and his heart like lead. In a few brief hours, how great, how terrible, how devastating the changes that had come upon Settlement Cliffs!

Attack, destruction, pestilence and flame had all worked their will there; and many a dream, a plan, a hope now lay in ashes, even like those smoldering cinder-piles across the river—those pyres that marked the death-field of the hateful, venomous, inhuman Horde!

Numb with exhaustion and emotions, he staggered up the path, knocked, and was admitted to his home by the old nurse.

He heard the crying of his son, vigorously protesting against some infant grievance, and his tired heart yearned with strong father-love.

"A hard world, boy!" thought he. "A hard fight, all the way through. God grant, before you come to take the burden and the shock, I may have been able to lighten both for you?"

The old woman touched his arm.

"O, master! Is the fighting past?"

"It is past and done, Gesafam. That enemy, at least, will never come again! But tell me, what causes the boy to cry?"

"He is hungered, master. And I—I do not know the way to milk the strange animal!"

Despite his exhaustion, pain and dour forebodings, Allan had to smile a second.

"That's one thing you've got to learn, old mother!" he exclaimed. "I'll milk presently. But not just yet!"

For first of all he must see Beatrice again. The boy must cry a bit, till he had seen her!

To the bed he hastened, and beside it fell on his knees. His eager eyes devoured the girl's face; his trembling hand sought her brow.

Then a glad cry broke from his lips.

Her face no longer burned with fever, and her pulse was slower now. A profuse and saving perspiration told him the crisis had been passed.

"Thank God! Thank God!" he breathed from his inmost soul. In his arms he caught her. He drew her to his breast.

And even in that hour of confusion and distress he knew the greatest joy of life was his.

CHAPTER XXIX

ALLAN'S NARRATIVE

The week that followed was one of terrible labor, vigil and responsibility for Stern. Not yet recovered from his wounds nor fully
rested from his flight before the Horde—now forever happily
wiped out—the man nevertheless plunged with untiring energy
into the stupendous tasks before him.

He was at once the life, the brain, the inspiration of the
colony. Without him all must have perished. In the hollow of his
hand he held them, every one; and he alone it was who wrought
some measure of reconstruction in the smitten settlement.

Once Beatrice was out of danger, he turned his attention to
the others. He administered his treatment and regimen with a
strong hand, and allowed no opposition. Under his direction a
little cemetery grew in the palisade—a mournful sight for this
early stage in the reconstruction of the world.

Here the Folk, according to their own custom, marked the
graves with totem emblems as down in the Abyss, and at night
they wailed and chanted there under the bright or misty moon;
and day by day the number of graves increased till more than
twenty crowned the cliff.

The two Anthropoids were not buried, however, but were
thrown into the river from the place where they had been shot
down while rolling rocks over the edge. They vanished in a tumbling, eddying swirl, misshapen and hideous to the last.

With his accustomed energy he set his men to work repairing
the damage as well as possible, rearranging the living quarters,
and bringing order out of chaos. Beta was now able to sit up a
little. Allan decided she must have had a touch of brain-fever.

But in his thankfulness at her recovery he took no great
thought as to the nature of the disease.

"Thank God, you're on the road to full recovery now, dear!"
he said to her on the tenth day as they sat together in the sun
before the home cave. "A mighty close call for you—and for the
boy, too! Without that good old goat what mightn't have happened? She'll be a privileged character for life in these diggings."

Beta laughed, and with a thin hand stroked his hair as he bent
over her.

"Do you remember those funny goat-pictures Powers used to
draw, a thousand years ago?" she asked. "Well, he ought to be here

now to make a sketch of you handing one to our kiddums? But—it was no joke, after all, was it? It was life and death for him!"

He kissed her tenderly, and for a while they said nothing. Then he asked:

"You're really feeling much—much better today?"

"Awfully much! Why, I'm nearly well again! In a day or two I'll be at work, just as though nothing had happened at all."

"No, no; you must rest a while. Just so you're better, that's enough for me."

Beatrice was really gaining fast. The fever had at least left her with an insatiable appetite.

Allan decided she was now well enough again to nurse the baby. So he and the famous goat were mutually spared many a *mauvais quart d'heure.*

Tallying up matters and things on the evening of the twelfth day, as they sat once more on the terrace in front of Cliff Villa, he inventoried the situation thus:

1—Twenty-six of the Folk are dead. 2—H'yemba is disposed of—praise be! 3—Forty still survive—twenty-eight men, nine women, three children. Of these forty, thirty-three are sound. 4—The Pauillac is lost. 5—The bridge is destroyed, and eight of the caves are gone. 6—The entire forest area to the northward, as far as the eye can reach, is totally devastated. 7—The Horde is wiped out.

"Some good items and some bad, you see, in this trial balance," he commented as he checked up the items. "It means a fresh start in some ways, and no end of work. But, after all, the damage isn't fatal, as it might easily have been. We're about a thousand times better off than there was any hope for."

"You haven't counted in your own wounds just healing, or the terrific time you had with the Horde," suggested Beatrice. "How in this world you ever got through I don't see."

"I don't either. It was a miracle, that's all. From the place where I descended for a little repair work, and where they suddenly attacked us, to the colony, can't be less than one hundred and fifty miles. And such hills, valleys, jungles! Perfectly unimaginable difficulties, Beta! Now that I look back on it myself, I don't see how I ever got here."

"They killed both the men you had with you?"

"Yes; but one of them not till the second day. You see, the carburetor got clogged and wouldn't spray properly. I realized I could never reach Settlement Cliffs without overhauling it. So I scouted for a likely place to land, far from any sign of the cursed signal-fires.

"Well, we hadn't been on the ground fifteen minutes before I'm blest if one of my men didn't hear the brushwood crackling to eastward.

"'O Kromno, master!' said he, clutching my arm, 'there come creatures—many creatures—through the forest! Let us go!'

"I listened and heard it, too; and somehow—subconsciously, I guess—I knew an advance-guard of the Horde was on us!

"It was night, of course. My search-light was still burning, throwing a powerful white glare into the thicket about a quarter-mile away, beyond the sand-barren where I had taken earth. I turned it off, for I remembered how much better the Folk could see without artificial light in our night atmosphere.

"'Tell me, do you see anything?' I whispered.

"The other fellow pointed.

"'There, there!' he exclaimed. 'Little people! Many little people coming through the trees!'

"For a moment I was paralyzed. What to do? There was no time now for a getaway, even if the machine hadn't been out of order. My mind was in a whirl, a rout, an utter panic. I confess, Beatrice, for once I was scared absolutely blue—"

"No wonder! Who could have helped being?"

"Because you see, there was no way out. Lord knew how many of the little fiends were closing in on us; they might be on all sides. The country was much broken and absolutely new to me. I had no defenses to fight from, and it was night. Could anything have been worse?"

"Go on, dear! What next?"

"Well, the Horde was coming on fast, and the darts beginning to patter in, so I saw we couldn't stay there. I had some vague idea of stratagem, I remember—some notion of leading the devils away on a long chase, outdistancing them and then swinging round to the machine again by daylight, and possibly fixing it up in time to skip out for home. But—"

"But it didn't work out that way?"

"Hardly! I emptied my automatics into the brown of the advancing pack, and then retreated, flanked by my two men. They were keen to fight, the Merucaans were—always ready for a mix—but I knew too much about the poisoned arrows to let 'em. We stumbled off through the woods at a good gait, crashing away like elephants, while always, apelike, creeping and hideous, the little hairy beast-people stole and slithered among the palms."

Beatrice shuddered.

"Heavens!" she exclaimed. "I—I'd have died of sheer fright!"

"I didn't feel like dying of fright, but I infernally near died of rage when in about five minutes I saw a flicker of flame through the jungle, and then a brighter glare."

"They burned the Pauillac?"

"I guess so. I never went back to see. They probably burned the planes, and tried to batter up the rest of it with rocks and things. They wrecked it all right enough, I guess. That was for the attack we made on 'em from its safe elevation at the bungalow. Well—"

"What then?"

"I can hardly remember. We trekked south, as near as I could reckon it, or south by east, with New Hope River as our objective-point. Oh, what's the use trying to tell it all? You know the jungle at night?"

"Wild beasts, you mean?"

"And snakes, Beta! Some sensation to step on a copperhead and then leap off just in time to miss the snap of the fangs, eh?"

"Oh, don't Allan! Don't!"

"All right; I'll skip that part. Anyhow, we hiked till daybreak, when my men began to complain of severe pain in the eyes. I had to stop and rig up some shields for them, and smear their hands and faces with mud to keep off the sun. Well, we managed to eat a little fruit and get a drink of water; but as for rest, there was none. For inside an hour, hanged if the darts didn't begin dropping again!"

"They'd come up with you!"

"Maybe. Or else it was another group of 'em. No telling. The whole country seemed to swarm with the devils. Anyhow, we had to mosey again. But—well—one of the darts got home on my best fighter. And—h-m!—he didn't last five minutes. He turned a kind of bluish-green, too. And swelled a good bit. I'll spare you the details, Beta. At any rate, we had to leave him. So there were only two of us now, and God knew where home was, or how many thousand of the hairy devils were lying in ambush on the way. So then—"

"What did you do?" she asked, shuddering.

"We hiked, and kept on hiking! All day we beat and trampled through the forest, and toward night there was no more go in us. So we decided to make a stand. Pretty objects we were, too, torn and bruised, mired from swamps clear to our waists, and a mass of scratches and bruises! Well, we hadn't long to wait when the attack was on again.

"I gave my one remaining man the spare automatic, and showed him how to handle it; and for about an hour we stood off the devils. But they flanked us, and all at once my man grunted and pitched forward. I'm damned if they hadn't driven a spear clean through his lungs!

"After that, good God! it was just a man-hunt, endless and horrible, through trackless wilds, over hills and mountains, through valleys, across rivers, Heaven knows where! But I always tried to keep my wits and beat to southward, hoping, ever hoping I might reach the New Hope. Well—now and then I could get far enough ahead to snatch a bite or a drink. Twice I slept—twice, in about a week; think of that, will you? Once in a hollow tree, and once under a rock-ledge. Only a few hours in all. But it helped. Without that I couldn't have got through."

She took his hand, and kissed and caressed it.

"My Allan!" she whispered, while in her eyes the tears started hot. "You suffered all that just to come home again?"

"What else was there to do? The last few days I hardly knew anything at all. It was a daze, a dream, a nightmare. There was so much pain in every part that no one part could hurt very much. The bushes pretty nearly stripped every rag of clothes off me—and the skin, as well. My sandals went all to pieces. I lost my sense of direction a hundred times, and must have often doubled on my tracks. I ate and drank what I could get, like an animal. Once, in a period of lucidity, I remember finding a nest of fledgling birds. I crunched them down alive, pin-feathers and all! Well—"

"My boy! My poor, lost, tortured boy!"

"When they wounded me I never even knew. All I know is that the spear wasn't one of the poisoned ones. Otherwise—"

"There, there! Don't think about it any more, darling! Don't tell me any more. I know enough. It's too awful! Let's both try to forget!"

"I guess that's the best way, after all," he answered. "I found the river somehow, after a thousand or two eternities. Instinct must have guided me, for I turned upstream in the right direction. And after that, all I remember is seeing the bridge across to Settlement Cliffs."

"And so you came home to us again, darling?"

"So I came home. Love led me, Beatrice. It was my chart and compass through the wilderness. Not even pain and hunger could confuse them. Nothing but death could ever blot them out!"

"And after all you'd been through, dear, you did what you did for us? Without resting? Without delay or respite?"

"That's life," he answered simply. "That's the price of the new world. He who would build must suffer!"

Her arms embraced him, her breath was warm upon his face, and in the kiss that burned itself upon his eager lips he knew some measure of the sweetness of reward.

CHAPTER XXX

INTO THE FIRE-SWEPT WILDERNESS

Less than three weeks after the extermination of the Horde, Stern had already completed important measures looking toward the rehabilitation of the colony.

The damage had been largely repaired. Now only some half-dozen convalescent cases still remained on the sick-list. What the colony had lost in numbers it had gained in solidarity and a truer loyalty than ever before felt there.

All the survivors, now vastly more faithful to the common cause than in the beginning, showed an eager longing to lay hold of the impending problems with Stern, and to labor faithfully for the future of the great undertaking.

The fishing, hunting and domestication of wild animals all were resumed, and again the sound of hammers and anvils clanked through the caves.

Under Stern's direction, half a dozen men crossed the pools in boats, descended the north bank of the river, and got hold of the cut bridge cables.

Stern shot a thin line over to them by means of a bow and arrow. With this they pulled a stouter cord across, and finally a strong cable. All hands together soon brought the bridge once more up the cliff, where it was lashed to its old moorings.

Barring a few broken floor-planks, easily replaced, only slight damage had been done. One day's labor sufficed to put it in repair again.

The parapet was rebuilt and a wall constructed across the end of the broken terrace. Work was begun on new cave dwellings, with great care not to weaken the strata and so invite another disaster.

Stern, very wise by now in gauging the barbarian mentality, undertook no direct punishment of such as had been led away by H'yemba. But he gathered all the Folk together in the palisade, and there—close to the mutely eloquent object-lesson of the little cemetery—he made them a charweg, a talk in their own speech.

"My people!" cried he, erect and strong before them all, "listen now, for this thing ye must know!

"The evil of your hearts, thinking to prevail against me and the Law, hath brought ye misery and death! Ye have rebelled against the Law, and behold, many are now dead—innocent as well as guilty. The landslide smote ye, and enemies came enemies far more terrible than the dreaded Lanskaarn ye fought in the Abyss! But a little more and ye had all died with battle and disaster. Only my hand alone saved ye—all who still live to breathe this upper air.

"Men! Ye beheld my doing with the earthquake and the Horde! Ye beheld, too, my answer to H'yemba, the evil man, the rebel and traitor. Him ye saw hurled, bleeding, from the parapet! That was my answer to his insolence! And if not he, then who can ever stand against me?"

He paused, and swept them with his glance, letting the lesson sink deep home. Before him their eyes were lowered; their heads bowed; and through them all ran murmurs of fear and supplication.

"My Folk! Rightly might I be angered with you, and require sacrifice and still more blood; but I am merciful. I shall not punish; I shall only teach, and guide, and help! For my heart is your heart, and ye are precious in my eyes.

"But, hark ye now, and think, and judge for yourselves! If any ever speak again of rebellion, or of treason, and seek to break the Law, on his head shall be the blood of all. For surely woe shall come again on us. In your own behalf I warn you, and ye shall be the judges. Now answer me, O my Folk, what shall be done unto any who rebels?"

"He shall die!" boomed the voice of Zangamon. The loyal fighter, now lean and gaunt with great labors, but still powerful, raised his corded hand on high. "Of a truth, that man shall die!"

"What death?" cried Stern.

"Even the death of H'yemba! Let him be cast from the parapet to death in the white rushing river far below!"

All echoed the cry: "Death to all traitors, from the rock!"

"So be it, then," Stern concluded. "Ye have spoken, and it shall be written as a Law. From Execution Rock shall all conspirators be cast. Now go!"

He dismissed them. While they departed and filed down the terraces to their own homes, he stood there with folded arms, watching them very gravely. The last one vanished. He nodded.

"They'll do now!" said he to himself. "No more trouble from that source! Another milestone passed along the road of self-control, self-government and communal spirit. Ah, but the road's a long one yet—a long and hard and stony road to follow!"

Next day Stern began making his plans for the recovery of the lost airplane.

"This is by far the most important matter now before the colony," he told Beatrice, watching her nurse the boy as they sat by the fire, while outside the rain drummed over cliff and canyon, hill and plain. "Our very life depends on keeping a free means of communication open with the mother-country of the Folk, so to call it, and with the city-ruins that supply us with so many necessary articles. No other form of transportation will do. At all hazards we must have an airplane—one at least, more later, if possible."

"Of course," she answered; "but why not make one here? Down there in your workshop—"

"I haven't the equipment yet," he interrupted; "nor yet the necessary metal, the wire, a hundred things. All that will come in time when we get some mines to work and start a few blast-furnaces. But for the present, the best and quickest thing to do will be to look up the old machine again."

"But," she objected, terrified at thought of losing him again: "but I thought you said the Horde wrecked it!"

"So they did; but beasts like that probably couldn't destroy the vital mechanism beyond possibility of repair. That is, not unless they heaped a lot of wood all over it, and heated it white-hot, which I don't think they had intelligence enough to do. In any event, what's left will serve me as a model, for another machine. I really think I'll have to have a try for it."

"Oh, Allan! You aren't going to venture out into the wilderness again?"

"Why not, dearest? You must remember the forest is all burned now; perhaps for hundreds of miles. And the Horde, the one greatest peril that has dogged us ever since those days in the tower, has been swept out with the besom of flame!"

"Which has also surely destroyed the machine, even if they haven't!" she exclaimed, using every possible argument to discourage him.

"I hardly think so," he judged. "You see, I left it in a wide sand-barren. I think, on the whole, it will pay me to make the expedition. Of course I shan't take less than a dozen men to help me bring it back—what's left of it."

"But Allan, can you find your way?"

"I've got to! That machine must positively be recovered! Otherwise we're totally cut off from the Abyss. Colonizing stops, and all kinds of hell may break loose below ground before I can build another machine entire. There are no railroads running now to the brink," he added smiling; "and no elevators to the basement of the world. It's the old Pauillac again or nothing!"

The girl exhausted all her arguments and entreaties in vain. Once Allan's mind was definitely made up along the line of duty, he went straight forward, though the heavens fell.

Four days later the expedition set out.

Allan had made adequate preparations in every way. He left a strong and well-armed guard to protect Settlement Cliffs. By careful thought and chart-drawing he was able to approximate the probable position of the machine. With him he took fifteen men, headed by Zangamon, who now insisted he was well enough to go, and ably seconded by Frumuos.

Each man carried an automatic, and six had rifles. They bore an average of one hundred cartridges apiece, and in knapsacks of goat-leather, dried rations for a week. Each also carried fish hooks and a stout fiber line.

The party counted on being able to supplement their supplies with trout, bass and pickerel from countless untouched streams. They might, too, come into wooded country, if the fire had left any to northward, and here they knew game would be plentiful.

One thing seemed positive in that new world: starvation could not threaten.

Cloudy and dull the morning was—yet well-suited to the needs of the Folk—when the expedition left Settlement Cliffs. The convoy, each man provided with eye-guards and his hands and face well painted with protecting pigment, waited impatiently in the palisade, while Allan said farewell to Beta and the little chap.

For a long moment he strained them both to his breast, then, the woman's kiss still hot upon his lips, ran quickly up the path and joined his picked troop of scouts.

"Forward, men!" cried he, taking the lead with Zangamon.

Some minutes later Beatrice saw them defiling over the long, shaking bridge.

Through her tears she watched them, waving her hand to Allan—even making the baby shake its little hand as well—and throwing kisses to him, who returned them gaily.

On the far bank the party halted a minute to shout a few last words to the assembled colonists that lined the parapet of the terrace.

Then they turned, and, striking northwest, plunged boldly into the burned and blackened waste.

Long after the marching column had disappeared over the crest of the second hill Beatrice still watched. Up on the cliff-top, with the powerful telescope at her eye, she followed the faint, drifting line of dust and ash that marked the line of march.

Only when this, too, had disappeared, merged in the somber gray of the horizon, did she sadly and very slowly descend the path once more, back to the loneliness of a home where now no husband's presence greeted her.

Though she tried to smile—tried to believe all would yet be well, old Gesafam, glancing up from her labors at the cooking-hearth, saw tears were shining in her beautiful gray eyes.

Barbarian though the ancient beldame was, she knew, she understood that after all, now as for all time, in every venture and in every task, the woman's portion was the harder one.

CHAPTER XXXI

A STRANGE APPARITION

At a good round pace, where open going permitted, the party made way, striking boldly across country in the probable direction of the lost airplane.

Some marched in silence, thoughtfully; others sang, as though setting out upon the Great Sunken Sea in fishing boats. But one common purpose and ambition thrilled them all.

A man less boldly resourceful than Allan Stern must have thought long, and long hesitated, before thus plunging into a desolated and unknown territory on such a hunt.

For, to speak truth, the finding of the needle in the haystack would have been as easy as any hope of ever locating the machine in all those thousands of square miles of devastation.

But Stern felt no fear. The great need of the colony made the expedition imperative; his supreme self-trust rendered it possible.

From the very beginning of things, back there in the tower overlooking Madison Forest, he had never even admitted the possibility of failure in any undertaking. Defeat lay wholly outside his scheme of things. That it could ever be his portion simply never had occurred to him.

As they progressed he carefully reviewed everything in his mind. Plans and equipment seemed perfectly adequate. In addition to the impedimenta already mentioned, a few necessary tools, a supply of cordage for transporting the machine, and three bottles of brandy for emergencies had been judiciously added to the men's burdens.

Each, in addition, carried a small flat water-jug, tightly stopped, slung over his shoulder. Allan counted on streams being plentiful; but he meant to look out even for the unexpected, too.

He had wisely taken means to protect their feet for the long tramp. In spite of all their opposition he had made them prepare and bind on sandals of goat's leather. Hitherto they had gone barefooted at Settlement Cliffs; but now that w as no longer permissible.

The total equipment of each man weighed not less than one hundred pounds, including tools and all. No weaklings, like the men of the twentieth century, could have stood the gaff marching under such a load; but these huge fellows, muscular and lithe, walked off with it as though it had been a mere nothing.

Allan himself bore an equal burden. In addition to arms and provisions he carried a powerful binocular, the spoil of a wrecked optician's shop in Cincinnati.

Underfoot, as the column advanced in a long line, loose dust and wood-ashes rose in clouds. The air grew thick and irritating to the lungs.

Now and then they had to make a detour round a charred and fallen trunk, or cut their way and clamber through a calcined barricade of twisted limbs and branches. Not infrequently they saw burned bones of animals or of Anthropoids.

Here and there they even stumbled on a distorted, half-consumed body—a hideous reminder of the vanquished enemy—the half-man that had tried to pit itself against the whole-man, with inevitable annihilation as the only possible result.

The distorted attitudes of some of these ghastly, incredibly ugly carcasses told with eloquence the terrified, vain flight of the Horde before the all-consuming storm of fire, the panic and the anguish of their extinction.

But Allan only grunted or smiled grimly at sight of the horrible little bodies. Pity he felt no more than for a crushed and hideous copperhead.

The country had been swept clean by the fire-broom. Not a living creature remained visible. Moles there still might be, and perhaps hares and foxes, woodchucks, groundhogs and a few such animals that by chance had taken earth; but even of these there was no trace. Certainly all larger breeds had been destroyed.

Where paradise-birds, macaws and paroquets had screamed and flitted, humming-birds darted with a whir of gauzy wings, serpents writhed, deer browsed, monkeys and apes swung chattering from the liana-festooned fern-trees, now all was silence, charred ashes, dust—the universal, blank awfulness of death.

Naked and ugly the country stretched away, away to its black horizon, ridge after ridge of rolling land stubbled with sparse, limbless trunks and carpeted with cinders.

A dead world truly, it seemed—how infinitely different from the lush, green beauty of the territory south of the New Hope, a region Stern still could make out as a bluish blur, far to southward, through his binoculars.

By night, after having eaten dinner beside a turbid, brackish pool, they had made more than twenty miles to northwestward. Stern thought scornfully of the distance. In his Pauillac he would have covered it easily in as many minutes.

But now all was different. Nothing remained save slow, laborious plodding, foot by foot, through the choking desolation of the burned world.

They camped near a small stream for the night, and cast their lines, but took nothing. Stern gave this matter no great weight. He thought, perhaps, it might be a mere accident, and still felt confident of finding fish elsewhere.

Even the discovery of three or four dead perch, floating belly up, round and round in an eddy, gave him no clue to the total destruction of all life. He did not understand even yet that the terrific conflagration, far more stupendous than any ever known in the old days, had even heated the streams and killed there the very fish themselves.

Yet already a vague, half-sensed uneasiness had begun to creep over him—not yet a definite presentiment of disaster, but rather a subconscious feeling that the odds against him were too great.

And once a thought of Napoleon crossed his mind as he sat there silently, camped with his men; and he remembered Moscow, with a strange, new apprehension.

Next morning, having refilled their canteens, they set out again, still in the same direction. Stern often consulted his chart, to be sure they were proceeding in what he took to be the proper course.

The distance between Settlement Cliffs and the machine was wholly problematical; yet, once he should come within striking distance of the scene of his disaster, he felt positive of being able to recognize it.

Not far to the south of the spot, he remembered, a very steep and noisy stream flowed toward the east, and, off to northwest of it rose a peculiarly formed, double-peaked mountain, easily recognizable.

The sand-barren itself, where he had been obliged to abandon the machine, lay in a kind of broad valley, flanked on one hand by cliffs, while the other sloped gradually upward to the foot-hills of the double mountain in question.

"Once I get anywhere within twenty miles of it I'm all right," thought Allan, anxiously sweeping the horizon with his binoculars as the party paused on a high ridge to rest. "The great problem is to locate that mountain. After that the rest will be easy."

At noon they camped again, ate sparingly, and rested an hour. Here Allan brought his second map up to date. This map, a large sheet of parchment, served as a record of distances and directions traveled.

Starting at Settlement Cliffs he had painstakingly entered on it every stage of the journey, every ridge and valley, watercourse, camp and landmark. Once the goal reached, this record would prove invaluable in retracing their way.

"If the rest of the trip were only indicated as well as what's past!" he muttered, working out his position. "One of these days, when other things are attended to, we must have a geodetic survey, complete maps and plans, and accurate information about the whole topography of this altered continent. Some time—along with a few million other necessary things!"

The third day brought them nowhere. Still the brule stretched on and on before them, though now, far to right, Allan occasionally could glimpse a wooded mountain-spur through the binoculars, as though the limits of the vast conflagration were in sight at least in one direction.

But to left and ahead nothing still showed but devastated land.

The character of the country, however, had begun to change. The valleys had grown deeper and the ridges higher. Allan felt that they were now coming into a more mountainous region.

"Well, that's encouraging, anyhow," he reflected. "Any time, now, I may sight the double-peaked mountain. It can't heave in sight any too soon to suit me!"

There was need of sighting it, indeed, for already the party had begun to suffer not a little. The perpetual tramping through ashes had started cracks and sores forming on the men's feet. Most of them were coughing and sneezing much of the time, with a kind of influenza caused by the acrid and biting dust.

The dried food, too, had started an intolerable thirst, and water was terribly scarce. The canteens were now almost always empty; and more than one brook or pool, to which the men eagerly hastened, turned out to be saline or hopelessly fouled by fallen forest wreckage, festering and green-slimed in the cooking sun.

In spite of the eye-shields and pigments, some of the men were already suffering from sunburn and ophthalmia, which greatly impaired their efficiency. Their failure to take fish was also beginning to dishearten them.

Allan pondered the advisability of suspending day travel and trekking only by night, but had to give over this plan, for it would obviate all possibility of his sighting the landmark, the cleft mountain. Though he said nothing, the pangs of apprehension were biting deep into his soul.

For the first time that night the idea was strongly borne in upon him that, after all, this might be little better than a wild-goose chase, and that—despite his desperate need of the Pauillac engine—perhaps the better part of valor might be discretion, retreat, return to Settlement Cliffs while there might still be time.

Yet even the few hours of troubled sleep he got that night, camped in a blackened ravine, served to strengthen his determination to push on again at all hazards.

"It can't be far now!" thought he. "The place simply can't be very far! We must have made the best part of the distance already. What madness to turn back now and lose all we've struggled so hard to gain! No, no—on we go again! Forward to success!"

Next morning, therefore—the fourth since having left New Hope River—the party pushed forward again. It was now a strange procession, limping and slow, the men blinking through their shields, their hands and faces smeared with mud and ashes.

Painfully, yet without a word of complaint or rebellion, they once more trailed over the fire-blasted hills on the quest of the wrecked Pauillac.

Hour by hour they were now forced to pause for rest. Some of the impedimenta had to be discarded. During the forenoon Allan commanded that most of the fishing-gear and part of the cordage should be thrown away.

Toward mid-afternoon he sorted out the tools, and kept only an essential minimum. Now that they had seen no possible need for ammunition, he decided to leave half of that also.

The tools and ammunition he carefully cached under a rock-cairn and set a tall, burned pole up over it, with a cross-piece lashed near the top. The position of this cairn he minutely noted on his map. Some day he would return and get the valuables again.

Nothing could be spared from the provision packets, but these were much lighter, anyhow. This helped a little. But Allan could see that the strength of his men, and his own force as well, was diminishing faster than the burden.

So, with a heavy heart, now half inclined to abandon the task and turn back, he surveyed the horizon for the last time that night in vain search for the landmark mountain of his hopes.

Morning dawned again pitilessly hot and sun-parched. By five o'clock the party was under way, to make at least a few miles before the greatest heat should set in.

Allan realized that this must be the crucial day. Either by nightfall he must sight the mountain or he must turn back. And with fever-burning eagerness he urged his limping men to greater speed, chafed at every delay, constantly examined the horizon, and with consuming wrath cursed the Horde which in its venomous hate had brought this anguish and disaster on his people.

Just a little past eight o'clock a cry suddenly burst from Zangamon, who had left the line during a pause to look for water in a near-by hollow.

Stern heard the man's hoarse voice unmistakably resonant with terror. To him he ran.

"What is it, Zangamon?" he cried thickly, for his tongue was parched and swollen. "What have you found? Quick, tell me!"

"See, O Kromno! Behold!" exclaimed the man, pointing.

Stern looked—and saw a human body, charred and distorted, face downward on the blackened earth. Up through the back something projected—something hard and sharp.

He stooped, wide-eyed, staring at the thing.

"A spear-head, so help me!"

Then he realized the truth. They had found one of his slaughtered companions of the terrible flight from the Horde!

Stern recoiled. Shocked though he was, yet a certain joy possessed him. For now he knew he could not be far from the path of success. The wrecked machine, he knew, could not lie more than one or two days' march ahead. If the party could only last that long—

The others came hobbling. When they, too, saw the mournful object and knew and understood, a deep silence fell upon them. In a circle they surrounded the corpse of their murdered comrade, and for a while they looked on it with woe.

Allan realized that he must not let inaction, thought and fear prey on them, so he commanded immediate burial of the body.

They therefore dug a shallow grave in the baked soil, and, taking good care not to touch the poisoned spear-head, carefully laid their companion to rest. Over the filled-in grave they heaved rocks.

"Does anybody know his name?" asked Allan.

"He was called Relzang," answered Frumnos. "I knew him well—a metal-worker, of the best."

"That's so—now I remember," assented Stern. "What was his totem?"

"A circle, with a bird's head within."

"Let it be placed here, then."

Their best stone-cutter roughly hewed the mark in a great boulder, which was set on top of the pile. Then nothing more remaining to do, the exploring party once more pushed forward.

But Allan could sense that now even its diminished strength

had greatly lessened. Discouragement and forebodings of certain death were working among the men.

He knew he could not hold them more than a few hours longer at the outside.

During the noonday halt and rest, under a low cliff, he made a charweg, saying:

"O my people, barring the matter of the patriarch's death, I have always spoken truth to you. Now I speak truth. This shall be the last day. Ye have been brave and strong, uncomplaining in great trials, and obedient. I shall reward ye greatly. But I am wise. I will not drive ye too far. The end is at hand.

"Either I see the cleft mountain by tomorrow night or we return. I shall push no farther forward than the march of one day and a half. After that I shall either have the flying boat or we shall go quickly to our safe home at Settlement Cliffs.

"Be of good heart, therefore. The return will be much easier and shorter. We can follow the picture of the way that I have made. Despair not. All shall be well. I have spoken."

They greeted his promise with murmurs of approbation, but made no answer, for body and soul were grievously tried. When he gave the order to advance again, however, they buckled into the toil with a good heart. Their morale, he plainly saw, had been markedly improved by his few words.

And, now filled with hot, new hope, once more he led the painful march, his binoculars every few minutes swinging round the far horizon in a vain attempt to sight the longed for height.

But other events were destined and were written on the book of fate. For, as they topped a high ridge about five o'clock that afternoon—dragging themselves along, parched and spent, rather than marching—Allan made a halt for careful observations from this vantage-post.

The men sank down, eager to lie prone even for a few minutes on the ash-covered soil, to hide their eyes and pant like hard-run hunting dogs.

Allan himself felt hardly the strength to remain upright; but he forced himself to stand there, and with a tremendous effort held the glass true as it slowly scoured the sky-line to north and west.

All at once he uttered a choking cry. The glass shook in his wasted hands. His eyes, staring, refused their office, and a strange purple blur seemed to blot the horizon from his sight.

With the binoculars he stared at a point N. N. W., where he had thought to see the incredible apparition; but now nothing appeared.

"Hallucinations, so soon?" he muttered, rubbing his eyes. "Come, come, buck up! This won't do at all!"

And again he searched the place with his powerful lenses.

"My God! but I do see them—and they're real—they're moving, too!" he exclaimed. "No hallucination, no mirage! They're there! But—but what—What can this mean? Who can they be?"

Tiny and clear against the dazzling background of the afternoon sky he had perceived a long line of human figures trekking to southeast over the distant hill-top, almost directly toward the point where his exhausted troop now lay inert and panting.

CHAPTER XXXII

THE MEETING OF THE BANDS

Convinced though Stern now was of the reality of the amazing sight he had just witnessed through his binoculars, yet for a long moment he remained silent and staring, utterly at a loss for any rational explanation of the remarkable apparition.

Exhausted in body and confused in mind, he could hit upon no answer to the riddle.

Might these be some detached and belated members of the Horde? No; for their figures and their gait, as he now for the third time studied them through the glass, were unmistakably human.

But if not Anthropoids, then what? Enemies? Potential friends? Some new and strange race, until now undiscovered?

A score of possible explanations struggled in his mind, only to be rejected. But this was now no time for questions, analysis, or thought. For, even as he looked, the end of the line came to view, then vanished down the blackened hillside.

Invisible, now that they no longer stood silhouetted against the sky-line, the strange company had disappeared as though swallowed up by the earth. Yet Stern well knew that they were coming almost directly down upon him and his little party. Already there was pressing need for swift decision.

What should he do? Advance to meet these strangers? Risk all on a mere chance? Or turn, retreat and hide? Or ambush them, and kill?

He found himself, for the moment, unable to make up his mind. Yet, should a pinch arise and the last contingency become necessary, he felt a powerful advantage. He was positive his little band, armed as they were, could easily wipe out this column. But, after all, must he fight?

His questions all unsettled and his mind confused from the terrible exhaustions of the march, he waited. He surveyed the neighborhood, with a view to possible battle.

On his left rose a ridge that swung to northward between the advancing column and his own position. On his right an arroyo or gully, choked with fallen tree-trunks and burned forest wreckage, descended in an easterly direction toward a rather deep valley. In this gully he saw was ample hiding-place for his whole force.

"Men!" he addressed them; "it is strange to tell, but there be others who come against us there!" He pointed at the far crest of the sawlike highlands, where now he thought to see a hazy, floating pall of dust.

"Until we know their purpose and their temper we must have care. We must hide ourselves and wait. Come, then, quickly! And prepare your guns against the need of battle!"

His words aroused and heartened his exhausted men. The prospect even of war was welcome—anything in place of this unending trek through the burned wilderness.

Zangamon cried: "Where be those that come, O Kromno? And what manner of men?"

"Yonder," indicated Stern. "I know not who, save that they be men. Wait but a little and you shall know. Now to the ravine!"

All got up, and with more energy than they had shown for some time, they trailed to the gully. Here they were soon well entrenched, with weapons ready. Stern now felt confident of the situation, however it might turn.

They waited. Some little talk trickled up and down the line, but for the most part the men kept quiet, watching eagerly.

Now already the dust of the advancing column had grown unmistakably visible, drifting downwind in a thin haze that ever advanced more and more to the southeast, came nearer always, and rose higher in their view.

"Be ready, men," cautioned Stern. "In a few minutes, now, the foremost will pass over that blackened hilltop there ahead of us!"

Higher and thicker grew the dust. A far, shrill cry sounded; and some minutes later the breaking of wood became audible as the column cut through a charred barrier.

Stern was half standing, half lying in the arroyo, only his head projecting over a charcoal mass that once had been a date-palm.

His weapon hung, well balanced, in his hand. All along the edge of the gully other pistol and rifle barrels were poked through debris. Forgotten now were sore and wounded feet, thirst, hunger, ophthalmia, discouragement—everything. This new excitement had wiped all pain away.

Suddenly Allan started, and a little nervous thrill ran down his spine. Over the top of the hill they all were watching a moving object had suddenly become visible—a head!

Another followed, and then a third, and many more; and now the shoulders and the bodies had begun to show; and now the whole advance guard of the mysterious marching column was plainly to be seen, not more than a quarter-mile away.

Allan jerked the binoculars to his eyes, and for a long moment peered through them.

His eyes widened. An expression of blank amazement, supreme wonder and vast incredulity overspread his face.

"What?" he exclaimed. "But—it's impossible! I—it can't be—"

Again he looked, and this time was forced to believe what seemed to him beyond all bounds of possibility.

"Our own people! The Folk!" he cried in a loud voice. And before his men could sense it he was out of the ravine.

His first thought was a relief expedition from Settlement Cliffs; but how could there be so many? Those who had remained at the colony were only twenty-five, all told, and in this long line that still at a good pace was defiling down the hillside already more than fifty had come to view, with more and ever more still topping the rise.

Utterly at a loss though he was, incapable of seeing any clue to the tremendous riddle, he still retained enough wit to hail the column, now passing down the slope some three or four hundred yards to westward.

"Ohe, Merucaan v'yolku!" he shouted between hollowed palms. "Yomnu! Troin iska ieri!"

Already his men had scrambled from concealment, and were waving hands and weapons, cloaks, burned brush wood, anything they could lay hands on, to attract attention. Their shouts and hails drowned out the master's.

But the meaning of the words mattered little. For the column on the hillside, understanding, had stopped short in its tracks.

Then suddenly, with yells, it dissolved into confusion of its component parts; and at a run the People of the Abyss swarmed to the greeting of their kinsmen and their own, the colonists.

Barbarians as the folk still were, they met with a vociferous affection. A regular tangi, or joy-wailing, followed, and all crowded vociferously about Stern, with hails of "Kromno! Long live our Kromno, our great chief!" in their own speech.

But Allan, dumfounded by this incredible happening, broke the ceremony as short as possible. The sight of these unexpected reenforcements dazed him. He managed to keep some coherence of thought, however, and flung rapid questions, to which he got scant answers.

Amazed, he stared at the newcomers, now shouting with their relatives from the colony in wild abandon. To his vast astonishment he saw that they had contrived eye-shields similar to those of his own party, and that they had likewise painted their faces.

They had supplies as well-dried fish, seaweed, crated waterfowl, and even fresh game. Allan's astonishment knew no bounds.

He laid a compelling hand on the shoulder of one, Rigvin, whom he remembered as a mighty caster of the nets on the Great Sunken Sea.

"Oh, Rigvin!" he commanded. "Come aside with me. I must have speech at once!"

"I come, O Kromno. Speak, and I make answer!"

"How came ye here without the flying boat? How did ye escape from the Abyss? Whither went ye? Tell me all!"

"We waited, Kromno, but you came not. Did you forget your people in the darkness?"

"No, Rigvin. There has been great distress in Settlement Cliffs. The flying boat is lost. Even now we seek it. Enemies attacked. We destroyed them, but had to sweep the world with fire, as ye see. Many things have happened to keep me from my people. But how came ye here? How have ye done this strange thing, always deemed impossible?"

"Harken, master, that I may tell it in few words! Later, when we reach the colony whereof you have spoken, we can make all things clear; but now is no time for a great talking."

"Go on quickly!"

"Yea, I speak. We waited for you many days, O Kromno; but you came not again. Days on days we waited, as you measure time. Sleepings and wakings we waited eagerly, but no sign of you was seen. Then uneasiness and fear and sorrow fell upon us all."

"What then?"

"We held a great charweg there at the Place of Bones, near the Blazing Well, to take thought what was best to do. For you were our chief; and our very ancient law commands that if any chief be in distress, or deemed lost, the Folk must risk all, even life, to save and bring him once more to his own.

"For many hours our wisest men spoke. Some declared you had deserted us, but them the Folk cried down; and barely they escaped the boiling vat. We agreed some calamity had befallen. Then we swore to go to rescue you!"

"Ye did?" exclaimed Stern, much moved. "Gods, what devotion! But—how did ye ever get out of the Abyss? How find your way so straight toward Settlement Cliffs?"

"That is a strange story, and very long, O Kromno! All our elders took thought of what ye had told us so often, and they made a picture of the way. We fashioned protections for the eyes and skin, as ye had said.

"Then the wise men recalled all the ancient traditions, which we had long deemed myths. They looked, also, upon certain records graven in the rock beyond the walls, past the place of burial. They decided the way might still be open past the Great Vortex and through the long cleft, whereby our distant fathers came.

"But they said it might mean death to try to pass the Vortex. They forced none to go. Only such as would need try."

"A volunteer expedition, eh?" thought Allan. "And look at the size of it, will you? These people are without even the slightest understanding of fear!"

"Thus it was arranged, master," continued Rigvin. "Eight score and more of us offered to go. All things were quickly made ready, and much food was packed, and many weapons. In fifteen long canoes we started, after a great singing. Men went in each canoe to bring back the boats—"

"They didn't even wait for you? But if ye had been lost, and sought to return, what then?"

"There was to be no return, master. All swore either to find you or die!"

"Go on!" exclaimed Allan, deeply moved.

"We sailed across the Sunken Sea, O Kromno, and reached the islands of the Lanskaarn. There we had to fight and thirty were killed. But we kept on, and in two days, watching for the quiet time between the great tempests, entered the Vortex."

"You all got through?"

"No master. There was not time. Many were lost; but still we kept on. Then on the fourth day we reached the great cleft, even as our traditions said. And here we camped, and sang again, and once more swore to find you. Then the boats all returned, and we pushed forward, upward, through the cleft."

"And then?"

Rigvin shook his head and sighed.

"O Kromno," he answered, "the story is too long! We be weary, and would reach the place whereof ye have told us. Later there will be time for talk. But now we cannot tell it all!"

"Ye speak truth, Rigvin!" he exclaimed. "I, too, have many things to tell. It cannot be this day. We will lead ye to the colony. We, too, need rest. My men are in sore straits, as ye see!"

He gestured at the groups gathered along the edge of the ravine. A great noise of talking rose against the heated air; and food and water, too, were being given to the Settlement men by the newcomers.

Stern knew the day was saved. Deep gratitude upwelled in his heart.

"Nothing that I can ever do will repay men like these!" thought he. Then, all at once, a sudden hope thrilled him, and he cried:

"Oh, Rigvin, one thing more! Tell me, in your long journey from the brink, have ye chanced to see a cleft mountain with two peaks on either hand?"

"You mean, master—"

"A mountain; a high jut of land, with two tops, side by side—like two grave-mounds?"

Rigvin stood a moment in thought, his soot-smeared brows wrinkled with the effort of trying to remember. Then all at once he looked up quickly with a smile.

"Yea, master!" he cried. "We saw such!"

"Where, where? For God's sake, where was it?" ejaculated Stern, gripping him by the arm with a hand that shook with sudden keen emotion.

"Where was it, master? Thus one day's marching."

Rigvin wheeled and pointed to northwestward.

"And ye can find it again?"

"Truly, yes. Why, master?"

"There, near that mountain, lies the wreck of the vlyn b'hotu, the flying boat, Rigvin! Lead us thither! We must find it. And then Settlement Cliffs!"

Through all his exhaustion and his pain he knew that now the goal was close at hand. And beyond toil, suffering and hardship once more beckoned prosperity and peace and love.

CHAPTER XXXIII

FIVE YEARS LATER

Long before daybreak that morning, the thriving village of Settlement Cliffs, capital and market-town of the New Hope Colony, was awake and astir.

For the great festival day was at hand, the fifth anniversary of the founding of the colony, to be celebrated by the arrival of the last Merucaans from the depths of the Abyss.

The old caves, now abandoned save for grain, fruit and fish storehouses were closed and silent. No labor was going forward there. The nets hung dry. From the forges, smithies and work-shops along the river-bank at the rapids arose no sounds of the accustomed industry.

The road and bridge-builders were idle; and from the farms now dotting the rich brule across the river—each snug stone house, tiled with red or green, standing among its crops and growing orchards—the Folk were coming in to town for the feast-day.

The broad wooden trestle-bridge across the New Hope echoed with hollow verberations beneath the measured tread of two and four-ox teams hauling creaking wains heaped high with meats, fruits, casks of cider, generous wines, and all the richness of that virgin soil.

On the summer morning air rose laughter from the youths and maidens coming in afoot. Sounded the cries of the teamsters, the barking of dogs, the mingled murmur of speech—English speech again; and the fresh wind, bearing away a fine, golden dust from the long roads, swayed the palm-tops and the fern-trees with a gentle and caressing touch.

All up and down the broad, well-paved street of the village—a street lined with stone cottages, bordered with luxuriant tropic gardens, and branching into a dozen smaller thoroughfares—a happy throng was idling.

Well clad in plain yet substantial weaves from the vine-festooned work-shops below the cliff, abundantly fed, vigorous and strong, not one showed sickness or deformity, such as had scourged the human race in the old, evil days of long ago.

Loose-belted garb, sandals and a complete absence of hats all had their part in this abounding health. Open-air life and rational food completed the work.

No drugs, save three or four essential ones, and no poisons, ever had crept in to menace life. Wine there was, rich and unfermented; but the curse of alcohol existed not. And in the Law it was forever banned.

On the broad porch of their home, a boulder-built cottage facing the broad plaza where palms shaded the graveled paths, and purple, yellow and scarlet blooms lured humming-birds and butterflies, stood Beatrice and Allan.

Both were smiling in the clear June sunlight of that early morning. A cradle rocked by Gesafam—a little older and more bent, yet still hardy—gave glimpses of another olive-branch, this one a girl.

The piazza was littered at its farthest end with serviceable, home-made playthings; but Allan, Junior, had no use for them today. Out there on the lawn of the plaza he was rolling and running with a troop of other children—many, many children, indeed.

As Beatrice and Allan watched the play they smiled; and through the man's arm crept the woman's hand, and with the confidence of perfect trust she leaned her head against his shoulder.

"Whoever could have thought," said he at last, "that all this really could come true? In those dark hours when the Horde had all but swallowed us, when we fell into the Abyss, when those terrible adventures racked our souls down beside the Sunken Sea, and later, here, when everything seemed lost—who could have foreseen this?"

"You could and did!" she answered. "From the beginning you planned everything, Allan. It was all foreseen and nothing ever stopped you, just as the future beyond this time is all foreseen by you and must and shall be as you plan it!"

"Shall be, with your help!" he murmured, and silence came again. Together they watched the holiday crowd gradually congregating in the vast plaza where once the palisade had been. Now the old wooden stockade had long vanished. Cleared land and farms extended far beyond even Newport Heights, where the Pauillac had first come to earth at New Hope.

Well-kept roads connected them all with the settlement. And for some miles to southward the primeval forests had been vanquished by the ever-extending hand of this new, swiftly growing race.

"With my help and theirs!" she rejoined presently. "Never forget, dear, how wonderfully they've taken hold, how they've labored, developed and grown in every way. You'd be surprised—really you would—if you came in contact with them as I do in the schools, to see the marvelous way they learn—old and young alike. It's a miracle, that's all!"

"No, not exactly," he explained. "It's atavism. These people of ours were really civilized in essence, despite all the overlying ages of barbarism. Civilization was latent in them, that's all. Just as all the children born here under normal conditions have reverted to pigmented skin and hair and eyes, so even the grown-ups have thrown back to civilization. Two or three years at the outside have put back the coloring matter in every newcomer's iris and epidermis. Just so—"

A sudden and quickly-growing tumult in the plaza and down the long, broad street interrupted him. He saw a waving of hands, a general craning of necks, a drift toward the north side of the square, the river side.

The shouts and cheers increased and cries of "They come! They come!" rose on the morning air.

"Already?" exclaimed Allan in surprise. "These new machines certainly do surprise me with their speed and power. In the old days the Pauillac wouldn't have been here before noon from the Abyss!"

Together, Beatrice and he walked round the wide piazza to the rear of the bungalow. The home estate sloped gently down toward the cement and boulder wall edging the cliff. In its broad garden stood the stable, where half a dozen horses—caught on the northern savannas and carefully tamed—disputed their master's favor with the touring car he had built up from half a dozen partly ruined machines in Atlanta and other cities.

Up the cliff still roared the thunder of the rapids, today untamed by the many turbines and power-plants along the shore. But louder than the river rose the tumult of the rejoicing throng: "They come! They come!"

"Where?" questioned Beta. "See them, boy?"

"There! Look! How swift! My trained men can outfly me now—more luck to them!"

He pointed far to northwestward, over the wide and rolling sea of green, farm-dotted, that had sprung up with marvelous fecundity in the wake of the great fire.

Looking now out over the very same country where, five years and a month before, she had strained her tear-blinded eyes for some sign of Allan's return, Beatrice suddenly beheld three high, swift little specks skimming up the heavens with incredible velocity.

"Hurrah!" shouted Allan boyishly. "Here they come—the last of my Folk!"

He ran to the corner of the piazza and on the tall staff that dominated the canyon and the river-valley dipped the stars and stripes three times in signal of welcome.

And already, ere the salute was done, the rushing planes had slipped full half the distance from the place where they had first been sighted.

A messenger ran down the gravel driveway and saluted.

"O Kromno!" he began. "Master—"

"Master no longer!" Allan interrupted. "Brother now, only!"

The lad stared, amazed.

"Well, what is it?" smiled Allan.

"The Council of the Elders prays you to come to help greet the last-comers. And after that the feast!"

"I come!" he answered. The lad bowed and vanished.

"They aren't going to let me out of it, after all," he sighed. "I'd so much rather let them run their own festival today. But no—they've got to ring me in, as usual! You'll come, too, of course?"

She nodded, and a moment later they were walking over the fine lawn toward the plaza.

On the far side, in a wide, open stretch that served the children sometimes as a playground, stood the great hangars of the community's air-fleet. Beyond them rose workshops, their machinery driven by electric power from the turbines at the rapids.

Even as Allan and Beatrice passed through the cheering crowd, now drifting toward the hangars, a sound of music wafted down-wind—a little harsh at times, but still with promise of far better things to be.

Many flags fluttered in the air, and even the rollicking children on the lawns paused to wonder as swift shadows cut across the park.

On high was heard the droning hum of the propellers. It ceased, and in wide, sure, evenly balanced spirals the great planes one by one slid down and took the earth as easily as a gull sinks to rest upon the bosom of a quiet sea.

"They do work well, my equilibrators!" murmured Allan, unable to suppress a thrill of pride. "Simple, too; but, after all, how wonderfully effective!"

The crowd parted to let him through with Beatrice. Two minutes later he was clasping the hands of the last Folk ever to be brought from the strange, buried village under the cliff beside the Sunless Sea.

He summoned Zangamon and Frumuos, together with Sivad and the three aviators.

"Well done!" said he; and that was all—all, yet enough. Then, while the people cheered again and, crowding round, greeted their kinsfolk, he gave orders for the housing and the care of the travel-wearied newcomers.

Through the summer air drifted slow smoke. Off on the edge of the grove that flanked the plaza to southward the crackling of new-built fires was heard.

Allan turned to Beta with a smile.

"Getting ready for the barbecue already!" said he, "With that and the games and all, they ought to have enough to keep them busy for one day. Don't you think they'll have to let us go a while? There are still a few finishing touches to put to the new laws I'm going to hand the Council this afternoon for the Folk to hear. Yes, by all means, they'll have to let us go."

Together they walked back to their bungalow amid its gardens of palm-growths, ferns and flowers. Here they stopped a moment to chat with some good friend, there to watch the children and—parentlike—make sure young Allan was safe and only normally dirty and grass-stained.

They gained their broad piazza at length, turned, and for a while watched the busy, happy scene in the shaded street, the plaza and the playground.

Then Beta sat down by the cradle—still in that same low chair Allan had built for her five years ago, a chair she had steadily refused to barter for a finer one.

He drew up another beside her. From his pocket he drew a paper—the new laws—and for a minute studied it with bent brows.

The soft wind stirred the woman's hair as she sat there half dreaming, her blue-gray eyes, a little moist, seeing far more than just what lay before them. On his head a shaft of sunlight fell, and had you looked you might have seen the crisp, black hair none too sparingly lined with gray.

But his gaze was strong and level and his smile the same as in bygone years, as with his left hand he pressed hers and, with a look eloquent of many things, said:

"Now, sweetheart, if you're quite ready—?"

CHAPTER XXXIV

HISTORY AND ROSES

Allan sat writing in his library. Ten years had now slipped past since the last of the Folk had been brought to the surface and the ancient settlement in the bowels of the earth forever abandoned. Heavily sprinkled with gray, the man's hair showed the stress of time and labors incredible.

Lines marked his face with the record of their character-building, even as his rapid pen traced on white paper the all but completing history of the new world whereat he had been laboring so long.

Through the open window, where the midsummer breeze swayed the silken curtains, drifted a hum from the long file of bee-hives in the garden. Farther away sounded the comfortable gossip of hens as they breasted their soft feathers into the dust-baths behind the stables. A dog barked.

Came voices from without. Along the street growled a motor. Laughter of children echoed from the playground. Allan ceased writing a moment, with a smile, and gazed about him as though waking from a dream.

"Can this be true?" he murmured. "After having worked over the records of the earlier time they still seem the reality and this the dream!"

On the garden-path sounded footfalls. Then the voice of Beatrice calling:

"Come out, boy! See my new roses—just opened this morning!"

He got up and went to the window. She—matronly now and of ampler bosom, yet still very beautiful to look upon—was standing there by the rose-tree, scissors in hand.

Allan, Junior, now a rugged, hardy-looking chap of nearly sixteen—tall, well built and with his father's peculiar alertness of bearing—was bending down a high branch for his mother.

Beyond, on the lawn, the ten-year-old daughter, Frances, had young Harold in charge, swinging him high in a stout hammock under the apple-trees.

"Can't you come out a minute, dear?" asked Beatrice imploringly. "Let your work go for once! Surely these new roses are worth more than a hundred pages of dry statistics that nobody'll ever read, anyhow!"

He laughed merrily, threw her a kiss, and answered:

"Still a girl, I see! Ah, well, don't tempt me, Beta. It's hard enough to work on such a day, anyhow, without your trying to entice me out!"

"Won't you come, Allan?"

"Just give me half an hour more and I'll call it off for today!"

"All right; but make it a short half-hour, boy!"

He returned to his desk. The library, like the whole house now, was fully and beautifully furnished. The spoils of twenty cities had contributed to the adornment of "The Nest," as they had christened their home.

In time Allan planned even to bring art-works from Europe to grace it still further. As yet he had not attempted to cross the Atlantic, but in his seaport near the ruins of Mobile a powerful one hundred and fifty-foot motor-yacht was building.

In less than six months he counted on making the first voyage of discovery to the Old World.

Contentedly he glanced around the familiar room. Upon the mantel over the capacious fireplace stood rare and beautiful bronzes. Priceless rugs adorned the polished floor.

The broad windows admitted floods of sunlight that fell across the great jars of flowers Beta always kept there for him and lighted up the heavy tiers of books in their mahogany cases. Books everywhere—under the window-seats, up the walls, even lining a deep alcove in the far corner. Books, hundreds upon hundreds, precious and cherished above all else.

"Who ever would have thought, after all," murmured he, "that we'd find books intact as we did? A miracle—nothing less! With our printing-plant already at work under the cliff, all the art, science and literature of the ages—all that's worth pre- serving—can be still kept for mankind. But if I hadn't happened to find a library of books in a New York bonded warehouse all cased up for transportation, the work of preservation would have been forever impossible!"

He turned back to his history, and before writing again idly thumbed over a few pages of his voluminous manuscript. He read:

"March 1, A. D. 2930. The astronomical observatory on Round Top Hill, one mile south of Newport Heights, was finished today and the last of the apparatus from Cambridge, Lick, and other ruins was installed. I find my data for reckoning time are unreliable, and have therefore assumed this date arbitrarily and readjusted the calendar accordingly.

"Our Daily Messenger, circulating through the entire community and educating the people both in English and in scientific thought, will soon popularize the new date.

"Just as I have substituted the metric system for the old-time chaotic hodge-podge we once used, so I shall substitute English for Merucaan definitely inside of a few years. Already the younger generation hardly understands the native Merucaan speech. It will eventually become a dead, historically interesting language, like all other former tongues. The catastrophe has rendered possible, as nothing else could have done, the realization of universal speech, labor-unit exchange values in place of money, and a political and economic democracy unhampered by ideas of selfish, personal gain."

He turned a few pages, his face glowing with enthusiasm.

"April 15—The first ten-yearly census was completed today. Even with the aid of Frumuos and Zangamon, I have been at work on this nearly two months, for now our outlying farms, villages and settlements have pushed away fifteen or twenty miles from the original focus at the Cliffs, or 'Cliffton,' as the capital is becoming generally known.

"Population, 5,072, indicating a high birth-rate and an exceptionally low mortality. Our one greatest need is large families. With the whole world to reconquer, we must have men.

"Area now under cultivation, under grazing and under forests being actively exploited, 42,076 acres. Domestic animals, 26,011. Horses are already being replaced by motors, save for pleasure-riding. Power-plants and manufacturing establishments, 32. Aerial fleet, 17 of the large biplanes, 8 of the swifter monoplanes for scout work. One shipyard at Mobile.

"Total roads, macadamized and other, 832 miles. Air-motors and sun-motors in use or under construction, 41; mines being worked, 13; schools, 27, including the technical school at Intervale, under my personal instruction. Military force, zero—praise be! Likewise jails, saloons, penitentiaries, gallows, hospitals, vagrants, prostitutes, politicians, diseases, beggars, charities—all zero, now and forever!"

Allan turned to the unfinished end of the manuscript, poised his pen a moment, and then began writing once more where he had left off when called by Beatrice:

"The great monument in memory of the patriarch, first of all our people to perish in the upper world, was finished on June 18. Memorial exercises will be held next month.

"On June 22 the new satellite, which passes darkly among the stars every forty-eight hours, was named Discus. Its distance is

3,246 miles; dimensions, 720 miles by 432; weight, six and three-quarter billion tons.

"On July 2, I discovered unmistakable traces either of habitations or of their ruins on the new and till now unobserved face of the moon, hidden in the old days. This problem still remains for further investigation.

"July 4, our national holiday, a viva-voce election and Council of the Elders was held. They still insist on choosing me as Kromno. I weary of the task, and would gladly give it over to some younger man.

"At this Council, held on the great meeting-ground beyond the hangars, I again and for the third time submitted the question of trying to colonize from the races still in the Abyss. If feasible, this would rapidly add to our population. The Folk are now civilized to a point where they could rapidly assimilate outside stock.

"In addition to the Lanskaarn, a strong and active race known to exist on the Central Island in the Sunken Sea, there remain persistent traditions of a strange, yellow-haired race somewhere on the western coasts of that sea, beyond the Great Vortex. Two parties exist among us.

"The minority is anxious for exploration and conquest. The majority votes for peace and quiet growth. It may well be that the Lanskaarn and the other people never will be rescued. I, for one, cannot attempt it. I grow a little weary. But if the younger generation so decides, that must be their problem and their labor, like the rebuilding of the great cities and the reconquest of the entire continent from sea to sea.

"In the mean time—"

At the window appeared Beatrice. Smiling, she flung a yellow rose. It landed on Allan's desk, spilling its petals all across his manuscript.

He looked up, startled. His frown became a smile.

"My time's up?" he queried. "Why, I didn't know I'd been working five minutes!"

"Up? Long ago! Now, Allan, you just simply must leave that history and come out and see my roses, or—or—"

"No threats!" he implored with mock earnestness. "I'm coming, dearest. Just give me time—"

"Not another minute, do you hear?"

"—to put my work away, and I'm with you!"

He carefully arranged the pages of his manuscript in order, while she stood waiting at the window, daring not leave lest he plunge back again into his absorbing toil.

Into his desk-drawer he slid the precious record of the community's labor, growth, achievement, triumph. Then, with a boyish twinkle in his eyes, he left the library.

She turned, expecting him to meet her by the broad piazza; but all at once he stole quietly round the other corner of the bungalow, his footsteps noiseless in the thick grass.

Suddenly he seized her, unsuspecting, in his arms.

"My prisoner!" he laughed. "Roses? Here's the most beautiful one in our whole garden!"

"Where?" she asked, not understanding.

"This red one, here!"

And full upon the mouth he kissed her in the leaf-shaded sunshine of that wondrous summer day.

CHAPTER XXXV

THE AFTERGLOW

Evening!

Far in the west, beyond the canyon of the New Hope River—now a beautifully terraced park and pleasure-ground—the rolling hills, fertile and farm-covered, lay resting as the sun died in a glory of crimson, gold and green.

The reflections of the passing day spread a purple haze through the palm and fern-tree aisles of the woodland. Only a slight breeze swayed the branches. Infinite in its serenity brooded a vast peace from the glowing sky.

A few questing swallows shot here and there like arrows, blackly outlined with swift and crooked wing against the vermilion of the west.

Over the countryside, the distant farms and hills, a thin and rosy vapor hovered, fading slowly as the sun sank lower still.

Scarcely moved by the summer breeze, a few slow clouds drifted away—away to westward—gently and calmly as the first promises of night stole up the world.

An arbor, bowered with wistarias and the waxen spikes of the new fleur de vie, stood near the woodbine-covered wall edging the cliff. Among its leaves the soft air rustled very lovingly. A scent of many blossoms hung over the perfumed evening.

Upon the lawn one last, belated robin still lingered. Its mate called from a sycamore beyond the hedge, and with an answering note it rose and winged away; it vanished from the sight.

Allan and Beatrice, watching it from the arbor, smiled; and through the smile it seemed there might be still a trace of deeper thought.

"How quickly it obeyed the call of love!" said Allan musingly. "When that comes what matters else?"

She nodded.

"Yes," she answered presently. "That call is still supreme. Our Frances—"

She paused, but her eyes sought the half-glimpsed outlines of another cottage there beyond the hedge.

"We never realized, did we?" said Allan, voicing her thought. "It came so suddenly. But we haven't lost her, after all. And there are still the others, too. And when grandchildren come—"

"That means a kind of youth all over again, doesn't it? Well—"

Her hand stole into his, and for a while they sat in silence, thinking the thoughts that "do sometime lie too deep for tears."

The flaming red in the west had faded now to orange and dull umber. Higher in the sky yellows and greens gave place to blue as deep as that in the Aegean grottos. The zenith, a dark purple, began to show a silver twinkle here and there of stars.

A whirring, roaring sound grew audible to eastward. It strengthened quickly. And all at once, far above the river, a long, swift train, its windows already lighted, sped with a smooth, rapid flight.

Allan watched the monorail vanish beyond the huge north tower of the cable bridge, sink through the trees, and finally fade into the gathering gloom.

"The Great Lakes Express," said he. "In the old days we thought seventy miles an hour something stupendous. Now two hundred is mere ordinary schedule-time. Yes—something has been accomplished even now. The greater time still to be—we can't hope to see it.

"But we can catch a glimpse of what it shall be, here and there. We must be content to have built foundations. On them those who shall come in the future shall raise a fairer and a mightier world than any we have ever dreamed."

Again he relapsed into silence; but his arm drew round Beatrice, and together they sat watching the age-old yet ever-new drama of the birth of night.

Half heard, mingled with the eternal turmoil of the rapids, rose the far purring of the giant dynamos in the power-houses below the cliff. Here, there, lights began to gleam in the city; and on the rolling farmlands to northward, too, little winking eyes of light opened one by one, each one a home.

Suddenly the man spoke again.

"More than a hundred thousand of us already!" he exulted. "Over a tenth of a million—and every year the growth is faster, ever faster, in swift progressions. A hundred thousand English-speaking people, Beta; a civilization already, even in a material sense, superior to the old one that was swept away; in a spiritual, moral sense, how vastly far ahead!

"A hundred thousand! Some time, before long, it will be a million; then two, five, twenty, a hundred, with no racial discords, no mutual antipathies, no barriers of name or blood; but for the first time a universal race, all sound and pure, starting right, living right, striving toward a goal which even we cannot foresee!

"Not only shall this land be filled, but Europe, Asia, Africa and all the islands of the Seven Seas shall know the hand of man again, and own his sovereignty, from pole to pole!"

His clasp about Beatrice tightened; she felt his heart beat strong with deep emotion as he spoke again:

"Already the cities are beginning to arise from their ashes of a thousand oblivious years. Already a score of thriving colonies have scattered from the capital, all yet bound to it with monorail cables, with electric wires and with the ether-borne magic of the wireless.

"Already our boy, our son—can you imagine him really a man of thirty, darling?—elected President on our last Council Day, guides a free people—a people self-reliant and strong, energetic, capable, dominant.

"Already the inconceivable fertility of the earth is yielding its bounties a hundred fold; and trade-routes circle the ends of the great Abyss; and all the vast territory once the United States has begun to open again before the magic touch of man!

"Of man—now free at last! No more slavery! No more the lash of hunger driving men to their tasks. No more greed and grasping; no lust of gold, no bitter cry of crushed and hopeless serfdom! No buying and selling for the lure of profit; no speculating in the people's means of life; no squeezing of their blood for wealth! But free, strong labor, gladly done. The making of useful and beautiful things, Beatrice, and their exchange for human need and service—this, and the old dream of joy in righteous toil, this is the blessing of our world today!"

He paused. A little, swift-moving light upon the far horizon drew his eye. It seemed a star, traveling among its sister stars that now already had begun to twinkle palely in the darkening sky. But Allan knew its meaning.

"Look!" cried he and pointed. "Look, Beatrice! The West Coast Mail—the plane from southern California. The wireless told us it had started only three hours ago—and here it is already!"

"And but for you," she murmured, "none of all this could ever possibly have been. Oh, Allan, remember that song—our song? In the days of our first love, there on the Hudson, remember how I sang to you:

"Stark wie der Fels, Tief wie das Meer, Muss deine Liebe, Muss deine Liebe sein?"

"I remember! And it has been so?"

Her answer was to draw his hand up to her lips and print a kiss there, and as she laid her cheek upon it she felt it wet with tears.

And night came; and now the wind lay dead; and upon the

brooding earth, spangled with home-lights over hill and vale, the stars gazed calmly down.

The steady, powerful droning of the power-plant rose, blent with the soothing murmur of the rapids and the river.

"Seems like a lullaby—doesn't it, dearest?" murmured Allan. "You know—it won't be long now before it's good-by and—good night."

"I know," she answered. "We've lived, haven't we? Oh, Allan, no one ever lived, ever in all this world—lived as much as you and I have lived! Think of it all from the beginning till now. No one ever so much, so richly, so happily, so well!"

"No one, darling!"

"But, after toil, rest—rest is sweet, too. I shall be ready for it when it summons me. I shall go to it, content and brave and smiling. Only—"

"Yes?"

"Only this I pray, just this and nothing more—that I mayn't have to stay awake, alone, after—after you're sleeping, Allan!"

A long time they sat together, silent, in the sweet-scented gloom within the flower-girt arbor.

At last he spoke.

"The wonder and the glory of it all!" he whispered. "Oh, the wonder of a dream, a vision come to pass, before our eyes!

"For, see! Has not the prophecy come true? What was then only a yearning and a hope, is it not now reality? Is it not now all even as we dreamed so very, very long ago, there in our little bungalow beside the broad, slow-moving Hudson?

"Is this not true?"

I see a world where thrones have crumbled and where kings are dust. The aristocracy of idleness has perished from the earth.

I see a world without a slave. Man at last is free. Nature's forces have by science been enslaved. Lightning and light, wind and wave, frost and flame, and all the secret, subtle powers of earth and air are the tireless toilers for the human race.

I see a world at peace, adorned with every form of art, with music's myriad voices thrilled, while lips are rich with words of love and truth—a world in which no exile sighs, no prisoner mourns; a world on which the gibbet's shadow does not fall; a world where labor reaps its full reward—where work and worth go hand in hand!

I see a world without the beggar's outstretched palm, the miser's heartless, stony stare, the piteous wail of want, the livid lips of lies, the cruel eyes of scorn.

I see a race without disease of flesh or brain, shapely and fair, the married harmony of form and function; and, as I look, life lengthens, joy deepens, love canopies the earth—and over all, in the great dome, shines the eternal star of human hope!

THE END